blue
rider
press

MARY COIN

ALSO BY MARISA SILVER

Alone With You

The God of War

No Direction Home

Babe in Paradise

MARY COIN

Marisa Silver

blue rider press

a member of Penguin Group (USA) Inc.

New York

blue
rider
press

Published by the Penguin Group
Penguin Group (USA) Inc., 375 Hudson Street,
New York, New York 10014, USA

USA / Canada / UK / Ireland / Australia / New Zealand / India / South Africa / China

Penguin Books Ltd, Registered Offices: 80 Strand, London WC2R 0RL, England
For more information about the Penguin Group visit penguin.com

Library of Congress Cataloging-in-Publication Data
Silver, Marisa.
Mary Coin / Marisa Silver.
p.   cm.
ISBN 978-0-399-16070-7
1. Women migrant labor—Fiction.   2. Women photographers—Fiction.
3. Depressions—1929—Fiction.   4. Photojournalism—United States—History—
20th century—Fiction.   5. Rural poor—United States—Fiction.   I. Title.
PS3619.I55M37   2013   2012039861
813'.6—dc23

Printed in the United States of America
3   5   7   9   10   8   6   4

BOOK DESIGN BY SUSAN WALSH

For Henry and Oliver

If you stand right fronting and face to face to a fact, you will see the sun glimmer on both its surfaces, as if it were a cimeter, and feel its sweet edge dividing you through the heart and marrow, and so you will happily conclude your mortal career. Be it life or death, we crave only reality.

HENRY DAVID THOREAU

PART ONE

Walker

1.

Porter, California, 2010

There is something gripping to Walker about a town in decline. As he drives down the streets of his youth, he feels as if he were looking at faded and brittle photographs of a place lost to time. The gap between what exists and what once was creates a sensation of yearning that feels nearly like love. The old residential section of town with its stripped and weathered homes and the buckled remnants of what were once tree-lined sidewalks is like a dead star, history and time lost in its collapse. All newness, all brightness, has moved to the outskirts, where there is a Taco Bell and a Kmart housed in an ersatz Spanish Colonial mall. Still, Porter cannot escape its past. It is surrounded by the fields of California's Central Valley, which are as old as Walker's family, who have owned them for a hundred and thirty years, as old as the Yokut tribes who roamed them long before that, paying spiritual tribute to a land that sustained them. Which is all Walker's ancestors ever wanted from this place to begin with: the assurance of a future.

Walker drives past his old high school. A marquee posts the results of the state proficiency exams, which are apparently good enough to merit four exclamation points. He passes the football field, its green dulled and yellowed by the late-summer sun. He remembers his string of desultory athletic failures—the dropped relay baton, the single basket scored after the final buzzer—high school shames he buried with a biting and sarcastic intelligence and a studied apathy that enraged his father. Walker makes a point of telling his children all his foundational stories, no matter how humiliating. He wants to front-load Isaac and Alice with a sense of their history so that they will not feel as unmoored as he does now, driving toward his father's house, toward his father, who is dying.

Walker is astonished by how little he knows about his father's childhood. The few stories he was told have had to pull duty as the narrative of an entire life and have taken on outsized and probably erroneous metaphorical significance. He knows that George let his brother convince him to climb to the roof, only to have Edward pull out the ladder from under him, leaving George dangling from the rain gutter until the groundskeeper rescued him. He knows that his grandmother died giving birth to his father and that Edward is not really George's brother at all but his half brother. Walker knows that his father lettered in archery, that he had a dog who grew drunk off a grape arbor and staggered home reeking like a town derelict, that he shined his shoes with an electric shoeshine, had his nails manicured once a week at the barbershop downtown, and that he smoked one cigar a year after all the crops had yielded. He knows that his father ate a baloney sandwich and tomato soup for lunch every day of his life. Walker knows these things not from his father's having told him but from gleaning information from family acquaintances and household staff or by observing the man whose translucence created in

Walker an obsessive if wary curiosity. As Walker drives, he shuffles these random bits of information around, trying to work out an arrangement that completes the picture of his father. But there are too many missing pieces. George Dodge was uninterested in sharing his past when there was so much future to exploit. He turned the century-old fruit groves into a successful family-owned corporation, shipping oranges from Porter—as well as melon and lettuce from his farms on the west side of the valley—all over the country. And if there is one truism about farming it is that the business is one of futures, of growth and harvest and planting and growth and on and relentlessly on. A person who gets mired in the past sees his crops grow brown and useless, and other growers swoop in to capture market share. "You're missing your future, boy," George pronounced, when Walker was eighteen and told his father that he wanted no part of farming but that he preferred to study history.

"History?" George said, his mouth twisting into an expression of disbelief.

"Understanding the mistakes of the past so we don't repeat them," Walker answered in a tone that, twenty-three years later, he cringes to recall. Such arrogance. A right of youth, he supposes, a necessity. How else is it possible to face the terrifying void of your unformed self except by claiming absolute intelligence?

"History will get you nowhere," George said.

Well, it has gotten him somewhere, Walker thinks. He is a social historian. He teaches university classes during the school year and takes the summer months to perform his field research in towns just like Porter, where he is continually drawn to the buried and forgotten

stories, to the molecules of the past that are overlooked by most tradi-
tional academics. He trolls through newspaper morgues and attics
filled with dusty and forgotten photo albums. He studies the ephem-
era: the grocery lists and obscure diaries, the death notices and high
school honor rolls, looking for the clues hidden within these random
pieces of information that might tell how history actually happened to
people. He leaves it to others to interpret treaties and battles. Walker
wants to know what people wore, how they dried their clothes, what
they served at their weddings, how they buried their dead. He needs
to answer these small, seemingly insignificant questions in order to
answer the larger ones. How did the unusual uptick in suicides in a
rural midwestern town give the lie to the romantic notions of pastoral
bliss touted during the Industrial Revolution, when cities were soot-
filled and disease-ridden factories of human attrition? Walker spent
three years traveling to a town in Minnesota to answer that question.
At his best, his work achieves a psychological portrait of a place and a
time. At his worst—well, his work has been accused of being beside
the point and subjective. *History will get you nowhere.*

Walker turns into the driveway of his childhood home. The
once venerable Queen Anne that has been the Dodge family
seat for one hundred years has grown saggy with age, its white coat
dingy as old teeth. The wraparound porch is pocked with wood rot.
He had hoped to arrive early enough to spend time with his father,
but the situation must have worsened in the last few hours; the ambulance has already arrived. Angela, George's home nurse and the
daughter of Beatriz, who was once Walker's childhood *niñera,* stands

at the door as the EMTs wrestle the gurney down the porch steps. Walker's mother has been dead for ten years, and he misses her often and especially at times like this. She was a wife of the old school, a Mills College graduate who used a refined intellect to manage all the contrapuntal temperaments in the household as if she were conducting an unruly elementary school orchestra. If she were still here, Walker imagines, somehow she would find a way to make the situation feel normal, the situation of a once tenacious and unyielding man being helplessly borne toward his end.

2

P rofessor Dodge? Sir?"

Walker looks vaguely around his classroom. The students watch him curiously, at least the ones not texting or trolling the Net on their computers. "I'm sorry?" he says.

He is back home, in San Francisco. It has been a week since he left his father at the hospital in Fresno, but he still feels unsteady, as if he has just stepped off a boat. Walker settled George into a private room, met the nursing staff, bought a sad bunch of dyed carnations from the gift shop and put them in a plastic water jug by his father's bedside. As George slept, Walker studied the small, twitching motions of his eyeballs beneath their veined lids as if he might infer something about his father's thoughts. Despite the fact that George slept under a blanket of morphine, his face was tense, his jawbone prominent, as if he were gritting his teeth, steeling himself for the oncoming disaster. Knowing that he might not see his father alive again, Walker wanted to say something, but he thought it would be cruel to wake him. The choice had felt selfless, but now Walker realizes he had simply been a coward; he had not known what to say.

It is September and the beginning of his semester-long class, which is called "Images: Codes and Democratic Valuation" in the university's course catalog but which he privately refers to as "Teaching Them How to Look at Stuff." The students are either edge-of-the-seat eager or hoodie-enshrouded nervous as he clicks through a PowerPoint display. He must have asked a question before he became distracted. He calls on a student now.

"Connotatively speaking, the image suggests bravery and victory," a boy says about the photograph of the flag-raising at Iwo Jima.

Walker suppresses a sigh. Those words: *structuralist, syntactical, punctum* . . . They have become signifiers in their own right of a certain analytical bent that Walker is, more and more, finding beside the point. He'd just like the kids to say what they think when they see the pictures. But he also knows that the students are like foals trying out their legs, and that these words make them feel powerful and adult. He will not deny them these moments of muscle-flexing self-regard.

"Well—Topher, is it?" Walker says. The boy wearing fashionable glasses preens, thrilled that his name has registered so quickly with his professor. "That's a good start. Anybody else?"

A girl raises her hand. Walker thinks her name is Sally. He's still working out his mnemonics. Funny hats = Sally. Orange puffy hair = Andre.

"Like, all for one and one for all?" Sally says.

"Okay. So what we're talking about—bravery, victory, collective effort—these are the first layers of meaning. But now we need to look beneath those layers."

The class is quiet.

"What we have talked about so far is the information that's there for the taking. The text, if we were speaking in literary terms. Now let's look at the subtext."

Blank faces. Worried faces. How-will-I-get-an-A-in-this-class? faces.

"Think about what an image represents on a subconscious level," Walker continues.

The class shifts uncomfortably, but he doesn't interrupt the silence. Silence, like boredom, can be a great instigator. And then: a hand rising, stealthy as a periscope.

"Yes? Remind me of your name?" Walker says.

"Elvis, sir."

Elvis. Lord. "Yes, Elvis?"

"I'm thinking about maybe that it has to do with what people wanted to think about the war."

Walker nods. "Keep going."

"They didn't want to think, like, it was a waste of time."

"Okay. You're on a good track here. Anyone want to jump in?"

Hands pop up. Some wave back and forth, a grade-school habit that never fails to charm Walker, reminding him how young his students are and how much he enjoys teaching them.

"Everyone wanted to feel like we'd saved the world from the Nazis," someone says.

"Well, this is a photograph from the Pacific, but you've got the right idea."

"I heard it was posed," a girl says. He thinks her name is Elsie. Doubting Elsie. Good. He needs a doubter.

"So what do we make of that?" Walker says. "What if the photographer posed the picture?"

"Then it's, like, made up?" someone calls from the back of the room.

"So it's a fiction?" Walker asks.

"But the battle really happened. They really won."

"What if it were a painting?" Walker says.

"That would be made up," Elvis says.

"So we expect a photograph to tell us the truth."

The class is silent in the face of the conundrum.

Walker remembers when he taught his children how to decode the Saturday-morning advertisements. Alice and Isaac had thought the world was filled with toymakers and cereal companies dedicated to inventing what children dreamed of. To find out that their desires were simply the function of corporate manipulation, and that Alice wanted an Easy-Bake Oven because she was told to want one and not because she had ever fantasized about baking small, rubbery-tasting cakes—her sense of betrayal was heartbreaking. Lisette had been furious. Why didn't he just blow the whistle on Santa Claus and the Tooth Fairy while he was at it?

He changes the projected image, and now an obscure photograph appears: a woman herding a yak through a rice field. Sunlight shimmers on the watery landscape. This is a photograph taken during the same war, not far from where battle was waged. "So tell me about this one," he says.

Confronted with an unfamiliar image of no obvious importance, the students have less to say. Some stare at their notebooks, hoping he will mistake their inability to answer for thoughtful preoccupation.

It will be a few weeks before they begin to understand how their own perceptions are blunted by images whose meanings have been narrowed by repetition, how their responses are, in many ways, as codified as their fancy words. For some it will take a whole semester to look at pictures they recognize and see them as strange.

"This is not a class about looking," Walker says, "which is what you do when you see a photograph you've been told is objectively important. You look. You agree with what you have been instructed to think." He mimes a caricature of an intellectual—serious frown, hand stroking goatee, nodding sagely, as if there is nothing he does not already know. The kids laugh. "But then you look away and you stop thinking. You stop imagining," Walker continues. "This is a class about seeing. And seeing is something else altogether. Seeing is about looking past surfaces of predetermined historic and aesthetic values. Seeing is about being brave enough to say: This unimportant image or piece of information that no one cares about? Well, there is a story here, too, and I'm going to find out what it is."

He takes a breath. "For your first assignment, I want you to choose five things from your dorm room and describe them."

"Just, like, describe?" someone says.

"As if you were a historian trying to piece together a moment of time from what you see around you. Objects tell stories. I want you to make connections between the items in order to come up with some idea of what they represent."

"Don't they represent us?" Elvis says.

Walker smiles. "Well, that's the question, isn't it?"

On his way back to his office, he checks his phone. Lisette has called three times in the last hour, which means that something is going on with Alice. It is a horrible feeling to think that if he hadn't noticed the messages, then whatever turbulent moment is playing itself out in Petaluma would pass and he would hear about it only as a story tied up neatly by an ending: Alice having skirted some emotional danger zone yet again. Really, Walker thinks in silent argument with his father, it is not the future he avoids but the present, which vexes with its roils of impetuous emotions, its lack of perspective, its unobscured now-ness. The present provides neither the gentling amber light of nostalgia nor the bright possibility of hope. It requires that a person take a look at himself in an unforgiving mirror and say, *This is all that I am: a marginally respected academic, a failed husband, a deserter of children.* Two years ago, Lisette moved on to another marriage and a town north of San Francisco. Walker worries that Alice's defiance and bitterness is something more insidious than typical teenage anger, and that Isaac's equanimity is the mask of a boy trying to be the one who doesn't cause trouble in a troubled house. When Walker publishes, Alice and Isaac attend his talks with unconcealed misgiving. They cannot figure out exactly why their father has spent two months in a town in Minnesota collecting photographs of dead babies in their Lilliputian coffins and studying the death rolls of an insane asylum, or why he can become obsessed with a photo album discovered in an attic in Idaho that belongs to a family that is not his own. Walker has placed a flattering monograph about his work on the coffee table in his apartment in the city the way his mother once left *The Joy of Sex* on his bed. But he doesn't think either Alice or Isaac has read it. Perhaps it is difficult to see their father written about in terms that don't apply to their small intimacies and frustrations with him. Or maybe the work suggests that he has an emotional life they have nothing to do with, which the divorce has made abundantly clear.

"Harry had to pick her up downtown," Lisette says, as soon as she answers her phone. "She was plastered."

"It's good that she called you instead of driving," he says.

"She didn't call. Some guy called."

"At least she has decent friends."

"The same decent friends who buy a sixteen-year-old booze."

"That's what a teenager would call good friends."

Lisette exhales heavily; she's not ready for jokes. "She graces us with her presence Monday through Thursday nights. All bets are off on the weekend unless she needs money. I have no idea what she's doing out there. I don't know who she is."

Walker can hear the panic in Lisette's voice. She has a mind that races from fact to disaster in mere seconds. It is his job to slow her down, to remind her how many steps there are between Alice, their difficult teen, and Alice, the drug-addled streetwalker.

"How is Isaac?" he says.

"Fine when Alice is not around. When she's home, he basically lives in his room with his close personal companion, MacBook Pro."

"Is he looking at porn?"

"Probably."

"Do you check his history?"

"I'm not going to do that. I don't think I want to know his history."

They are silent for a while. They never disagree about the children. They both feel powerless in the face of the popular culture that has kidnapped Isaac's and Alice's attention. Neither of their children reads books. Alice plays a three-note bass in a variety of quickly disintegrating bands. Isaac knows how to create apps for his smart phone. At least they aren't sitting at home playing Nintendo, Walker and Lisette weakly reassure each other. But of course Nintendo is a dated and benign fear. As hard as they try to keep up, Walker and Lisette fall further behind their kids, like two people chasing a train.

"Why don't you make Alice come home at least one weekend night?" he suggests. "Tell her she has to have dinner with you and Harry and Isaac."

"Because, quite honestly, it isn't so pleasant to sit at the table and watch her scowl." She lets out a pale laugh and then a sigh full of resignation.

"I know," Walker says.

"Tell me she's going to be okay," she says.

"She's going to be okay."

They are quiet. Of course neither of them knows if this is true.

"She threw up all over Harry's car," Lisette says. "He told her to clean it out or pay for the detailing herself."

"That's good."

"Needless to say, she's making a production out of the whole thing. She's got Isaac running back and forth with wet paper towels."

"He shouldn't have to do that."

"He wants to."

"Tell him to stop."

"I'm on top of it, Walker," she says, her tone snapping to attention.

Their amicable post-divorce relationship takes these sudden sharp turns that he is never prepared for, where he comes face-to-face with her dissatisfactions. Although the dots don't quite connect, he knows this zinger refers to a time when he and Lisette were still married and his frequent absence from his family's life provoked her. Her resentment made his attempts to parent when he was around feel hollow, as if he were a bad actor. His work preoccupied him so much that sometimes he sat at the dinner table looking at Lisette and the children as if they were a photograph some future historian would discover and place in a social and economic context. While he was following his intuition, digging through the leavings of forgotten lives, not promoting his career in any straightforward way, Lisette was raising children, teaching high school physics, and, as he learned, having an affair with Harry, who is now her very decent and very present husband.

"Should I talk to her?" he asks, the formulation an admission that he is ancillary to the family, a semi-useful acquaintance who can be called on if necessary. At any rate, it's a rhetorical question. They can each lecture Alice and cajole Alice and threaten Alice. But in the end, there is nothing either of them can do.

3.

Two nights later, Walker is woken from a thick sleep by the phone. His father has died. The combination of being semiconscious and hearing the words he has been anticipating finally spoken as blunt, stupid fact makes him feel a confused sense of emergency. He throws on yesterday's clothes, gets in his car, and drives through the predawn hours until he is back in Porter. It is only when he pulls up to the house, where the rising sun is just beginning to flare against the windows, that he realizes he has come to the wrong place. His father's body is still at the hospital. For the first time in more than a century there is no Dodge living in this home.

During the next few days, his sisters, Evelyn and Rosalie, fly in from Chicago and Houston. His brother, Matthew, who has taken over the company, drives down from Fresno, where he runs Dodge Holdings from its corporate office. The meeting with the lawyer is short and unsurprising. George's assets are tied up with the company, and he has left only small amounts to each of his children. The Dodges were always and only about the land.

Walker and Lisette decide that Alice and Isaac do not need to come to the memorial service of a man at whose behest they visited only on Christmas and Easter. Now that the day has come, though, and Walker enters the church alone, he wishes they were with him. He sits next to Angela and her mother. Beatriz is a tiny woman, and her feet do not meet the ground when she sits in the pew. He remembers how proud he was—how proud they both were—when he grew taller than his *niñera*. For years she had promised to treat him to dinner when the blessed event occurred and she kept her word, taking him to her brother's taquería, where Walker gorged himself on carnitas and happily received the congratulatory pats on the shoulder of every patron who entered the place—most of them employees of Dodge Farms. Beatriz is seventy-five, George's age, although she looks ten years younger, her face barely lined, her short and thick waist giving her a robust aspect. She cries softly through the service with a lack of embarrassment that Walker envies. The muscles of his face ache from the effort of trying to keep himself under control.

That the mayor is at the service along with other town dignitaries does not surprise Walker, but he is taken aback by the numbers who come from the groves. Foremen and field managers fill the pews, along with their wives and children. When the service is over, they wait to speak to Walker and his siblings. As they share stories of George's generosity during a particularly dry season, or recount how he sent a week's worth of food when one of the men lost his wife, Walker feels his father growing less distinct until, having assumed the shape of this benevolent and thoughtful *patrón*, he becomes virtually unrecognizable. Walker is disheartened when none of the employees come back to the house for the small reception Evelyn and Rosalie have organized. He would like to talk more to them, to hear the stories they might tell that would fill in the many blanks of his father's life. But either his sisters didn't extend the invitation or the men and their wives do not feel comfortable coming to the *casa grande*, a title that is both frankly descriptive and queasily suggestive of plantation hierarchy.

A tall, older man still in possession of an erect posture crosses the living room and greets Walker with a firm handshake. "Which one are you?" he says.

"Walker."

"The oldest boy."

"That's right," Walker says. He loves the way the elderly see everyone else as permanent children.

"Well, son, I'm sorry for your loss."

"I'm afraid I don't remember you," Walker says.

"No reason why you would. I'm Edward Dodge."

Walker is taken aback. "Uncle Edward?"

"I guess you could call me that, too."

Edward and George had not spoken since their father's death, when the will revealed that the entire operation had been handed down to George. Now Edward's vitality seems like a rebuke, the winning move in a chess game of dynastic family madness.

"Funny to be back here," Edward says. "Place hasn't changed a bit."

Walker looks around foolishly, as if he had not noticed this before. He feels unaccountably embarrassed in front of this man, as if he should apologize for the fact of his father's luck.

"Your dad and I used to come in so muddy that one of the ladies would have to carry us straight to the bath or Mother would raise a fit," Edward says.

"My father never talked much about his childhood," Walker says.

"He ever tell you about the boxing ring?"

"No."

"Well, you know he was a serious boy, your dad. Skinny and not much for fighting. Then I come along like a bat out of hell, and I'm bigger even if I'm three years younger. Once I find out how little it takes to get your dad to cry, well . . ." He smiles at the memory. "So your granddad, he gets some of his men to build a boxing ring out back, wooden floor and ropes—the works—and he buys us each a set of boxing gloves. And then comes this man down from Monterey with muscles the size of cantaloupes. Says he was an amateur boxer, although who knows? Probably he got into a bar fight now and again up there with those fellows from the canneries. Well, it turns out Dad has hired this man to teach us how to box. And lo and behold, the first time George and I step into that ring, George throws me down with one punch. So Dad pays the boxing coach and sends him home, has the workers take down the ropes and pull up the floor, and that's the end of that." He lets out a bark of a laugh.

"Can I ask you something?" Walker says.

"Fire away."

"Why did Grandfather cut you out of the business?"

Edward smiles in a way that suggests a private history. "He took the answer to that question to his grave."

"You must have been angry."

"Confused, mostly," he says. "But I never imagined myself as any sort of farmer. I guess he knew that. And George was special to him."

"Why?"

Edward thinks for a moment, and then laughs. "You know what?

I never asked him. That's the way of it, isn't it? You always ask the wrong questions."

Later, Walker stands on the porch watching the guests leave. He has the feeling that the people are taking away fragments of his father—a story or a joke or a friendly game of five-card draw played one August night when the windows were flung open against the still heat and the cicadas sang and his father wiped a sweating tumbler of Scotch against his brow.

Just before the EMTs lifted the gurney carrying his father into the ambulance, Walker caught a glimpse of George's expression. It was etheric, trapped somewhere between living and dying. Walker had a sudden, awful feeling that his father thought he was making the journey to the hospital alone. "Dad. I'm here," he said. "I'm going to drive right behind the ambulance. I'll see you very soon."

George reached up a hand and grasped Walker's wrist with surprising force. Walker heard his father's struggling wheezes, smelled the sour, spent odor of George's mouth, seventy-four years of food and saliva and sucked-back tears and sucked-back feelings stored in the nooks between yellowed teeth. His eyes darted with a wild, unruly energy.

"Burn me up," he whispered.

4

When Walker and Lisette split, they sold their house in the Sunset District, and he now lives in an apartment in the Mission, which he has not decorated with much more personality than the motel rooms he occupies during his fieldwork. He knows he ought to pay more attention to his place and try to make it a proper second home for Alice and Isaac. But their weekends are filled with activities, and they want to be close to their friends, so they rarely visit him in the city. During the school year, Walker drives to Petaluma to see them—sometimes twice a week—taking the kids out to dinner, or Isaac to his soccer practice or to an orthodontist appointment. Alice recently got her license, so it is a challenge to invent her need for him unless Lisette has impounded her car keys for one reason or another. Walker's visits have the quality of courtship. He takes great pleasure in dressing, in planning the activities, in the nervousness he feels as he nears the highway exit, the adrenaline kick when he pulls to the curb outside Lisette and Harry's yellow cottage. He honks and waits for the door to open and for his kids to appear. They are shy and petulant as they ford the turbulent distance between the house and his car. There is something sweet and tentative about the way the awkwardness of the encounters makes it impossible for any of them to take the time for granted, even though the kids complain to their mother about "having" to see Dad and sit heavily into the car and do not speak for a few minutes, or even fifteen minutes. Once Alice managed to go a whole night without saying a word. Her reticence is sometimes physically painful for Walker, who can still feel the sensation of her warm body against his chest when he lifted her from her crib each morning. Still, the discomfort is worthwhile for the pleasure he feels when Isaac inadvertently hums a song or when Alice delivers the first of her thrusts, which Isaac does not have the requisite aggression to parry—when they cannot help but be themselves.

He is taking them on a fishing trip to Humboldt County for a long weekend. Isaac says he is excited to go, but Walker suspects the only reason Alice has agreed is that hanging around the pot capital of California will give her bragging rights with her friends. The kids are particularly sluggish when he picks them up. Alice drags her unrolled sleeping bag down the front walkway, a nasty, lolling tongue of girlish purple and pink meant to reassure him of her absolute disinterest in this vacation. Upon seeing his contrary, difficult girl, Walker realizes how much he has missed her and her dedication to her misery, as well as her intelligence, which shines despite her valiant attempts to hide it. He loves her tangled blond hair and her wide face. The small mole on her cheek is probably a point of intense scrutiny and the locus of a vague unhappiness, but he thinks it distinguishes her, and that, in time, some boy or man will tell her that it is something he loves about her. She dresses in a combination of clothes that Walker recognizes as the province of hip kids everywhere: thrift-shop finds jumbled together in mismatch, a kind of assertive ugliness, as if she is daring others to locate the beauty she cannot yet find in herself.

Isaac comes out of the house in his usual state of akimbo—shoelaces undone, his cartoonish bubble of blond hair flattened from sleep, bright pimples sprayed across his forehead. He wears the fishing vest Walker bought for him the previous Christmas and carries his fishing pole. Walker feels grateful to his son for willingly entering into the possible charade of this trip. Alice turns back to Isaac and says something Walker can't hear, but he can tell by the way Isaac's shoulders drop that she has nailed him for his enthusiasm or his outfit or both. Her brother's lack of cynicism enrages her. Isaac continues to the car, struggling underneath the double burden of his camping equipment and his sister's judgment. Walker reminds himself that despite the divorce and the move and a sister whose emotional vicissitudes dominate, Isaac is still a boy who bends toward happiness. And Alice, if he wants to relieve himself of the burden of guilt for a split second, is no different from who she was at two, when she seemed less child than highly reactive substance that Walker and Lisette handled gingerly, fearing unexpected explosions. He imagines that she has learned to playact apathy as a way of protecting against the crisis of feelings that attend her barely hidden anxieties.

"Are we gonna stop for lunch?" Alice says when they have been driving for barely an hour.

"I made sandwiches," Walker says. "In the cooler."

He watches in the rearview as the kids find the food. Isaac takes a huge, trusting bite while Alice checks between the bread.

"Nutella and bacon!" Isaac exclaims. It is a favorite combination that health-minded Lisette refuses to indulge.

"On white bread!" Walker adds, and to his relief Alice gives him an ironic thumbs-up.

He pulls off the road at Fortuna.

"Why are we going here?" Isaac says.

"Redwoods."

"Jesus. We've seen redwoods, Dad," Alice says.

"The coast redwood towers over all other trees in the world," Isaac intones as if he is quoting a science video from school. *"Exceptional trees can reach a height of three hundred and fifty feet or more."*

"Oh, my God!" Alice groans. "The fucking redwood report!"

In the mirror Walker sees her glance his way, wondering how he will react to her language. When he says nothing, he can't tell if she is triumphant or disappointed. He remembers when each of his kids was in the fifth grade. Along with the report on the California missions, which required that he and Lisette spend weekends with saws and glue guns and boxes of sugar cubes, the redwood report was a rite of passage. Lisette, a Bostonian, objected to the entire curriculum. She could not understand why the children were learning about Father Junípero Serra and the Chumash Indians and redwoods instead of the Pilgrims and the Iroquois and the sorts of trees that might grow outside Emily Dickinson's door.

"California kids learn California history," Walker told her.

"If I'd known my kids were going to be Californians, I would never have married a bum like you," she answered flirtatiously. "I guess I didn't think it through."

No one thinks it through, he muses now, as he drives into the state park. He imagines there must be some genetic predisposition to do the opposite, to be impulsive and unreasonable. Otherwise how would the race survive?

I t does not take them long to hike past the glut of visitors who cluster near the trailhead and to wander deep into the forest. The temperature drops. Modern noises cut out and are replaced by the sounds of birds and the crunch of leaves underfoot and the gentle sawing of branches scraping against one another. Neither child complains. Alice stops at one point and leans back in order to stare at the canopy of trees. Walker refrains from offering banal narration—*Isn't this fantastic?* or *Wow, how beautiful!*—the parental equivalent of a sideline cheer. If Alice is having any sort of transfiguring moment, the last thing she wants is her father sharing it.

Walker slides his pack off his back, unzips it, and pulls out a cardboard box. It was delivered two weeks after George died, and Walker has not yet had the heart to open it. He takes his apartment key from his pocket and uses the jagged edge to slice through the packing tape.

"What's that?" Isaac says.

"It's Grandpa," Walker says.

"Jesus fucking Christ," Alice yells.

"No. Just my father."

"Ha, ha," she says wryly. She comes closer, her horror turning to a shy curiosity that he finds touching. Walker pulls a plastic baggie filled with his father's ashes from the box.

None of his siblings seemed eager to participate in any kind of ritual, but Walker feels that his father's final, unexpected wish to be cremated will not be completely honored until his ashes are spread. He can still bring to mind the furiously energized look in his father's eyes when George made his last request. At the time, Walker wondered if there was some psychotic aspect to the drugs he was being given. George could hardly have been called a spiritual man, and he was too discreet to have visions of his body feeding the next round of orange trees. It occurs to Walker that George's decision not to be buried in the Dodge plot at the edge of the original orchard was a choice against the family, that some part of his dying wish, for whatever reason, was to be finally released.

"It's so little for a whole person," Alice says, cupping her hands as if she were holding the bag.

"I thought we'd spread him here," Walker says.

"Is that against the law?" Isaac says.

"Probably." Alice's eyes flash at the idea of subversion, and Walker looks around for dopey dramatic effect. "I don't see anyone."

"Me neither," she says, forgetting to belittle him.

Both children are quiet as he unknots the closure and shakes some of the ashes onto the forest floor.

"We should do it around," Alice says. "Like not dump it all in one place."

Walker and Isaac and Alice roam the forest, sprinkling ashes in the spots each one feels are particularly beautiful or quiet, or where a bird trills or a butterfly has landed. It is a half hour of extravagant closeness that makes Walker feel his separation from his children more acutely.

When they are finished, he holds the empty baggie.

"It looks like a used condom," Alice says, returning to form.

"Thank you for that enduring image," he says.

They walk back through the woods toward the parking lot.

"We never really knew him," Isaac says.

"Some people don't want to be known," Walker says.

"That's stupid," Alice says. "Everyone wants to be known. Otherwise it's just fucking depressing."

Of course she is right. Everyone wants to be known. Perhaps the ones who conceal themselves most of all. The question is: Who is foolhardy enough to go in search of them?

The following days are a struggle. There is intermittent rain and it is cold. The cabin Walker rented is small and damp. After an initial burst of excitement about fishing, Alice gives up and spends long hours sitting on rocks by the edge of the Trinity with a blanket wrapped around her or lying in the infrequently appearing splashes of sun. Isaac is a valiant fisherman, but Walker has the feeling his son is summoning interest for his sake. Walker gives in to an emergency trip to the nearest mall and movie theater and an unnecessarily expensive sweater purchase meant to endear him to Alice. When the weekend is finally over, he drives the children back to Petaluma. The rigors of so much concentrated time together sap all three of them, and the quiet in the car has the quality of surrender. Isaac gives Walker a tight hug before dragging his backpack and fishing gear to the house. Alice's kiss is as frictionless as a bug's wing. As he watches her walk away, Walker remembers when she was thirteen.

He had casually tickled her back only to feel her unexpectedly stiffen. It turned out that she had been wearing her first bra. He supposes the complications of the moment—Alice taking on the habits of womanhood while he tried to drag her back to her childish, sexless self—were too much for her, but the removal stung him just as it does now. The screen door closes before she can get her sleeping bag inside. As she struggles, she sees that he is watching her. Her face forms into a mask of scorn, as if this were his fault, too.

Mary

5.

Tahlequah, Oklahoma, 1920

Her mother told her that she looked at people too hard. "It's like you're a robber trying to break inside a person's skin," Doris said, as she threw a ball of dough against the table and attacked it with her big hands and the strength of her broad shoulders. "It makes you strange."

"I'm not strange," Mary said, although she liked the idea that she might come to possess Toby unawares simply by the power of her gaze. She watched him in the next field over, guiding the horse and plow through the rows, the dirt turning dark as he passed, as if he were pulling a blanket over the raw earth. She watched him hoist bales of hay, wondering how his rattlebone frame could counter the weight of the dried grasses. Toby Coin, "that sickly boy," as all the mothers referred to him for years, shaking their heads sadly as if already committing him to a collective memory. He'd managed to outwit all expectation just by staying alive, beating back whooping cough and measles and scarlet fever so that he became a miracle boy as well. Mary saw how people looked at him in town, their eyes narrowing as if they didn't trust that he was quite human. His cheeks were sunken below their bones, and Mary sat in church and thought about tracing those sharp ridges with her finger, and then her tongue. As the preacher exhorted the congregants sitting shoulder to shoulder on the hard wooden benches to believe against the odds of bad planting seasons and poorer harvests, telling them they should feel special for having been chosen by God to withstand his insults, she felt something reach down to the deepest part of her, as if a hand were touching her there, the way she sometimes touched herself at night, holding her breath, careful not to wake Betsy and Louise, who lay next to her, or her brothers, who slept on the other side of the house's single room. All the land: acres of chocolate dirt and golden lashes of wheat, the blue Cookson Hills tangled with trees and networks of undergrowth, and the distant Ozarks, which seemed to Mary a mountain range big enough to cover the world. Yet, in their churches and houses, in their schools and even in their beds, people were always huddled in a bunch as if they had to mass together against the threat of too much freedom.

Doris gathered the flattened yellow disk into a ball and pounded it with the meat of her fist. "Do this three times," she said. "Three. Not two."

"Should I write that down?" Mary said.

"Don't be smart."

"That's not likely." Mary knew how to read and write, and Mrs. Petit told her she was the best at sums in the whole class. But when Mary turned sixteen, her mother pulled her out of school. As far as Doris was concerned, Mary knew nothing of any real use.

"Someone'll shoot you for looking at them that hard. Or worse," Doris muttered.

"What worse?" But Mary knew the answer. She could tell that her mother sensed something moist and wanting in Mary's parted lips. "You trying to catch flies?" she'd say when the two of them walked through town. Mary was narrow-hipped, with barely a chest, but it was something else about her that caught men's attention, a sultry drag to her gait, as if she were waiting for someone to step into her path and make her change direction.

Her mother was right: she looked hard at the men who walked into the Last House, which sat at the edge of town, far enough from the stores and saloon, the hotel and the two churches that it resembled a child excluded from a schoolyard game. Men entered through the doorway, their shoulders bent low as if they were expecting some unseen hand to yank them away from their sinful intention. She watched those same men when they came out again, too, their mouths as soft as bruised pears, their awareness adjusting to their sudden exposure. She watched the boys she'd known at school, too. They were nearly men now, a state of almost, which made what they had been and what they were becoming tantalizingly present at the very same time. The being of a thing was most powerful when it was seconds from extinction. A flower about to drop from its stem, a shot rabbit twitching its last. She studied the way these boys walked down the street, their inward-turning toes lending their movements the same lumbering intensity of a baby just learning to walk.

But it was Toby Coin who drew her eyes the most, as if he were one of the trick cartoons in the newspaper where a woman's hat was actually a bird or a white man had one Chinaman eye. The fact of Toby's survival in the face of lifelong weaknesses suggested a persistence she craved more than she desired the obvious strength of the other boys who would start wrestling with one another at a moment's notice as if they couldn't think what else to do with all that fire inside them. Toby was like a spindly tree that had miraculously outlasted a tornado, left stripped and bare of leaves but still standing while houses and barns lay in ruins.

She had touched him once. She was six years old, her father not yet dead of being so drunk he fell off a cart and let a horse crush his chest. A traveling carnival stopped in Tahlequah for a hot August week, and Mary was given enough money for two rides. She joined the line for the Maze of Mirrors, and an Indian with an empty eye sewn up in jagged stitches took her ticket. "Whatever you do, don't take yer hand off the wall," he instructed her, "or you might never come out the other side." Mary stepped into a dark tunnel that was lined with mirrors. Candles had been placed in holders along the ground, and Mary saw herself reflected in their glow. It seemed as if the world contained hundreds of Marys, girls who looked exactly like she did, who had the same cut on their knee from where they'd tripped playing four square, and who wore her favorite blue smock, the one her mother told her she had better keep clean for church. Remembering the Indian's warning, she dragged her right hand along the wall as she turned a corner. There she was again, only this time she was a hundred short fat girls whose necks had disappeared and whose legs were the size of the feed sack her brothers filled with hay and strung from the barn rafter to use as a punching bag. She didn't like those girls at all, so she turned around. There she was again, only this time she was as long and stretched out as a string of spit and her head was so small she could not see her eyes. She tried to make her way back to the first room where she had been normal, but the crowd behind her was laughing and screaming and pushing her forward, and when she turned the next corner her hand broke free of the wall. Now there were mirrors on all sides and hanging on the tent ceiling, too, and she could no longer tell which way was forward or what was up or down. She turned around looking for a way out, but she became more confused and scared. Only moments before, she'd been a girl begging a penny ticket from her father, a girl who went to school and fed the chickens, who was a skinny half-breed the white boys called Pocahontas, patting their mouths with their hands, hopping twice on one foot, then the other, *hiya hiya ho ho*. But now she was too many Marys and she was no one at all, lost and never to come out the other side, just like the ugly Indian had said. She started to cry for her mother, but people moved around her and paid no attention. She began to sink to the ground when she felt a hand grab hers and pull her through the maze. When she finally emerged into daylight, she shut her eyes against the sudden brightness as the hand slipped away from hers. When her eyes adjusted, she saw the sickly Toby Coin look back at her once before he disappeared into the crowd. The half-dead boy who missed more school than he attended had held her hand so tightly that his sweat was still on her palm.

William Coin's first wife died when Toby and his older brothers were young, and he raised them as he did the livestock on his farm. He fed them and threw water on them every so often when they were dusty and put a switch to their hindquarters when they didn't work fast enough. Three years ago he went to Tulsa and came back with a new wife, a woman he referred to as "the spinster," although she was not yet thirty, and whom he quickly filled with babies. Now that Mary was no longer in school, she was sometimes called to help the newly pregnant Carlotta Coin with her housework. Doris was happy for the money, but Mary was more excited to be in close proximity to Toby.

"Did you hear me?" Doris said. She was holding a fresh ball of dough and wiping the sweat from her face with her forearm.

"Three times, not two," Mary said.

Doris looked at her dolefully. "You must have left your brain in bed this morning. I said we're out of sugar."

"I'll go," Mary said. Anything to get away from the house and her mother's critical gaze.

Doris put more corncobs into the fire beneath the iron stove then slid the loaves inside. The stove heated the sod house to an intolerable degree, but outside was worse, the Indian-summer air dry and cracking like Doris's skin. Doris was thirty-nine, and her braid of jet hair was already laced with gray. Her face reminded Mary of the shape of a flower vase, the planes of her cheeks rising up at a gentle incline to her prominent cheekbones, features Mary had inherited, although not her mother's nut-brown Cherokee coloring or her coal-black eyes. Mary wondered how long it would take to inherit her mother's calloused hands and matching nature. Her brothers worked the field with Titus, the hired man, but, as her mother was quick to point out when the boys complained, she'd be happy to trade places with them and let them cook and try to clean a house made of dirt.

"Wash these up before you go," Doris said, handing Mary the rolling pin and mixing bowl.

As Mary plunged the dishes into the wash bucket, she studied the house's only decoration, a framed newspaper photograph nailed to the wall. The dirty glass fuzzed an already indistinct image of her grandfather, whom the accompanying headline proclaimed as "The Cherokee Murderer," as if there were only one of them across all of history. Mary leaned in close to read the article she'd read a hundred times before. Her grandfather had been chased down and killed for the murder of a white man. He'd built a house within a house, one wall of sod protecting the other, where he'd hid with his family until the posse attacked with dynamite. Mary imagined lit sticks dropping down like shooting stars while women and children, her mother among them, ran out into the night, shrieking the stumbling syllables of Cherokee that the old people who shuffled along Main Street still spoke when they were drunk or telling secrets. She'd memorized the final sentence of the article. *The condemned man walked calmly into the night, the house in flames behind him, accepting his dastardly fate.* Mary wondered what it would be like to walk toward death. Would her mind leap forward to a place where the dying had already happened so that she could feel herself in heaven even before she got there? Or could she stop time with the power of her mind just like the photograph did? Her grandfather was already dead when the picture was taken, his body propped against a door. Someone had settled a rifle in his lifeless arms. Mary tried to figure out exactly what got subtracted from a man when he died so that even if he was made to pose like the living, there was nothing vital about him. She'd seen animals die— lame horses her brothers shot to be merciful, her old dog, Pete, lying down one day in a circle of sun and letting go. In each case, what struck her was how quickly life fled, as if it didn't want to be collared and dragged back. And what was left? Just the shape of something that could not be called a horse or a dog, just as her grandfather in the photograph could not be called a man.

W hen Mary arrived in town, she was surprised to see that the doors of the Indian school were already open and half the town was on the street in front of Crew Drugs, clustered together as if they were waiting for Mr. Anderson to call out the winner of one of his store's prize drawings. Two years ago she had won a tin of mercolized wax complexion cream, which she had hidden from her sisters in the ring hole of a sawtooth walnut tree and used so sparingly she still had some left. But Mary did not see Mr. Anderson. Instead, a tall stranger stood at the center of the commotion. Despite the heat, he wore a full suit and a hat.

"What's going on?" Mary said, when she found Betsy and Louise in the crowd.

"We better go home," Betsy said.

"Something's finally happening in this town and you want to leave?" Mary said.

"Mama will be mad."

"Hang Mama."

"I'm going to tell her you said that."

Mary looked at her prissy sister with her neat braids and her pursed, disapproving expression. "Your mouth is going to get stuck that way if you don't watch out," she said.

The man held a purple scarf over his head. "Pure silk, ladies. And a color to offset even the darkest of complexions."

A wave of excitement swelled as he tossed the scarf into the air. Women and girls lunged as if he'd thrown a handful of gold coins. Next he drew a feathered boa out of the trunk, waved it around in a circle, then released it to the crowd. Then came hats with brims the size of serving platters and elbow-length gloves. The man held up a soldier's jacket.

"See this bullet hole, boys? Put your nose to it and inhale," he said, bringing the material to his sunburned face. The man's accent was precise and clipped, each word finished off completely, just the way Mrs. Petit instructed her students to speak, because she said good diction would prove their education. "That sweet odor," the man said. "Does it smell a little bit like cinnamon? Does it remind you of your father's cigar? That's gunpowder, boys. Straight from Appomattox. Hand over my heart." He held the jacket out to the children, who fell into a reverential hush. "Fifty cents to get your picture taken wearing this," he said.

As the crowd groaned, and someone shouted that the man ought to take his business someplace where people had money to waste on a picture they could see by looking in the mirror, Mary noticed another, younger man in shirtsleeves made translucent by sweat who was busy setting a camera on a tripod.

"You've got it backwards, sir," the older man said. "I'm offering to pay *you* good money if you'll allow me the honor of taking your photograph."

The noise of the crowd shifted up an octave as nearly all the men, women, and children put themselves forward, the women patting their hair and pinching color into their cheeks, the men drawing themselves up tall and hitching their pants above their waists. Mary watched the photographer take his time scanning the willing, making a show of indecision. Finally, he chose a short, pillowy Indian woman lacking most of her teeth who wore her hair in two long braids that framed heavy jowls and a grim expression. He held out a hand as if asking the old woman to dance. As if in a daze, she allowed him to lead her into the clearing at the center of the crowd. He then reached into the trunk and pulled out a clutch of garments, including a shell-and-bone headdress. The whites in the crowd, seeing what the man was after, began to drift away to the business of the day while the Indians closed in around the trunk.

"We don't wear them clothes no more, mister," someone said.

"It's just for the photograph," the man said, handing an embroidered blouse to the old woman.

"This here's Choctaw," she said. "I ain't no Choctaw." She nodded once as if agreeing with herself and walked away. There was general grumbling, and people began to disperse.

"One dollar for a picture!" the photographer called out. "Now, that's a fair deal no matter where you come from."

Titus, Doris's hired man, came forward. He was a six-foot-tall full-blooded Cherokee with a chest strong enough to drag a hoe through root-clotted dirt faster than a mule. The photographer pulled a breastplate from the trunk, and Titus hung it over his dirty work shirt.

"Perhaps without the shirt," the photographer said.

"Show me your dollar," Titus said.

The photographer took four quarters from his pocket but held on to them. "Without the shirt," he said.

Titus pulled off his shirt. His bare breasts rose up in small hillocks of muscle stained with the dark ink of his nipples.

"We have a warrior here, Elvin," the photographer said to his assistant. "A bona fide Indian chief." He took a position behind the tripod, drawing the dark cloth over his head. "Don't look at the camera," he called from underneath his tent. "Pretend I'm not even here."

"You better be here, or who's giving me my money?" Titus said, and the crowd laughed.

"You are absolutely right, sir," the photographer said. "Now, if you'll just look off there." He pointed, his head still shrouded by the cloth.

"What am I looking at?"

"Nothing."

"Then why am I looking?"

"You're a warrior just back from battle. You're thinking of recent victory."

"I ain't no fool," Titus said, and began to lift the breastplate over his head.

The photographer came out from behind his camera. "Look here. I'm sure I can find someone else to take this money off my hands."

Titus stared at the photographer for a long while. Mary could tell by the expectant quality of the silence that people were hoping for a fight. Finally, Titus straightened the breastplate, looked off to the left, and didn't move an inch or even blink an eye.

A general squealing of girls erupted just as Toby Coin emerged from the hardware store carrying a wrinkled sack, but the excitement was not on his account. The photographer's assistant held up a doeskin dress, a slight piece of fawn-colored material barely larger than a dishrag.

"We don't raise our girls to parade around in their knickers," a woman scolded.

Mary hoped Toby would look her way, but he hitched his bag higher in his arms and headed toward his horse and wagon.

"I'll do it," she said. She snatched the piece of cloth from the man's hand and pulled it on underneath her dress the way she did when it was winter and too cold to strip off her nightgown before her day clothes were in place. She shimmied out of her sleeves and snaked her hand through the single armhole of the doeskin, leaving her dress in a puddle on the ground. The crowd fell silent as though it had been mystified by a magician's trick. Mary noticed a familiar slack-jawed expression in the faces of the men as they took in her bare shoulders. She felt the queer nature of her power, the way it made her feel both strong and diminished at the same time.

"I'm gonna tell Mama." Betsy hissed, pushing Louise behind her as if to protect her from their sister's degeneracy.

Well, Betsy was a rule-following prig, Mary thought, and her life-long derision of her sister and the fact that Toby was now studying her from his seat high up on his wagon wiped away more subtle confusions of the moment.

The photographer's assistant positioned her so that she stood sideways to the camera. "Stiff like a statue," he said.

The photographer studied Mary. "She does not have an authentic look," he said.

"You are awfully light-skinned," the assistant said to her. "Are you sure you're Indian?"

"My grandfather was the Cherokee Murderer," she said. A few people in the crowd laughed.

"Young lady," the photographer said. "Please do not waste my time."

"Think of something Indian," the assistant said.

But all she could think of was Toby's eyes on her naked shoulder.

"Think of rain dances," the young man continued.

But where was he? He had turned the cart around and, along with Titus, who now sat in the seat next to him, was driving out of town. Uninterested. Or disgusted. She had made herself ridiculous in front of him, her sisters, in front of the entire town.

"Or papooses," the young man said. "Or—"

She spun around to face the camera. "Or scalping?"

"Don't move!" the photographer said, and she stood, frozen by her mortification. The wait seemed interminable. She wanted to flee, to run into the hills and disappear until everyone who had witnessed her humiliation was dead and gone. Finally, the man emerged from beneath the black cloth. "Perfect!" he said. "Pack up, Elvin," he instructed his assistant. "I've got what I need."

"What do I do now?" Mary asked the assistant.

"You give us back that costume."

"What about the picture?"

"Some rich man back East is going to put it on his mantel and tell all his friends he saw a real Indian princess on a trip he never even took."

"But I'm not a princess."

"Now you are."

By the time Mary arrived home, Betsy had already told Doris the entire story. Doris held out her hand, and when Mary put the quarters in it, that same hand caught Mary by surprise and she cried out as the money clattered to the floor. For days afterward there was a mark on Mary's chin from where her mother had slapped her with the rough edges of the coins.

6.

A cricket was buried in the wall next to her bed. Mary heard the trilling as if the bug were inside her ear. The sod walls of the house were alive with worms and centipedes and colonies of ants, and after the sun went down and the world beyond the windows became black, it was sometimes possible for Mary to imagine that her family lived underground, and that the house was nothing but a cave dug into dirt. Her mother had left the door open to bring in the night air, and the locusts sang and bugs flew into the screen where they died. It was late October, but the summer heat had still not let up. Mary's senses flattened out during the day, numbing themselves to withstand the onslaught of sun and the squalls of hot wind that moved the dry dirt off the ground into busy whorls that just as quickly settled. She would discover grit in the most unlikely places—between the pages of a book or underneath the lid of a jar of tomatoes. But at night, her eyes and ears came alive, and distinct noises seemed menacing to her, as if they were warnings of some kind.

The cricket chirped, and she put her hand over the place on the wall where she thought it might be, as if the weight of her palm would comfort it. But the noise continued, and she realized the insect had probably become stuck and that it would stop its desperate song only when it died. She felt sorrow for the witless thing that was trying to attract a mate where no mate could ever find it. Doris would laugh at that, as she laughed about Mary's attachments to a particular chicken or a young tree. Doris warned her children of the dangers of lazy sentiments. She believed such softness would weaken them and make it impossible to survive in a place whose terms were not negotiable. Mary considered trying to dig the cricket out of its entrapment. But the wall was covered with insulating newsprint, and her mother would notice.

A candlestick sat on the floor by Mary's side of the bed. The wax had melted down to a nub, but the wick sustained a desultory flame. She held the candle close to the wall. She'd read nearly every inch of newsprint covering the house. Stories a decade old or more were glued next to pieces about the war in Europe, so that it seemed to Mary that time did not so much progress as circle back on itself, the past and present forming a different kind of relationship than *before* and *after*. She read about a famous tenor who performed Verdi in New York City in 1912. Mary's father had been alive then. He'd put her to sleep to the songs his Russian mother had sung to him, *Bayu-bayushki-bayu, ne lozhisya na krayu,* his breath pickled by drink. His voice, low and graveled like distant thunder, was comforting the way a storm could be before it arrived, making the world feel small, its boundaries defined by anticipation. She stared at the faded newspaper photo-graph of the portly singer, his fur coat barely closing around his gut, the flesh of his face forming a bloated cushion on which his features rested. She did not know who or what Verdi was, and the fact that there was no explanation made her aware that there were words and ideas meant only for people who already knew them. Lifting her candle higher, she scanned the advertisements directed toward fashionable city women who wore fox stoles with glass beads set into the eye sockets and claws still intact. She read news of the war dead, who were never named, as if one body were like any other. She wondered what happened to their names now that they were only labels for memories that would fade and disappear. Where her mother had recently patched a corner, Mary read local news about wheat prices and articles about the new tractors that could cut and thresh in a third of the time it took a man and a mule to do the job. Her mother claimed these machines were no better than your own two hands, but Mary knew that her mother decided something old was better than something new only to bury want. The newsprint was a savior on days when Mary had nothing to look forward to but hours of helping her mother with cooking or sewing or killing a chicken, or on nights like this when she could not sleep. But the news was a rebuke, too. She was as trapped as that cricket, stuck in this house filled with the sweet smell of rotting earth.

The bug's incessant bleating drilled into her head. She felt every cell of her body helplessly drawn into the compulsive task of paying attention, trying to find a rhythm and a meaning to every scritch and trill until her nerves were on fire. She stood up, careful not to jostle the bed and wake her sisters. She slipped on her boots then crossed the hardpack of the floor, holding her candle low so that the light would not rouse her brothers, who slept on the other side of the room, and so that it would not create shadows on the screen her mother placed around her own bed each night for privacy. Mary thought she could remember hearing that iron bed creak as the panels of muslin shifted, but she could not be sure what was true memory and what was just a story she'd invented to remind her that Doris had once had softness in her and might still, although she was loath to show it. Mary could no longer recall her father's face and could reconstruct it only by looking at her brothers and finding what was common to them, the way the corners of their mouths stretched downward, the shared cleft in the chin—features that were not her mother's but could not be random, showing up on both boys as they did.

A swarm of mosquitoes fluttered around the screen, attracted to the flame. Mary blew out the candle, waited for the bugs to fly away, and walked outside, careful not to let the door slam behind her. Her skin grew alert beneath her nightdress, her nipples hardening in the cooler temperature. The tops of her thighs rubbed smoothly against each other as she walked. It was awful, this wanting body of hers, horrible to always feel this urge to open, to unpeel, to expose hidden parts to light. She walked past the vegetable plot; past the shed, where the white leghorns shifted in their coop; past the barn, where Titus slept with the mules. The three cows stood in the corral near the hog pen, swaying gently against one another, their bells chiming lightly. She headed toward the dark line of red gum trees, the windbreak between her family's land and the Coins'. The trees' widespread branches overlapped, making them look like men with their arms around one another's shoulders, hunching drunkenly toward home.

The Coin house was dark; everyone would be sleeping, especially the two little children who were given a thimbleful of whiskey each night. The house was of a better grade than Mary's, built not of sod bricks but of cedarwood. It extended to four rooms and an attached mudroom, which they used as a larder. The floor was laid with raw planks of Ozark pine. The utilitarian furniture that suited a widower and his three motherless sons had been replaced with pieces Carlotta had brought to her marriage—a velvet love seat and a delicate rocking chair made of polished burled wood. The furniture was no match for the rough uses of a farmer. In three years the pieces had become gaunt and dulled like their owner.

Toby and his brothers worked the field for their father in exchange for room and board and the promise of inheriting the farm when the time came, but Carlotta wanted no part of another woman's family and demanded that the brothers live in the barn. They slept in the hayloft and took their meals outside when it was fair and with the horses and mules when it was not. When Mary worked for Mrs. Coin, she hardly saw Toby, who left for the fields before the first light and did not return until dark. But she searched him out in the bits and pieces of him that were left in the house. Dusting behind the beds, she found an old school ledger with his name marked on the cover in the careful, lip-bit print of a boy just learning to hold a pencil. There were half-empty medicine bottles stored in a box below the kitchen sink, which Mary imagined had been used to cure Toby's innumerable childhood illnesses. The amber-colored bottles bore the signature of Dr. Pallet, a man Doris considered a fool for the cathode-ray treatment he foisted on ignorant white women, telling them that a glowing tube inserted in private places would ease their monthly troubles when every Cherokee woman knew that black cohosh would do the trick.

Mary stood outside the barn, inhaling the sweet, overpowering scent of grass and manure and hide coming from the mucky stalls. She concentrated on Toby the way she concentrated on Carlotta's babies when she was called to take care of them, calming their tetchy cries by breathing slowly near their faces so they would catch her rhythm. *Come to me,* she thought, so hard that she could feel the words rise up in her throat and push at her lips. When she heard a cough and then movement, she tucked herself into the shadows of the roof's overhang, amazed by the power of her longing. Toby appeared at the door wearing nothing but long underwear bottoms. His chest was muscular but so thin as to look concave. Walking out into the open, he ran his hand through his hair, then reached into his long johns. A hard stream of piss arced into the air, followed by a mournful wheeze of gas. When he was done with his business, he continued to hold himself, moving his hand slowly and then faster. Mary no longer had the sensation that she was spying on him, and that he alone was the victim of the moment. Something more complicated was happening now. As Toby stroked himself, he leaned back and tilted his face to the night sky. With a strangled grunt, he was done. He tucked himself in and wiped his hand on his hip. He turned as if he was going to head back into the barn but stopped, facing her. She wanted to cry out, wave her arms, do anything to make the inevitable come more quickly. She would lose her job with Mrs. Coin; that was certain. She would have to explain everything to her mother, and her humiliation would be doubled. But Toby said nothing. Maybe he couldn't see her. Maybe he was walking in his sleep. Or perhaps she had been stupid and lucky at the same time, a combination her mother told her happened only once in a poor person's life, which was when they died. An abundance of dumb luck was for other people, Doris said, people whose paths had been smoothed before them by generations of dumb and lucky ancestors. Finally, Toby walked back into the barn. Mary ran home, across the line of gum trees, past the chicken coop and the pump, propelled by the withering knowledge of her cowardice: when the moment had come to claim what she wanted, she had only prayed to disappear.

7

Betsy's cough began with the first November frost as a minor irritation that embarrassed her during church sermons. By January, it had grown worse. Doris administered wormwood tea, but even that did not assure Betsy or anyone else a night of rest. Betsy's lips stayed dry no matter how much Mary swabbed them with a wet cloth, and she began to stoop all the time to try to lessen the effect of her spasms on the aching muscles of her chest. The girl's uppity expression became vague. Her eyes conveyed a rheumy abstraction uncharacteristic of the sister whom Mary had spent so much time despising for the fact that she never made their mother angry.

Doris did not credit illness. She had never paid much attention to the sniffles and small fevers of her children. She told them that they weren't sick when they complained that they were, as if disease were something you could decide about one way or another. She stood by the curative effects of disbelief. Doris made Betsy get out of bed each day along with the other children, put on her dress, her shoes, and her stockings, even though she was not allowed at school until her cough subsided. When Mary was not at the Coin farm helping with an increasingly pregnant and despondent Carlotta, and if the cold was not biting, Doris insisted she take Betsy with her when she did her chores. With each passing day, Betsy's ability to hold herself upright weakened in direct proportion to her mother's denial. If the girls were outside, Mary would put her arm around Betsy's shoulders and jostle her forward with her hip in case their mother happened to look out the window, so that she would not accuse them of lingering and avoiding work. Each evening, when Betsy sat at the table staring into her soup, Mary would wait until their mother's back was turned and dump some liquid onto the dirt floor where it would be quickly absorbed. The collusion brought the sisters closer, and every so often Mary was able to get a rise of laughter out of Betsy. Taking down the clothes from the line one morning, Mary wiggled a finger that had inadvertently poked through the flap at the front of her brother's drawers. Betsy covered her eyes in shock but she could not hide her broad grin.

During the third week of Betsy's illness, she took a turn. Her cheeks pinked and her sputum lost its greenish color. She managed to eat more of her food. Doris did not mention this recovery in the same way that she had not given words to the illness. One day, she simply stripped the girls' bed and washed the sheets, signaling that she was done with Betsy's illness and that everyone in the house ought to be as well. By this time, Mary's services were required each afternoon at the Coin farm to care for the younger children while Carlotta, hugely pregnant and full of associated miseries, rested. Carlotta was so impatient with the demands of being a farm wife that Mary imagined that her life in Tulsa must have consisted primarily of sitting in her once fancy chairs and drinking tea out of china cups while other people cooked her dinner or told her when to take her next breath. Carlotta insisted that her children dress in frilly white outfits meant for church even on regular days, and she alternately demanded that Mary take the children outside so that she could have some "time to think my own thoughts, for heaven's sake" and scolded Mary for letting them get dirty. She was quick to remind Mary that it was only due to her father's business misfortunes (gambling misfortunes, Mr. Coin was happy to clarify) that she had been passed over by more suitable men and was forced to marry a farmer. "I am not made for this" was her constant refrain as she stood in her fashionable dresses, which fell to her ankles in a hobble that made it impossible for her to take long strides and which, as the months passed, strained against her pregnancy. She kept a subscription to *Modern Priscilla,* and while Mary jostled and hushed the little ones and tried to content them with games of peekaboo, Carlotta studied the needlecraft magazine fiercely, as if she thought she could somehow enter the pictures and become a lady who had nothing better to do than stand around in a fancy gown while her fingers played with the lace veil of her hat. Whenever William Coin was in the house, an air of anxiety permeated, as if the rooms were holding their breath waiting for the inevitable explosion. That the children were too noisy and underfoot was his usual complaint. If he'd been in town drinking that day, the objection might become a sloppy, arm-swatting rage that often landed on Carlotta and occasionally on Mary if she was nearby. Mary knew the work she was really being paid for was to serve as a buffer between Mr. Coin's discontent and Carlotta's despair.

When Carlotta's labor finally commenced it was loud and angry. Like all things in her life, the pain was the fault of others—of her terrified and mewling children, of Mary, and of Mr. Coin, who fled the house as soon as the midwife arrived. The hours passed slowly, punctuated by Carlotta's violent moans. Mary played with the little girl and boy, and when night fell, she tried to put them to sleep by reciting the stories about Baba Yaga her father had told her, leaving out the part where the old witch ate the children. But each time they began to drop off, Carlotta would let loose with another howl, and they would startle and cry. Mary assured them that their mother didn't scream because she was sad but because she was happy, which was enough of a fairy tale to lure them back to sleep.

The baby was born long after midnight. Mr. Coin had returned by then, drunk but chastened by the birth and the officious midwife. He joined his wife in the bedroom and closed the door behind him. Mary heard laughter from within, a sound that made her feel embarrassed, the way it was humiliating to watch one person lie to another. After the midwife drove away in her car, Mary walked outside to the barn and pounded on the door. A few moments later, Toby appeared. His hair was tangled, and his face was imprinted with the crisscrossed pattern of loose hay.

"The baby came," she said.

"Is it alive?"

"So far."

"All right, then." He began to shut the barn door.

"Don't you people have manners?" she said.

"What's that?"

"It's the middle of the night. Somebody better take me home."

She was wrong about the hour. It was nearing dawn as Toby drove the wagon across the windbreak. The house seemed lifeless in the gray light. Her mother would be up soon to fix breakfast.

"It's a boy," Mary said as the cart bumped over the dirt clods. "In case you're interested."

"One more for him to knock around, I guess," he said.

"One more for her to dress up like a doll."

He laughed quietly. She had never heard his laugh, which was lower than his voice and smooth. She studied his hands as they gripped the leather reins and imagined them on her. The air tightened around them, and even though there was nothing strange about two people sharing a bench on a horse cart, she was conscious of every time her coat sleeve brushed against his. The arc of the sun surfaced above the fields, throwing the crop into momentary shadow before the light rose high enough to touch the braided tips of the new wheat, making them look like matches just catching fire. It was later than she thought, and yet there was no smoke from the chimney. Louise was not in the coop gathering eggs. Her brothers were not hitching the horse outside the barn.

"Oh!" She gasped, finally understanding the message hidden in all these clues.

A s the family hovered around Betsy's grave listening to the preacher, Mary thought her mother looked like a tree that had been struck by lightning. She seemed bent in some imperceptible way, as if she were blackened from the inside, her bones nothing more than char and deadness that would soon disintegrate into ash. Mary was aware that the rest of life was a feint, and that what people considered happiness was simply an avoidance of this grief.

Toby arrived one afternoon soon after the funeral to pay the Coin family's respects. He sat uncomfortably on a wooden chair that was too small for his lanky frame, eating the sympathy cake he had brought with him, the same one Carlotta had ordered Mary to bake a day earlier. Knowing that Carlotta would take credit, Mary had left out half the sugar and the butter, and the cake tasted like apple-flavored dirt. Still, Toby ate dutifully, moving his fork to his mouth in an unbroken rhythm. Doris's silence made any thought of small talk ridiculous, and the sound of Toby's fork on the plate and his swallowing noises were loud and uncomfortably intimate. When he was finished, he stood and set the plate on the table where it clattered awkwardly.

"They make you come here?" Mary said when she followed him outside.

"They didn't make me do anything."

The admission created a silence between them.

"I saw you that night," he said.

"I don't know what you're talking about," she said weakly.

"You could be arrested, sneaking around a person's house in the night like a common thief," he said.

"You're the one who should be thrown in jail. Doing what you did out there for God and everyone to see."

"Not everyone."

She could feel heat rise in her face. "Did you come here just to shame me?"

"Not really," he said.

8.

Tahlequah, Oklahoma, 1921

Not much of a day for marrying," Doris said, staring out at the low March sky, which threatened and then delivered heavy snow. "Too bad you couldn't wait for summer."

It was said without rancor. The bite had been taken out of her with Betsy's death the previous year. Sometimes Mary found her mother staring at the photo of the Cherokee Murderer, and Doris seemed to gaze beyond the plane of her father's picture, as if that dead man were just the start of a line of mistakes that all added up to her life. Doris continued to care for the house, to feed her remaining children and the hired man, to check on the health of the livestock and make sure that she got nothing less than top dollar for the crops. But every so often, Mary would catch her mother unawares, when Doris's obsidian eyes would shift about in a panic, as if she suddenly could not make sense of the people and animals who surrounded her.

Now she eyed the swell of Mary's stomach. From the back no one would have guessed Mary's condition—she was still as narrow as a teenage boy—but from head-on the situation was unmistakable: her belly sat in front of her like a balloon. One day Doris would give

Mary lanolin and instruct her to rub it on her skin to avoid the pale pleats that scored Doris's stomach and breasts. The next, she would look balefully at her daughter, shaking her head at the redundancy of life; Doris had held her firstborn in her arms and was already pregnant with the second when she wed Mary's father.

Mary had spent the last weeks collecting tins from neighbors and cutting them into thin strips. Now rollers hung off her head at uneven lengths so that she looked like a sadly decorated Christmas tree. She stepped into the dress she would be married in. It belonged to a cousin, a big girl with man-sized shoulders, but Doris figured correctly that with ten cents' worth of satin sash purchased from the Jew in town and tied high under Mary's bosom, the dress would do just fine, and the excess material would take care of her round middle. Mother-of-pearl buttons ran down the front of the dress from the neck to the waist, and when Mary finished fastening them, she looked at herself in the small mirror that hung above the dresser, leaning down to catch her image where the glass was pure.

"You look like a child in that thing," Doris said. "You are a child."

"What's the difference what age I'm at?" Mary said. "Whether it happens now or next year or five years from now. Making babies is what you raised me for."

"You're not a cow," Doris said.

"I sure look like one in this dress," Mary said. She thought she saw a trace of her mother's smile, but it vanished before Mary could draw it out. "What else am I raised for, then?" she said. "What am I supposed to be?"

"You'll know who you are when you start losing things," Doris said.

L ater that morning, Mary stood before the preacher and watched as a bead of sweat made its way down Toby's neck and stained the collar of his shirt. She remembered when they had lain at the edge of a field, surrounded by the tall grasses, the pink flowers from a dogwood drifting down onto their heads and arms. Toby had parted the two halves of her unbuttoned blouse and had traced spirals on her small breasts. He told her stories of his illnesses, which seemed to Mary to behave like impulsive little boys flinging rocks through windows, unaware of the havoc they produced. There were middle-of-the-night spiking temperatures and emergency trips into town to wake Dr. Pallet who had nothing to offer Toby's parents other than the advice to wait it out, meaning that Toby would either live or die and there wasn't much anybody could do about it either way. He suffered bouts of asthma where he could not get his breath. When his mother had been alive, she made him stay inside the house on the worst days. She would sit him over a pan of hot water and drape a towel over his head to open up his lungs. His father complained that she was turning him into a weakling and a shirker. After she died and Toby was pulled from school, he worked harder than his older brothers to prove his father wrong. To deal with the breathing problems, his father gave him a pack of Dr. Batty's Asthma Cigarettes, and when those expensive smokes ran out, he gave him Chesterfields. Mary thought Toby's childhood sickness accounted for the way he could seem like a ghost. He did not so much enter a room as appear in it, and she always had the unnerving sensation that he had been watching her for longer than she realized. When Toby slipped the band around her finger and put his lips to hers, his fevered breath went into her throat like liquor. She felt faint and sagged against him. He drew her close so that they were suddenly in an embrace that was much more private than either had intended, and the preacher reminded them that they were in God's house.

They stayed in the hotel in town that night, an extravagance that Toby insisted on. She was relieved since she was not ready to occupy the windowless larder that Carlotta Coin had finally agreed to set aside for the new couple. At first, Carlotta complained about Toby and Mary taking over the room, but when she realized that she could insist that Mr. Coin buy the four-door icebox with the nickel-plated hasps she'd had her eye on in the Sears catalog, she calmed down. Mary watched as Toby laid the dollar bills on the hotel registry desk one by one as if he had never handled money before. Watching the way he moved his lips as he carefully counted made her feel that she and Toby were too young and foolish to be paying for the hotel room and marrying and having a child. She waited for the clerk to laugh at them and tell them to get on home and stop playing dress-up games, but all he did was take the money and hand Toby a room key attached to a ball weight. It was this heavy object, more than any vow she had spoken that day, that caused Mary to fully understand what she had done.

The hotel room had a provisional quality meant for grain salesmen and the occasional traveling lawyer, not for anybody looking to have an experience to be remembered down through the years, one that might be called into service when a reinforced binding was required to hold a marriage together. The bed sagged. There was no rug to warm bare feet. Mary realized that far from feeling as though she and Toby were now joined as one, she felt more separate from him than ever. She was struck by the oddness of him, of any single human being, and all the ways he differed from her. She realized that she would now spend years noticing or deciding not to notice the strangeness of him, the way he held his head at a slight angle as if he were hard of hearing, or the way his teeth scraped against his fork when he ate, or how he cleared his nose in the morning. She didn't know if she could stand a lifetime of this kind of attention. It was an intimacy that would have the opposite effect: it would demand that she acknowledge her isolation and then somehow overcome it each day, every minute of every single day.

She clutched the small bag that held her nightdress and a change of clothes and watched while Toby closed and locked the door, then laid the heavy key on the night table. She panicked and tried to imagine how long it would take her to get that key in her hand, fit it into the lock, and run away. She could tell by the high color of his cheeks that his fever was still up, but when she asked him if he wanted to lie down or if she ought to get him a glass of water from the sink at the end of the hall, he only smiled in the sober way she had become familiar with that suggested he had long ago come to terms with the difficulties of his life.

"Take off your dress," he said, removing his coat and his jacket and hanging them over the bedpost. "I want to see you."

"You've seen me," she said. "I've got the belly to prove it." But this was not the truth. All the times they had been together there was always a slip hiked over a hip, underwear strangling her ankles, his belt buckle digging into her stomach. It had been easy in barns or fields or up in the hills, hidden by brambles so a stranger passing by would think the rustling was only a woodchuck or a vole. It had been easy with clothes on.

"Come on, honey," he said gently. He began to unbutton his shirt.

"If you want a show you can go down the street," she said, holding her coat closed around her. "I'm sure those ladies can take care of you just fine."

He said nothing and continued to undress. The muscles of his chest and arms moved smoothly against one another as he folded his shirt and placed it on the foot of the bed. He took off his pants and his socks and his drawers until he was naked. A train sounded in the distance. She looked out the window.

"What are you thinking about?" he said.

"I'm thinking about that train."

"What about it?"

"About what it would be like to be on that train going far, far away."

"Am I on it with you?"

"No," she said. She began to cry. "Aw, shit."

"Take off your clothes, Mary."

She took off her coat and laid it on the bed. Then she reached around and loosened the sash of her dress and watched it fall to the floor. She undid the button at her throat and then moved to the next, her hands working awkwardly. The dress was so big that the material slipped easily off her hips.

"And that," he said, motioning to her slip.

She reached down and picked up the hem and drew the material over her belly, her shoulders, and finally her head. She was embarrassed by her sagging and discolored undergarments. She crossed her arms over her bare breasts. "They'll do for milking," she said.

"Don't do that."

"Do what?"

"Make a joke out of us."

When she was finally naked, his body reacted to hers. He was her husband. She repeated the word to herself, trying to give it sense.

"Mary Coin," he said.

"Don't call me that."

"It's who you are."

She felt his gaze go right through her as if she were transparent. She was nobody yet. How could he not see that?

They lived in the larder as man and wife, but Carlotta still expected Mary to clean and sew and help with the three children. The only difference was that now that Mary was part of the family, there was no reason for Carlotta to pay her. One morning, lifting an armful of sodden clothing from the washing bucket, Mary felt something tear at her gut. She dropped the clothes. She was only in her seventh month.

"You move around and that baby will fall right out of you," her mother told her when she entered the house and took one look at her daughter's pale complexion. Carlotta had sent for Doris, not wanting to be part of early or dead babies. Doris, having taken stock of the silly furnishings in the Coin house, knew the woman would be useless. She instructed Mary to lie in bed or stretch out on Carlotta's love seat for the remaining two months of her term. Mary saw Carlotta begin to protest the loss of her maid and the ill use of her sofa, but a sharp look from Doris quieted her. The crisis of Mary's early labor and the useless frippery of the house where her daughter now lived resurrected some aspect of Doris's character, and Mary was relieved to see her mother grow mean and resourceful. Doris handed a pouch of herbs to Carlotta, ordering the dumbstruck woman to boil them and dose Mary morning and night.

Mary kept to her bed for much of the day. When she needed to get away from the house and breathe air that was not scented with the rancid smell of the cow chips Carlotta used to heat the stove, she would take a chair outside. On an unseasonably hot day, she sat on the porch and stared at the field, shielding her eyes from the sun's glare. Toby's brothers had both married and started families in the last year. Fed up with their father's penury and enticed by the newspaper advertisements promising jobs for men with grit and a sense of adventure, they had left for the sawmills of California. Toby worked the field alone now, a speck in the distance. The wheat had just begun to come in but it was stunted and patchy, and there was talk among the farmers of a dry season. But Toby refused to walk away from all the years of his hard labor and prove his father right. That night, he returned from the field, his skin so dry that it hurt him to chew his food. He lay in bed while Mary rubbed chicken fat into his chapped hands. She could sense by the way he flexed his fingers when she was done that he was proud of his body's ability to withstand such daily torment. He told her about things he'd seen that day—a red-tailed hawk soaring high, a pair of sand vipers twisting together in a mating dance. The light from a candle threw a shadow on the wall, and as he talked he interlaced his hands to show her the sinuous love duet of the deadly snakes.

When Mary began her eighth month, William Coin sold the farm.

"And the house, too?"she asked stupidly when Toby told her, but the news had made her instantly think of her coming child.

"Everything." He explained that his father had found an ignorant buyer just off a train from the East who knew nothing about patterns of drought. William Coin got the man drunk on whiskey and made the sale.

That night, Mary woke from an uncomfortable sleep. She reached for Toby, but he was not beside her.

"You're not supposed to be on your feet," he said when she found him at the edge of the field. Her feet were swollen in her shoes, and even the short distance she'd walked made her belly twinge. They stood side by side, facing the distant hills.

"I couldn't make it work," he said finally, his voice thick. He squatted down and scooped up a handful of dry dirt. "This land needed more than I knew how to do for it."

"You act like it's a person," she said.

"It's a person to me. I was here every day of my life. I talked to it." He laughed at himself, shaking his head. "Like the way you do a cow. I used to tell it what I wanted it to do."

"I married a crazy man."

"You married a farmer."

A week later, Mary watched as Toby packed everything they owned into the trunk of the old Hudson his father had grudgingly agreed to give him. Before heading west, they stopped off to see Doris.

"Hope that baby don't come in the car," she said.

"It won't," Mary said.

"Because you say so?"

"My baby minds me. Just like I minded you."

Doris let out a small grunt of disbelief. She took down the photograph of Mary's grandfather from its place on the wall. "Nobody else ever took notice of this but you," she said, putting it in Mary's hand.

"We'll come back, Mama."

"No, you won't," Doris said. "But there's nothing I can do about that, either."

As they drove away from the farms and lost sight of the familiar land, Mary closed her eyes. She was seventeen. Her husband was twenty-three. Living under the thumb of Carlotta Coin, she had felt too old, as if she had already lived through any newness her life might offer and the years would only present repetition. Now, trying to find a comfortable position on the barely cushioned seat, the few belongings of her life rattling against the walls of the trunk, she felt in possession of nothing and everything at the same time.

Three and a half weeks later, Mary stood up from the pallet where she and Toby slept, her body instantly alert as if she sensed an intruder. She looked for her mother sleeping behind the muslin curtain, and then for her sister, Louise, but they weren't there. Slowly, her confusion cleared and she remembered that she was in the cabin that Toby's brother Robert leased in a place called Millwood, in the state of California. She was living in a makeshift town as unfamiliar to her as those cities and countries she read about on the newspaper covering the walls of her mother's house. Mary realized there was no one breaking into the tiny home. The intruder was inside her. She stood and knocked her huge stomach against a wall as she felt her way through the dark, tiptoeing past Robert and Sarah and their little daughter and out the door.

The collection of buildings that made up the sawmill stood out against the dark night, shapes lit vaguely by a cloud-covered moon. During the day, the mill was an excitement of sound and energy— the grunts and squeals of the saws, the thick plumes of exhaust from the boiler, the heavy thunk of wood planks being stacked on top of one another, and above that din, the shouts of men. But she preferred the town as it was now—still and silent and expectant. She felt the edges of herself against the air, the weight pressing down on her crotch. She sensed the lumbering trees crawling up the Sierran foot-hills in the distance and the dark river that flowed nearby. She wanted to set this moment in amber so that she would remember it forever: she was living at the farthest edge of the country, surrounded by trees with trunks nearly as big as houses. Imagine, Mary thought, as if she were talking to her child—a land of storybook trees, and the rumor of an ocean after which there was a million miles of nothing and then the rest of the world.

A rush of warm liquid ran down between her legs. She reacted as if she were jumping out of the way of a glass of spilled milk. But there was no *out of the way*. She was in the way of what was happening to her. She *was* what was happening to her. She had not been able to envision this event when her mother described it, couldn't think how water that could slip through your fingers could also break as if it were a solid thing. Her organs knotted and seized with a force that made her whimper. She knew her body was beyond her now, and she could only stand by helplessly while it did what it would do. Carlotta Coin had taken a powerful dose of castor oil before she'd had her baby so that she would not soil herself in front of the midwife. This fussiness seemed laughable to Mary now. The contraction subsided, leaving only a backache, the dull throb she felt at the beginning of her monthly bleeding. She walked to the edge of the river where logs floated, indolently knocking against one another. Her feet slid over the lichen-covered rocks until her toes touched the cold water. A heron flew down and settled itself elegantly on the opposite bank. A second contraction gathered in her pelvis. She knew she ought to go back to the cottage and wake Sarah, who had birthed other babies in the camp. But she was not ready yet. She walked along the edge of the river until she found a place where the logs drifted apart from one another and she could see her dark form reflected in the water. Shedding her nightdress, she turned to the side and marveled at the incredible shape of her body.

"Mary?"

Toby was behind her, holding out a blanket. "What are you doing?"

"Look at me!" she said. It was the way she used to call her mother to watch her while she did a headstand or balanced on a fence, needing

Doris's gaze to make the moment real, to stamp it into history. "You'd like it if I spent my days watching you breathe," Doris used to say in exasperation whenever she was called, but she always came, her hands covered in flour or stained with pig guts, sanctioning these small victories with a terse nod.

"Are you dreaming, Mary?" Toby said.

"Yes!" she said. "No!" She laughed.

And at that moment, she felt as if a hand had reached up into her in order to turn her inside out. "Mama!" she cried.

9

B y 1925, there were three pulling at Mary's skirts, prancing circles around her, beating on her with their fists, and letting loose their pinched and plaintive whines because they wanted her attention while she was kneading dough for bread, silently reciting her mother's lesson: *Three, not two.* She stopped what she was doing for a moment and watched the torrent of Ellie, Trevor and June, mystified that she could have released so much sheer energy into the world. She and Toby had their own cabin now in exchange for a healthy cut of Toby's wages. The mill buildings sat down by the river, but the family cabins and the bunkhouse for the single men were tucked into the foot of the forested hills. To have a home of her own, to not be living under the gaze and judgment of another woman, was something Mary took pleasure in each day, no matter that the cabin's single window was cracked or that the walls were so haphazardly joined that the house was filled with flies during the day and with cold mountain air at night. She looked out of the window toward the mill. The men were too distant to make out, but every once in a while, she might see a lean, taut figure walking from one building to another with a board slung across one shoulder, and she would know that it was Toby. She did not see him now, but she noticed a crowd beginning to gather around the tracks that ran down from the mountain. A train whistled in the distance.

"Mama! Mama!" Trevor grabbed her hand and pulled. Ellie was already out the door, even though Mary had warned her not to leave the house without asking for permission. Aside from foreign men coming and going, there were other dangers at the mill. Children had been injured playing on unstable piles of wood. A boy had drowned trying to balance on a floating log. Trevor slipped his hand from hers and raced after his sister. June sat on the floor stacking the wooden blocks Toby had made, and Mary quickly picked her up, knowing that cunning Ellie would draw her trusting brother into some kind of trouble. Sure enough, as soon as Mary reached the tracks, she saw that Ellie had dared Trevor to see if he was brave enough to stand on an iron rail as the train pounded closer. Mary pulled him to safety and gave Ellie a smack on her arm.

The children fell into a reverent silence as the big Shay engine appeared trailing flatcars loaded with freshly cut logs. The train slowed to a stop, exhaling its vaporous breath. Then came the hurly-burly of activity as the men sprang into action, shouting orders as the long arm of the unloader began to sweep the logs off the train. The sugar pine and white fir and giant sequoia logs came out of the forest like newly injured soldiers, their sheared ends exposed and raw-looking. The wounds touched Mary in a way she knew was foolish, but she could not stop thinking of the trees as amputations. She imagined the stumps standing alone, filled with longing for their missing parts. She touched her stomach. Of course this was the next baby talking. Pregnancy made her wide open. She might be unaccountably moved by the sight of a dog crouched to do its business, the pathetic wobble of its hind legs, the still vacancy of its watery eyes. A month earlier, a crazed hummingbird had spent four days tapping on the window of the cabin. Ellie, an easily enraged girl of four, was furious with the bird and pounded her fist against the window, but Toby grabbed her hands and explained that something had gone wrong with the bird's mind and that it was mistaking the glass window for a tree. To Mary, the misperception seemed not crazy, only human, and she had wept.

The children did not want to go indoors. Mary took them to see the planer where their uncle Levi smoothed the newly cut planks so that running your hand along an edge you could mistake the wood for silk. The air was tangy with the wet, warm scent of cut logs combined with the acrid smell of the steam boiler that Uncle Robert tended. Four men carried a pale, debarked log to the long timber mill where Toby worked the spinning blade of the circular saw. Trevor begged Mary to let him see his father run the giant machine, but Toby had forbidden the family to watch him work. "I forget myself at the sight of you," he told Mary one night when they were in bed. He lay behind her, his mouth moving against her damp neck, his hand draped over her stomach, massaging the tight drum of her stretched skin. "You don't want a one-armed husband, do you?"

Mary coaxed the children back to the cabin with a promise to round up the cousins for a game of Run, Sheep, Run. While Ellie took charge, designating herself as fox king, Mary thought back to when she was a girl and she and Betsy had traced the attributes of their imagined husbands in the dust outside the chicken coop, erasing the words with their shoes as quickly as they wrote them so that Doris would not witness their silliness. Betsy had been practical: no farting, no burping, no false teeth. Now, as Mary sat outside the cabin on a three-legged stool trying to occupy June, she remembered her list: good singer, small ears, doesn't kick dogs. She realized that in some ways she had never been without Toby. She had conjured him, and then he had appeared as if her writing had released a messenger into the wind who had gone looking for those words as they existed in a single man. And here he was: handsome, kind, enough of a singer to soothe a miserable baby or make them all laugh when he struggled for the high notes of the birthday song, which he insisted on singing at top voice, holding the special boy or girl in his arms and waltzing them into their next year.

She wondered what Betsy's life would have been like if she had lived. She would probably not be spitting out children like water-melon pits. There were ways to avoid it. Mary's sisters-in-law swore by Lysol douches and had only two children each. Mary knew that Toby could arrange things so that he was outside of her. But when it got to that point, she could not bear the feeling of his withdrawal and she would hold him tightly. And these children—she could not imagine them before they came into being and now she could not imagine them not existing. Ellie, with her bossiness and her discontent; Trevor, with his wide eyes, who took everything his sister and his cousins told him on faith, a sweet gullibility that had landed him a quarter-mile away from the mill one day, searching for hidden treasure; June, who, though still a baby, would pitch a fit if Mary tried to get her into a dress. It was true Mary had cried when she fell pregnant for the fourth time. And there had been the undisguised fear in Toby's eyes the night she admitted it to him. But when she looked at her children playing their game of chase, she thought of them as a fist held up to fate. She'd met women at the mill who spoke longingly about the places they had come from—Arkansas, Kentucky, or Oklahoma. But Mary knew these women were reveling not so much in memories of a place as in recollections of their girlhoods, when there had been few demands upon their time and none on their bodies. She listened to their complaints, knowing that for her, each new child settling onto her breast for the first time was a confirmation, another puzzle piece locking into place.

Each afternoon, when Toby came home from his shift, he would hold June in his arms while Trevor and Ellie tried to claim his attention. For the first hour, his face assumed a gentle, uncomprehending smile because his ears were numbed deaf by the clang and roar of the mill's machinery. But once he got his hearing back, and the older children had gone off to their games or chores, he'd talk to June about what he'd seen during the day, about how it had taken twenty Chinese men to roll a huge section of red fir to the head saw, or how a sawyer had to be sent home because he was drunk on the job. He'd ask the little girl's opinion about whether their mother was the prettiest woman in the town or only the most beautiful.

"You're a fool for talking sense to a baby," Mary said two months later, after Della was born and he was regaling the infant with tales of his day.

"A baby understands everything right from the start," he told her, staring down at the bundle of blanket that was his newest daughter.

Each year found him holding on to the seat of a borrowed bicycle while Ellie, then Trevor, then each child in turn veered and fell, scraped and cried. Intimate with shame, Toby whispered instructions into their ears so as not to humiliate them in front of the neighbor children who had come out of their homes to watch. When June took off without a hitch as if she had been born to ride a bicycle, Toby stood back and watched her disappear down the road.

"There she goes," he said.

Mary heard the tremble in his voice and saw his jaw working against his feelings. "She's free now," she said, linking her arm through his.

"No such thing," he said.

B y the time their fifth child, Ray, was born, there were rumors from the east of men jumping out of the windows of tall buildings. Orders were down at the mill, and there was not enough demand for the foreman to run double shifts. Toby was one of the first to be let go, then Robert. Levi could get more cuts out of a log than any other man on the crew, and the boss offered to keep him. The brothers knew it would be harder for three men arriving at a new place looking for work than it would be for one, or even two, but having survived their father, they had a notion of their collective endurance, and they determined to stay together.

They moved from one mill to the next for as long as the work held out, and each new job was of a shorter duration than the one that preceded it. Mary learned how to quickly make a home. Familiarity had less to do with knowing your neighbors than it did with the unchanging seating arrangement at the dinner table and not letting up on chores out of sympathy for a tired or displaced child. Ellie and Trevor went to school the first day they arrived at a new town whether or not they were frightened by strange children and a stern teacher. June and Della did the small chores even if their efforts to carry laundry in from the line resulted in clean sheets being dragged through the mud. Ray was wakeful and demanded Mary's constant attention, which made her days all the more exhausting, having to hold him and charm him while she worked.

When James came three years later, they were living in Wilseyville. Luckily, he was a sleepy baby who was content to rest in his basket and stare up at the passing shadows on the ceiling. Each year brought fewer jobs and lower wages for the jobs Toby did manage to get, but Mary kept up her system, believing that order would see them through. She made sure her children knew the alphabet and how to write their names before they entered school so that they would not be held up to ridicule. There was a limit to what she could teach them, and when Ellie wanted to know what was in the Milky Way that made it milky, or how to spell the word *determination*, Mary silently cursed her mother even as she threw ash into pond water and watched the dirt sink to the bottom of the washtub, a trick Doris had taught her when the laundry had to get done and the well was dry.

"Mama, look! Mama, look!" Della cried out. "Look what we did!"

Watch me breathe, Mary thought, standing at the open door of the cabin, watching June and Della dress empty soda bottles in paper outfits. *Well, of course.*

After work dried up in Wilseyville, they moved to Calpine, and one town was not unlike the other: a company store, a post office, a schoolhouse—which was often nothing more than a room attached to the back of the store—a few churches, more saloons. The sharp, medicinal scent of the hillsides in the morning and then again at night. The particular damp cold that existed summer and winter because of the nearby forests. The feeling Mary had of being small. She had grown up accustomed to seeing great distances, so that if she ever needed to find a wandering cow, all she had to do was stand outside and turn in a circle and there it would be, set against the wide, white sky as if she had drawn a cow on a piece of paper. Now the cloak of the forest made her feel as hidden as the animals that haunted the undergrowth.

There was a movie theater in Jerseydale, and although they hardly had the money for it, Mary insisted that the children go to a show. When she was a girl, a movie had been projected on a sheet hung on the wall of the bank building in Tahlequah. A storm was brewing and the sheet was not secured properly, and when the wind kicked up, the images rolled and dipped over the billowing material until the screen became hopelessly tangled. Now, sitting in the dark theater, Mary watched how her children's initial awe was overtaken by helpless laughter. She remembered that long-ago night when the storm finally overtook the town and the projector was shut down, when everything that went wrong was a heart-quickening reminder that the world was not always what you expected it to be. Outside the theater, Trevor took to walking like the funnyman, toppling down the street with duck's feet and twirling a stick as if it were the actor's cane until he swacked Ellie in the face and opened a cut across her cheek.

"Will I have a scar forever?" Ellie wailed.

"Probably," Mary said, as she stanched the blood with the hem of her dress.

"I'll never be pretty," Ellie said, tears and snot clogging her words.

"Why do you need to be pretty when beautiful will do?"

"But I'm not beautiful, Mama! You're the beautiful one."

That night, music coming out of a saloon wound its way through the town and into the open window of the Coin house. Toby pulled Mary to him. The children sat on the beds and watched their parents dance in slow circles. Mary closed her eyes and let herself be carried away until she forgot where she was. When she opened them, she saw the small, grave faces of her children as they studied this performance of love, and she felt the immensity of her responsibility.

A sound exploded the stillness of the night. In her broken sleep, Mary thought the moon had fallen out of the sky and landed on her house. She screamed herself into consciousness to find that Toby was already up and dressed and pushing her shoes toward her. The windows glowed orange.

Outside was a confusion of flames and the crack and thunder of collapsing buildings. The steam boiler was a fountain of sparks. She and the children ran away from the mill while Toby rushed down to the river where men filled washbasins and buckets and even empty suitcases with water to throw on the fire. But one building caught and then another until the whole mill was engulfed. The smoke rolled through the town in great, eye-stinging billows. Mary pulled James's nightshirt off him and bit into the material, tearing off strips, which she fastened around the children's heads. Ellie refused her blindfold. Mary wished Ellie was like the others, content not to have to look at the destruction, but she knew the girl was too sharp to be tricked into ignorance by a simple eyeshade. She and Ellie watched as the bunkhouses caught, one after another, the final one igniting the cabins, which went down like dominoes. The walls of their house collapsed in what seemed an almost gentle curtsy.

A spark landed ten feet in front of Mary. She stared, unable to move, as it ignited a tuft of grass. The flame caught a bush and burned through the dry leaves in seconds, until what remained was only a skeleton of branches, which was then engulfed as well. She was entranced by the sudden beauty of the thing turned back on itself; time reversed. She thought about her grandfather who had walked calmly out of his double-walled bunker toward the guns that killed him. She thought, too, of her father in his coffin, Betsy in hers. All those deaths. It seemed only right that hers would be added to the list. What had her mother said? A person couldn't be dumb and lucky twice.

"Mama!" Ellie screamed.

A low-lying snake of fire slithered toward Mary and her children. She handed the baby to Ellie and pitched herself front-first on top of the flames until she suffocated them. And then all the women nearby began to do the same, racing to wherever they saw trouble begin and throwing themselves on top of that trouble before it did them and their children in.

The next day, Mary walked through the rubble of their destroyed house. They had never had anything but now they had nothing. Mary realized how different those two conditions were. A wind stirred the ashes on the ground. The air smelled of the turned-fruit odor of burned things. She searched for salvage while Toby packed what little there was—a few pots, a fork and spoon, the clawed end of a rake—in the Hudson, which had survived the blaze. A cough had settled into his chest from inhaling the smoke, a hard, dry sound that cut through the churchlike quiet that pervaded the town as people moved about, dazed by the quick violence that had been done to them. Toby lit cigarette after cigarette to open his lungs.

Mary thought she ought to cry, but crying seemed too general a reaction for the specific disaster that had occurred and the set of ramifications that unfurled from it. When she had gone to the Jew's store in Tahlequah before the wedding, she'd watched as he flicked the spool and the grosgrain ribbon fell to the floor in lazy figure eights. This was her future now, she thought. A flick of the wrist, a wayward spark, and the spool unwound.

10.

Corcoran, California, 1931

Mary had never thought much about her hands, but sometimes, when she needed to take a moment to ease out her back or to stare down the row of cotton to judge how long it would take her to work her way to the water wagon, she would catch sight of her ripped and ragged cuticles. She felt great sadness for them, as if they were not part of her but were some children she'd seen by the side of the road, waiting on parents who were, in turn, waiting on luck. She and Toby had each bought a pair of gloves, but it was impossible to pick the cotton off the stalks quickly enough with the thick material making their fingers clumsy. It was harder still to crack open the bolls to get at the late yield. She took a scissors to the gloves' fingertips. But even with this adjustment, the bulky protection was a hindrance.

They had driven down from the lumber mills where even in the heat of summer you had only to walk into a nearby grove to find some shade and where newly fallen pine needles provided a cool carpet for your feet. They'd worked wherever there was work, picking peaches, drying grapes for raisins, packing tomatoes. Now they were in a flat, inland town where there were few trees to break up the relentless glare of the sun. When they'd first arrived, Mary's eyes feasted on the even rows of white cotton, which seemed as soft and inviting as new snowfall and reminded her so much of home. But that siren loveliness revealed itself to be nothing more than a ruse, a pretty girl whose looks rope you in to a life of demand and perpetual inadequacy. Mary hated the cotton.

They lived at the pickers' camp in a tent Toby had bought with the last of his mill wages. Ellie, Trevor, June, and Della attended a school held in a shed where there were few books and pencils. The teacher was a picker's wife who said she'd been a schoolmistress in Arkansas, although Ellie complained her spelling was worse than half the kids'. While Mary worked the rows, James and Ray played alongside her. She told them to stay close, but inevitably Ray would run off, embroiled in some imaginary battle, slashing the air with a stick, and Mary would have to chase after him, losing valuable minutes and the pennies those minutes represented. Toby worked two rows over so that he would not have to mind the children and at least one of them would make a full day's wage. Mary tried to ignore his constant coughing, willing herself not to look up every time she heard his wet heaves and the sound of him hawking phlegm out of his lungs. But when he had a fit so powerful that it brought him to his knees, she went to him. She looked for the water truck, but there was at least a quarter mile of picking before they would reach the end of the row and Toby could get a drink. On particularly hot days, there were pickers who fainted, but the foreman would sooner replace a dehydrated worker than drive the water truck into the field and remove a crew's incentive to make it from one end of a row to the other. Toby recovered and told Mary she should get back to work. If she was caught dawdling, the foreman would yank her off the line. They had to work as fast and as hard as they could if they were to make enough that week to barely feed everyone. Mary returned to her row and adjusted her long white sack around her chest. A shout went out, and she heard the buzzing of a duster. She told James and Ray to put their heads down just as the plane flew low over the field, but James, entranced, stared up at the plane while Ray whooped and twirled in the falling powder. Mary bent over to fill her bag once more.

There was blood on Toby's pillow each morning. He could no longer hold his body upright much less haul a sack of cotton down a line or climb up the ladder onto the truck bed to weigh his take. Mary went to the fields each day and tried to increase her pace, but the sun and the heat and the problem of the little boys made that impossible. At night, she began to look away when Toby undressed because the sickness had ruined his body. His back was a rutted map of disks and bone. His skin was sallow and loose.

When a doctor finally visited the camp, he held a handkerchief over his nose and mouth and diagnosed tuberculosis. Mary spent the nights awake, holding Toby while he coughed, laying water-soaked rags over his forehead, cleaning the blood off his lips and chin. When the fever gripped him, she pressed her body on top of his to stop the shaking.

"What do I do? Tell me what I should do?" she said to him toward the end of the second week of fevers, when Trevor begged her to let him quit school and work in the fields to make up for his father's lost pay. Toby's eyes fluttered open. She wanted not just an answer for the present crisis but for every problem that might arise in a lifetime. When should Ellie be allowed to walk out with a boy? If June refused to put on a dress, should they just let her wear her brother's overalls? For the rest of her life? But how would she get a husband? She knew the questions were unimportant, and yet she realized that if she could manage to ask them all, the answers would amount to her and Toby's life together. If they could make every future decision ahead of time then it would be as if she had gotten all of him.

"James will be fine, don't you think?" she said one night as she knelt by his side, trying to cool his fever with a moist cloth. "I know he doesn't talk and people think he's not right. But there's a light in his eyes." Toby's breathing was so shallow that she had to put her ear to his mouth to know he was still with her.

"Fine," he mumbled, barely moving his cracked lips.

"He might be the smartest of them all. You don't have to be a loud-mouth to have a brain inside your head." She was babbling now, but she feared that if she stopped talking, he would forget to take his next breath. "Once James starts in school, we won't let him stop. Don't you think that's right? But if he wants to work like his brothers, then . . ."

"Fine," Toby exhaled.

"Which is it?" she said desperately. "Fine, he stays in school, or fine, he works? You have to tell me, Toby. You have to tell me right now."

His eyes drifted to the right. She turned to see what had caught his attention. When she looked back at his face, he was gone.

H e's been taken away," she said to her children, who were waiting outside the tent. And then she changed what she'd said, because right at that moment she stopped believing in God. "He's left us," she said. And that was not right, either, because it suggested that he had made a decision to abandon them. She sat down on the ground and let the children come to her. "We're alone," she told them. This is what it all amounted to in the end. Toby's brothers and their wives had been generous through the worst of the illness, making up for Toby's lost earnings by giving Mary extra potatoes or carrots, a bone for her soup. But they could not continue to cut into their own supplies to keep her and her kids going. And she couldn't bear to stay with them. It was too difficult to watch Robert's and Levi's children run to greet their fathers when the day was done. It made her angry to see gestures of affection pass between the couples or to lie in bed and hear the low murmurs and laughter coming from their nearby tents. And although they would never say as much, Mary's sisters-in-law counted Toby's death as her failure just as they thought her six children were her folly. Mary knew it was the meanness of the times that made them think this way. Each day, the camps were flooded with families, and there was not enough work to go around. People became competitive in all sorts of ways, as if a better dress or a laughing child or a living husband was proof that a person would make it.

Mary sustained the weight of sorrow that would descend on her freshly each morning when she woke up and had to remind herself all over again that her husband was gone. But what terrified her most was that she knew that what had happened to her had not really happened yet. Right now there was only waking and feeding and sending the big children to school and taking the little ones into the field and wiping sweat and filling a bag and standing on lines. A larger grief was still out there, waiting to overtake her when she was not looking. She had to be careful.

On the day they left the camp, she sat behind the wheel of the Hudson while the children settled themselves in their seats. Ellie took James on her lap, and Trevor took Ray on his.

"Tell me," Mary said, beginning the ritual she followed whenever they left a place.

"Lureen. She was nice," Ellie said, about a girl she'd met in the camp who had given her a bracelet made of red beads.

"Trevor?"

"I liked it when you let me work in the fields," he said softly.

June said she liked the schoolteacher, and Ellie said the schoolteacher was dumb as a turkey and didn't even know the times tables, but Mary shushed her. Della liked the new comb Mary had bought at the company store after she'd broken the old one trying to get a rat's nest out of June's hair. Ray said he liked the day Mary had found a swimming hole, and James said, "Everthin'," and they all laughed because everything was a lot for a boy who didn't say much.

"So that's how we'll remember Corcoran," Mary said, because it was important that a place stay in the mind as somewhere worthwhile.

"What about you, Mama?" June said.

"I'll remember the smell of sage. Some nights, after you all were asleep, I went outside and stood there and just . . . sucked it in."

"I'll remember Daddy," Ellie said.

Mary looked out the dusty windshield at the road ahead that narrowed and then disappeared over a small rise.

"Where will we go now?" Della said.

A man had told Mary that there were farms hiring to the east. Not cotton, she'd said. Anything but cotton. "There," she said now, gesturing with her chin.

"What's there?" Ellie said.

"Oranges."

Vera

11.

San Francisco, California, 1920

I t was a costume party to celebrate—well, no one really knew what
was being celebrated. The loose collection of artists and poets and
self-styled arbiters of taste Vera had befriended since moving to the
city often seemed to spend more time playing than working, the parties themselves being a form of *tableaux vivants*. Vera was meant to
wear something outrageous—she knew one man who was coming as
an orangutan, pink buttocks and all—but what she decided at the last
moment was that she would dress like the society women she had
begun to photograph in her studio on Sutter Street. These ladies were
much derided by Vera's crowd as boringly conventional and cor-
rupted by wealth, but they were the lifeblood of her work, and she
was frankly mesmerized by the ease with which they moved through
their lives. There was always a chauffeur-driven car following slowly
behind them as they shopped in case they became too tired to walk.
Tea in silver pots stood at the ready should they need refreshment. If
it began to rain, an umbrella would suddenly appear, held aloft by a
maid. Vera was devoted to these women because they paid for her
photographic services and recommended her to their friends and provided her with a living enough to rent a studio and eat out at a café on

Saturday nights if she stuck to home-cooked boiled onions and beef on weekdays. But there was something ineffable about them that captivated her beyond her economic pragmatism. Even the ones who had long noses or large foreheads held themselves as though these were the very attributes that defined elegance. The women knew they were rare prizes, and Vera had created a career of sorts taking photographs to prove them right. It would be interesting to try on that entitlement—at least for an evening.

Vera borrowed a dress from Mimi Van Der Mere, the daughter of a railroad manufacturer. A young woman besotted with all things artistic, Mimi was delighted when her photographer came up with the "marvelous idea" of dressing like her, her merriment a sure signal that she knew Vera could never pull off such a transformation. *My photographer.* Vera's clients often used the possessive—*my driver, my girl at Gump's*—as if Vera were one of a retinue, and, in fact, she supposed she was.

She stood in front of the mirror in the attic room she rented on Gough Street. The black velvet dress fell into a dangerous V down her back. The material gathered in loose folds over her chest and then again at her hips, ending mid-calf. It was the fashion of the day that Vera generally avoided, not because she was prudish but because she did not like to show her bum leg. But tonight she would be brave. Her limp could enhance the costume. It would lend her the air of insouciance she admired in her coterie of friends who walked down the street as if they had just been pulled from bed. Mimi had also lent her a string of false pearls, which Vera arranged as a choker with the extra length dangling down her back. When she moved, the pearls tapped against her spine like a man's searching fingers, a sensation that kept her focused on her purpose: she wanted sex. She was twenty years old, new to San Francisco, and her inexperience made her feel alone among people for whom sex was casual currency. Her little skirmish in New York—Bremmer fondling her while she painted photographs in his uptown studio, staining lips and blueing eyes—had been enough to convince her that her withered leg did not make her hideous to a man in need. But Bremmer was old, his kisses dry and craven. Even if she had been willing, he hadn't had the courage to do more than reach underneath her blouse while she rubbed her hips against him. Their encounter ended abruptly, with him slinking back into the studio, his hands covering the stain on the front of his trousers.

She reconsidered the party. It was foolish to think she could hide in an elegant outfit when her history was as plain as her plain face and was apparent to anyone the moment they saw her take a step. She could summon the exact details of her illness and its aftermath as if it had all just happened yesterday and not thirteen years before, when she was Vera Duerr, a seven-year-old in Hoboken, New Jersey. She'd woken in the center of night, feeling like she was balanced perfectly between dreaming and wakefulness. Her brother, Leon, was asleep in the bed next to hers; she could hear his adenoidal breathing, the slurp and effort of it. There was another person in the room, too, a dark shape by the closet door. She was not frightened the way she was when she had nightmares about kidnappers, only curious that a stranger should be standing near her closet, as if he wanted something to wear. She had always known there was a shadow world of ghosts and goblins and witches, known that life was made of things you could see and things that you couldn't, like your thoughts or wind. These ideas often absorbed her, and Miss Hildt had sent a note home saying that if Vera didn't learn to pay attention she would have to repeat the second grade. Her mother had given her a stinging *potch* on the fanny and said dreams were for sleep. Period. *Das Ende der Geschichte*. The end of the story.

Maybe the ghost wanted Vera's favorite dotted-Swiss dress with the embroidery around the hemline or maybe her new boater. She would tell the ghost that it was all right to take her nice things because her mother had told her that this was what Christian people did to let other Christian people know they weren't stingy. Vera started to speak, but she could not make her mouth form the words. When she tried to get out of bed, pain shot up her leg and spread through her chest, knocking her back against her mattress. And then the ghost disappeared, and there was her mother leaning over her, a mess of un-brushed hair and dangling hairpins, her eyes wide and her mouth pale and loose without the slash of lip rouge from the lovely enamel pot Vera coveted that her mother had promised to give her when it was finally empty.

"Shhh, shhh," her mother insisted, shaking Vera by the shoul-ders. She put her lips to Vera's forehead. "She's burning up!" she cried, and then she was screaming in German the way she did when-ever she argued with Vera's father about why he was home so late, and why he forgot to bring the fish she asked for, and then Leon woke up and started crying. Next, Vera was in her father's arms as he ran down the stairs of the apartment building. He wore only his night-shirt, even though it was winter, and she worried that maybe someone would see his thin, hairy legs and would laugh at him. Everything was odd and wrong and painful at the same time: to be awake at night when she had school the next day, to be visited by a ghost who wanted her dresses, to be sweating even though it was such a cold January that her mother had bought her a new pair of boots lined with lamb's wool, which cost too much and her mother didn't want to hear about it if Vera's toes started to push against the front of the boots before the winter was out because money didn't grow on trees. And now her father was running down the street with her in his arms, wearing his white nightshirt, which had once risen up when he reached for something on a high kitchen shelf, and she had caught a glimpse of his pink, wormy thing.

When she woke up the first time, she was alone. The unfamiliar room was a bright constellation of rectangles and squares that floated together and then drifted apart. She closed her eyes and slipped back into a dream of drowning. She struggled, working her hands against the heavy water and kicking her feet, only her legs wouldn't move and she was pulled down again. She pumped her arms until she could see daylight glimmering above the surface of the water, and then down again she went until she could not hold her breath any longer. She had to let it out and she knew she would die when she did, and then her head finally broke through, and she gasped. She was awake. Drowning had been a dream of a strange and terrifying place, but now she was in an even stranger place where the light was dirty. She thought someone should wash it and make it clean because her mother said a filthy home was a sign of being poor. And they were not poor. Vera's father had his own law office with Uncle Henrick. They had a maid named Grace who knew how to train Vera's hair into sausage curls.

She slept again, and when she woke there was no light at all. She reached out her hand but could not see her fingers. When she tried to get out of the bed, she felt as if someone had driven a needle into her knee. She collapsed onto the cold floor, her right leg crumpling beneath her as if it were made of sand.

The ward was full, but the nurses kept the curtains pulled around each bed so that Vera could not see the other children. She tried not to be frightened by their cries, or by the angry-sounding bells, or the fast patter of feet in the hallway as they drew close, a signal that something was terribly wrong, maybe terribly wrong with her. Nurses came and went, their bright, serious eyes glittering like her mother's jet necklace. Some were funny, their worn-out jokes blurry beneath their hygiene masks: *Why will you never starve in a desert? Because you can always eat the sand which is there!* She would smile and laugh, though it hurt to do those things. It hurt to eat and sometimes to breathe. Occasionally a nurse would sit in the chair by Vera's bed and complain about her sore feet or about her useless husband while she glanced worriedly over her shoulder because, she would admit with a wink and a whisper, she was playing hooky. Each morning, white-coated doctors drew aside the curtain around Vera's bed with a terrible whoosh, stared at her wordlessly, then turned toward one another and nodded while they muttered under their breath like the flock of albino pigeons, with their pink blind eyes, that pecked at the concrete of the schoolyard. When the nurses bathed and dressed her, Vera felt like someone was peeling off her skin. When she cried, the ladies would say, "Now, now," or warn her not to disturb the other children.

"There's no use you polios being in hospital," Nurse Peg said, two weeks after Vera had been admitted. "There's nothing we can do for you." Peg was the fattest and meanest of the nurses. She never played hooky and never told jokes. She changed Vera's sheets while Vera was still in bed because it took less time that way, even though being rolled back and forth was so painful that Vera had to stuff the corner of her pillow into her mouth so that she would not scream. Nasty as she was, though, Nurse Peg had a lovely way of talking, like the Irish who cleaned the gutters outside Vera's building on Washington Street, calling back and forth to the firemen at the station house in their spongy accents.

"Will my leg work again?" Vera asked.

"If you're lucky. But for sure you'll be lame, so," Peg said, as she stripped Vera's bed out from under her, the faster to make it up for the next patient. As she fussed and huffed, her wool stockings rubbed against each other, *shhh, shhh,* like Vera's mother, trying to hush the polio away as if it were an irritating child. *Lame.* It was a sweet word, buoyant like a runaway kite rising at an angle into the sky. As Vera waited for her father to come and collect her, she thought of the illustrations in *The Pied Piper of Hamelin* that showed children marching after the man in his ragged cloak. One little boy followed at a distance, slowed by a dragging leg, his crutch made of a split branch tucked under his arm. *For sure you'll be lame, so.*

Vera took the trolley to Russian Hill. The party was already dense and loud with the giddy hysteria manufactured for such evenings. She felt her hips slide against the cool material of her gown as she steadied herself in the high-heeled shoes she was so unused to wearing. It was impossible for her to believe that every man and woman in the room was not studying her, judging her wanting, pathetic, even. But of course they weren't looking at her when there were so many more magnetic, more dangerously self-aware people who did not wonder if they looked good in their outfits because there was no question that they did. She circulated among musicians she knew who were dressed as Indian pashas, and sculptors balancing high wigs and sporting beauty marks as though they were members of the Sun King's court. Women who otherwise spent hours in cafés complaining about the denigration of their sex were dressed like Elizabethan whores, their breasts pouring out of tight bodices. A Russian violinist wore nothing but a diaper and sucked on a baby bottle filled with vodka. A poetess was dressed in rags because, she said, no one paid anything for poetry.

"I cannot make out your getup at all." The voice behind Vera spoke in a slow, western slur. She turned and looked up—way up— at a tall man whose black cape was slung rakishly over one shoulder, revealing a frayed red lining. He held a cane that had a carved horse's head for a handle. His long, smooth fingers folded over the nostrils in a way that made the horse seem alive and his mastery of it a matter of course. Her eyes traveled down the length of the stick until they reached the points of the man's tooled boots. A cowboy? A magician? The man's face was narrow, his nose beaked, and he stooped slightly, a habit, she imagined, formed from a lifetime of leaning down to listen to a shorter world. He sported a horseshoe mustache along with the louche demeanor that she had become accustomed to in her new acquaintances in the city.

She hadn't thought of how to describe her costume. A privileged socialite? An elegant doyenne of the arts? She stumbled as she tried to think of the bon mot that would suggest that she was aware of the irony and wit of her choice, but what would come so easily to the sophisticates in the room eluded her. "I'm . . . I'm beautiful," she said. She was immediately embarrassed by what this man would obviously perceive as the radical difference between her pronouncement and the reality of her short, squarish body and what her mother had always assured her was a strong face.

"That's no costume at all," he said.

"You haven't seen me without it."

"I will."

"Clever," she said. She had only begun to be comfortable with this kind of flirtatious gamesmanship. Each time she saw a woman arrive at the party with one man and leave with another, or with two others, or nuzzling another woman's throat like a cat, she could not help but be mildly shocked. Casual infidelities and assignations were justified by theories of ownership or collectivism, or by the writings of an obscure French philosopher someone had met when he'd last been in Paris. It seemed that everyone was always going to or return- ing from Paris. She was not sure how anyone in this perpetually impoverished group could afford the trip, but the act of being about to go abroad seemed to be enough to suggest intellectual vigor and sexual adventurousness.

"Where is your magician's hat?" she said. "Where is your rabbit?"

"Excuse me?"

"You look like Houdini."

"I'm a painter."

"That's not much of a disguise in this crowd."

"What's your name?"

"Vera. Vera Dare." She had christened herself with this new last name after leaving the East, hoping that the alias would prove transformative.

"Well, Miss Vera Dare, I don't believe in disguises," he said. His height, combined with the intensity of his gaze and his unnervingly direct manner, gave her the impression that she was a mouse being sized up by a hovering owl.

When she woke up the next morning, she was alone. She had not noticed the painter's room the night before, but now she saw the canvases leaning against a small dresser. A few cups and dishes lay piled in a sink. The wood floor was covered with splotches of ocher and red and green paint. Light filtered through the scrim of dust on the bare window. The room was chilly the way so many in San Francisco were, as if the city's builders hadn't quite reckoned with the fact that this was not the sunny California of advertisements and postcards but a town whose skies could be as heavily lidded and grim as any in the East. Vera stood, wrapping a sheet around her. She was never comfortable naked; even when she was by herself she did not like to confront the disfiguring effects of her disease—her unmuscled leg that turned in on itself enough to be noticeable. *For sure you'll be lame, so.* She caught her face in the small mirror that hung above the painter's sink. Her party makeup was smeared, her eyes sunken, her pores large. Whatever allure she had convinced herself she possessed the night before had vanished. The effects of too many glasses of wine and the man's confident insistence on how the evening would go had made her forget herself, but now the memory of her illness's aftermath came at her like a warning finger.

Once she was brought home from the hospital, her mother spent an hour each day roughly kneading Vera's leg, pulling her foot and holding it to the count of twenty because it no longer sat perpendicular to her calf but drooped like a lady's limp handshake. Vera would bite her lips against the pain, but sometimes the agony was too much and she cried and begged her mother to stop.

"You don't want to be a cripple all your life," her mother said, pronouncing the word in the German: *Krüppel,* the guttural slosh in the back of her throat making Vera's debility more horrifying than it already was. She thought about the white-haired, legless veteran who sat on the sidewalk outside Ackermann's butcher shop begging passersby to drop money into his outstretched union cap. *He* was a cripple. Was she just like that man now?

Months later, she tried to get used to the new brace that forced her to swing her leg around in a semicircle in order to take a step forward. The straps chafed the back of her knee. The brace ran underneath her boot so that, even if she wore dark stockings to try to conceal the leather straps that crossed her calf, it was impossible to hide the shiny metal. When she walked down the street, people stared as if she had a dead rat attached to her leg and they gave her a wide berth. When her family took strolls in the spring sun and they passed a neighbor, her mother would hold her breath as if she could somehow trick those disapproving gossips into not realizing she was there, the way Vera and Leon held their breath when they ran past a graveyard. Vera had been a sociable girl up until then, a ringleader of neighborhood make-believe who always claimed the best parts—Mother, Queen, Prima Ballerina. But when she returned to school the following September, held back a grade since she'd missed most of the previous year, she was aware of the children staring at her as she struggled up the stairs or made her slow way down a hall, careful not to get knocked over by students racing to beat the school bell. She sat alone during yard games because, despite the fact that her father took her to the park on weekends and let her win at footraces and praised her speed, there was no possibility of letting her schoolmates see the way she had to lurch forward with her good leg, then make a little hop while hiking up her hip so that her braced foot could clear the ground. Each morning, she woke with a terrible stomachache. She and Leon would walk half the distance to school before she had to vomit onto the dirt surrounding one of the sidewalk trees or into a garbage can. If she got any sick on her clothing, she would spend the first class in the bathroom, scrubbing her blouse or running her sticky braids underneath the sink faucet. Tardy. Tardy. Tardy. The report card was filled with red X's.

"You cannot be mediocre," her mother said when Vera brought the offending document home. "You most of all."

And five years later, when she was twelve: "You see, *mein Kind*, you can't make mistakes. You have to be better than everyone else." Vera had gotten her first period during history class. She had spent the rest of the school day with her coat tied around her waist to cover the faint brown stain on the back of her dress. The rag she wore inside her underclothes only exaggerated her limp, and she knew that everyone at school could tell. They were watching her, always watching.

All except her father. Only when she was with him did she forget what she had become. He called her *meine Schnöheit, meine Liebe,* my princess. The evenings were spent catering to his playful whims— *Erika, einen Kaffee, bitte,* he'd call out to Vera's mother. *Leon, a unicorn, please! Vera, I'll have another pot of gold!* And when she was thirteen and learned to cook *Pfefferpotthast* and *rohe Kartoffelknödel,* she sat stiffly attentive at the dinner table, staring at her father while he ate. Her lips twitched between a smile and a nervous frown as he made the humming sounds that always accompanied his eating. He was unembarrassed by this noise just as he was not ashamed to belch or pick out the food that had become stuck between his teeth with his long pinkie nail, and Vera knew that these bodily gestures were simply forms of appreciation and that she had done well.

And then, one day, he simply did not come home from his law office, and she never saw him again. There were rumors that he and his brother had absconded with their clients' money and taken a boat back to Europe. There was talk of a woman, a *Polish* woman, a detail that, more than policemen knocking on the apartment door, proved his criminality as far as the neighbors were concerned. All Vera knew for certain was that the only person in the world who found her beautiful had gone away forever.

She leaned over the painter's sink and splashed her cheeks with cold water. Discovering a tin of toothpowder, she rubbed some on her teeth with her finger. She imagined that her lover would return, perhaps with a loaf of bread and a pot of jam. She brushed her fingers through her hair, then sat on a chair and arranged the sheet so it fell alluringly off her shoulders. *No.* It would be better if he found her in bed, waiting and willing. She settled herself on the lumpy mattress the way she sometimes had her clients pose, an arm languidly resting above her head, the other hand grazing her chest. She drifted off into the fantasy of the coming reunion. When she woke an hour later, she was still holding this position and she was still alone. She dressed quickly, feeling foolish for imagining that the night meant more than it did. He had kissed her lazy foot, stroked her atrophied calf. But she was nothing more than an oddity for him, a New Jersey provincial with a limp. A story to tell his worldly friends. She hurried home in her velvet dress, clutching her pearls in one hand, feeling cold and obvious among the warmly dressed Sunday strollers and the families heading to church.

I t was the arrogant scrape of his boots outside her studio door a week later that let her know instantly that it was he. She was preparing bills for her clients and she did not greet him when he entered. He wandered through the small room, taking note of the chaise, the throw pillows, the empty birdcage, and the urn filled with pussy willows she had arranged for an older client who was coming later in the day, a Levi Strauss cousin who would not be comfortable with Vera's preferred background of wall and corner, simple geometries of light. He leaned in to study the paintings and the small sculptures she had received in exchange for photographing other artists and their work.

"Do you know what I missed most about you?" he said, finally.

The low growl of his voice reached down into her belly. "I was not aware that you missed anything," she said, keeping her eyes on her papers.

"That place below your shoulder, that—" Now he was next to her, his finger tracing the declivity between her clavicle and her neck.

She stood, upsetting the papers on her desk. "Do you make a habit of this?" she said.

"Of what?"

"Of luring women to your room and then disappearing?"

He laughed. "I didn't disappear. And as far as I remember, I didn't lure."

"I'm accustomed to breakfast."

"Accustomed?"

She felt her face heat up. Had her virginity been that obvious? She had checked the sheets before she left. There was no blood. "I want you to leave now," she said, humiliated.

"I don't think that's what you want at all." That uncanny frankness she had been unmanned by at the party, as if they were not involved in a flirtation but were negotiating the terms of a contract.

"You know my mind better than I do, I suppose," she said.

"You only have to watch a body to know what the mind is about."

She looked down at her leg, wished she hadn't.

"You are glorious," he said.

12

E verett Makin was twenty years older than she and a foot taller. They walked the streets of the city, he in his cape, she in fanciful hats and thrifty ensembles meant to resemble what she imagined the women in Picasso's studio might wear—flamenco skirts and long scarves. He traveled to Utah and Arizona and returned with canvases filled with deserts and mountains, men on horseback, and steady-eyed Indians draped in blankets. "Two weeks," he told her whenever he left for one of his painting trips, although he was often gone a month or more. She was lonely during his absences. Lying in her bed at night, unable to sleep, she would convince herself that he had finally become disgusted by her physical imperfection and that he would not return. And yet, impossibly, he always did. And once with a ring, a simple band of silver carved with a Navajo design of an eagle. They hired a minister and invited two friends to her studio to witness the marriage. She lit a fire in the fireplace and tossed hot coals under the samovar. The steam and the threadbare Oriental rug and the ruby-red velvet of the chaise created the atmosphere of a seraglio that seemed to augur adventure and magic. Vera sent a telegram to her

mother: I HAVE MARRIED A PAINTER. The response: A PAINTER? STOP.
OF HOUSES? STOP.

N o nurses! No doctors! No white coats!" Everett said, and so, in
1924, Philip was born in the bedroom of their tiny house on
Russian Hill. Vera's labor began in the middle of a rainstorm that
lashed the windows and didn't let up for twelve hours, a hoary oper-
atic accompaniment to her pain. Everett, so enamored with the wild,
wanted his child born to it, and Vera agreed to squat in a doorway
and deliver her baby into his big hands while he coaxed her as he
might a mare in foal.

When it was over, she lay on the floor in a daze, as Everett gently
cleaned the screaming curd-covered baby. Watching him handle the
infant so expertly, she felt a familiar isolation and feared that she
would be unequal to her robust husband and her perfectly formed
child. But after an initial burst of caretaking enthusiasm, Everett
declared that it was time for him to head to Nevada for a painting
trip, and she was drawn into the baby's need in a way that dissolved her insecurities. She liked the feeling of nursing Philip, how
it made her woozy and pleasantly vacant, the way time seemed to
stretch beyond its limits while he sucked. She was surprised and
proud that she was a capable mother and that despite her impediment
she could carry and diaper and feed and bounce just like all the other
mothers who huffed strollers up and down the steep hills or along the
paths of Golden Gate Park.

As soon as Philip could walk, Everett took the family on camping trips to the Sierras where they would pitch a tent by a river, strip off their clothes and fall into the cold, clear water as if it was a nutrient they had been deprived of. Everett called Vera his "city lass" when she was frightened by a noise in the night, or when she followed Philip around the campsite, worried he might eat a dangerous berry. But she could build a fire and cook a meal on it, and she learned to identify animals from their scat. She was pleased that he wanted her to share this world he so often escaped to and that she could conquer it despite her silly walk and her customary comforts. Their second boy, Miller, was conceived in a field of tangerine-colored wind poppies. Nine months later, when her pains began at a campsite along the shore of the American River, he might have been born in the wilderness, too, if Everett had gotten his way. But she refused to give birth in a tent while her three-year-old was free to wander near the treacherous rapids. They hurried home, the car jerking and shuddering along the rough mountain roads so furiously that she spent the entire ride certain that a strong jolt would knock the baby out of her. Once back at the house, she lay in bed waiting for the contractions to speed up. Exhausted by the drive and the worry, she fell asleep. When she woke, it was already morning. Her contractions were gone and she was still pregnant. The doctor called it false labor, and it went on this way for two weeks.

"No baby?" Everett would say when they woke each morning after a night of writhing pain.

"No baby," she'd say, and get up to face another day of waddling after Philip and attempting to get work done in her studio.

"Hello in there," Everett said one night, lying between her legs and calling toward the unborn child. "Come on out. We're not monsters."

When their laughter subsided, she was in tears.

"Now, what's this?" Everett said.

"Maybe the baby doesn't want to be born."

"What are you talking about?"

"Maybe it knows it will be like me."

"And what's so wrong with you?"

"This!" she said, pointing at her withered calf.

"The child can't catch a sickness you had twenty years ago."

"But maybe—" She finally admitted to him her deepest and most humiliating secret: that her disfigurement did not feel like the effect of a disease but like something inbred, some cellular fault that she could pass on to a child. The sense of impairment was as much of a trait as her hazel eyes or her light brown hair. Philip was unscathed, but it was impossible to believe that she would not be punished for imagining that she could have the love of a handsome, gregarious man and that she could give birth to two unblemished babies.

"What if we do wrong by these children?" she said.

"But we absolutely will! Just like your father did wrong by you and probably his father did wrong by him for one reason or another. That's the way of it, darling. That's the fun of it."

"Tell it to this baby," she said, somehow reassured by Everett's irrepressible confidence.

"THAT'S THE FUN OF IT!" he yelled between her legs.

Twenty-four hours later, Vera squatted and Everett made a perfect catch. Miller was born.

13.

San Francisco, California, 1930

The young woman sat on the chaise and struck a pose. She folded her slender hands and placed them awkwardly in her lap where they looked more like plaster casts of hands than like useful appendages. She held her mouth in a strange, pursed attitude. Vera knew at once that she had practiced posing in front of a mirror, and that this was an expression she thought made her seem alluring or intelligent or mysterious or all three. The somber mood following the stock market disaster of the previous year was evident in the dour grays and browns Vera noticed all about her on the street. Still, women like Eleanor Cunningham, this inheritor of a brass fittings fortune, continued to arrive at Vera's studio in their new Parisian wardrobes. These fashionable ladies had given up the drop-waist dresses of the last decade, and Eleanor wore a smartly slim coral-colored evening gown that hugged her lithe figure. She fooled with the cloth flower affixed to her shoulder, unhappy with the lie of its petals. She was nervous. She was lovely, too, with a delicate nose and pale skin and gray eyes that rose up at the corners like a Siamese cat's.

"I don't really know what you want me to do," Eleanor said. Her voice was high and feathery. She was not a woman whose future would require her to be loud. The photograph was being made to mark her twenty-first birthday.

"There's no 'should' about it, really," Vera said. She was tired. Everett had been gone a month on a painting trip to Arizona, or was it Nevada?—she couldn't remember what he'd told her. She'd stopped listening when he announced his departures because it didn't matter where he went, only that he was gone. And she didn't want to argue with him about the point of making more and more art when his paintings were not selling. They could barely afford their nursemaid, and if one of them had to stay home to mind the children, Vera felt it ought to be the person who was not making money. Philip and Miller, six and three, had both come down with colds. They were especially clingy this morning when she had left the house. They had cried and fought their way out of Mei Ling's arms and run down the rickety wooden porch steps, begging Vera not to leave. She had to peel them off her and finally use harsh words, which she regretted all the way to the studio. She had little patience for a rich girl with a lack of confidence.

"Just get comfortable," Vera said.

Eleanor tried to arrange herself in a suggestion of relaxation, but the result was a pose as stiff as a child awaiting a doctor's visit.

"You know," Vera said, "I have to fiddle with my camera for a moment. Why don't you just have a look around the studio?" The young woman needed distraction so that she would forget herself. Otherwise, they'd be here all day.

Eleanor studied the objects on the shelves, the Mexican Day of the Dead diorama made out of painted bread dough, the porcelain dolls Vera had begun to collect, all of them castoffs missing a leg or an arm or an eye so that they were both pathetic and ghoulish in ways that always provoked conversation. Eleanor picked up a nude African figurine with an erect and outsized phallus.

"Can you imagine?" Vera said.

Eleanor giggled. The strategy was working. Her shoulders had softened. Her face was unguarded and alive. She put the statue back in its place and leaned in to look at a small painting of a horse that Everett had made for Vera when they first began seeing each other.

"Your husband is the painter," Eleanor said, as if she were informing Vera of the fact.

"I believe that's true," Vera said.

"He came to our home once. My father admires him very much."

"Your father admires him, but you don't?"

"Oh," Eleanor said, her face coloring. "I didn't mean—"

"I'm teasing," Vera said.

The gaffe made Eleanor become self-conscious again. Vera walked across the studio pretending she needed something on her desk, exaggerating her limp. Often, if she accentuated the imperfection, she could put her more anxious clients at ease. She did not stand in judgment of them; after all, she was nothing but a cripple.

"What are you fond of?" Vera said casually.

"What do you mean?" Eleanor said.

"Well, I like cherries, for instance. I live for cherries, actually. Each year I wait, and when they come in season I go mad for them. And you know the thing about a cherry is that the taste is so elusive. You can't quite fix on it when you bite into one. It's a mischievous fruit, the cherry. And so you have to have another and another and—"

"Nectarines," Eleanor cut in.

"It's like biting into a sunset."

"Yes," Eleanor said excitedly, "exactly."

"And?"

Eleanor looked up expectantly.

"What else do you like?"

"I like to have my hair brushed," the girl said slowly. "I would like to have my hair brushed by a man."

Something loosened in her. She was no longer a daughter of wealth entering society, trained to organize lunches and servants and to join charity clubs. She was another kind of girl coming into her womanhood, someone who was a mystery to herself. Vera stood behind her camera.

"Sit down," she said. "Let's begin."

Later, after Eleanor was driven back to Pacific Heights in her chauffeured car, Vera stayed at the studio to develop the film. She knew she ought to go home to the children, but there was something about the girl that compelled her—those gray eyes, the way she tilted her head back against the bare wall as if she intuited how the light would bisect her face.

As Vera worked, she was snagged by a feeling of melancholy. Sometimes the darkroom brought back memories of her grandmother's cramped apartment where Vera and Leon and their mother had moved once it became clear that Vera's father would not return. Grossmutter Bauer was a tiny, bitter woman who dressed in full mourning even though her husband had been dead for ten years.

She kept the curtains of her home drawn in order to protect her heavy mahogany furniture. The sepulchral atmosphere of the apartment made Vera feel as if she and her family had been buried alive.

Vera's mother found work at a library across the river in Manhattan and she transferred Vera to a school on Hester Street. No one knew Vera there, and she was relieved not to have to suffer the excruciation of being a castoff in a place where she had once belonged. She was a legitimate outsider now, a gentile from New Jersey, and it was no longer her limp or a brace that marked her, or the fact that her father had disappeared or that her family was suddenly poor. At the new school she was different because she celebrated Christmas and did not understand when the children said *Du bist a narish goy*, or they thought she didn't understand, anyway. At the end of each school day, Vera had to wait two hours before she met her mother in front of the library for the ferry ride across the Hudson. Rather than use the time to study in order to keep up with the impossibly bright students, she wandered the streets of the Lower East Side, looking for her father.

At first he appeared to her as familiar backs: broad, dark-coated, slightly hunched. She followed these men from Hester to Forsyth to Grand. She grew more certain with each passing block that the peculiar cant of the shoulders or the bristles of hair furring the nape of a neck were proof. Her heart sped up as she dared to run closer, anticipating the moment when she would see her father's face. He would smile with relief as though he had found her after months of searching. But when she was finally confronted with a stranger's expression of curiosity or irritation, she felt a terrible emptiness, as if there was nothing inside her but dark wind. An awful sensation, but one that became familiar and even comforting just the way it was pleasant to wiggle a bad tooth and prick the nerve to a bearable degree of pain. She had forgotten the sound of her father's voice, his laugh, the noise of him gargling and spitting into the sink after brushing his teeth, and this renewable heartbreak was now the only feeling she could associate with him.

As she searched, she discovered the city. She watched the fishmongers on Fulton Street flinging one slick body on top of another, rubbing their cold noses with the heel of a hand and then digging into a vat to bring out another black-eyed tuna or a waggling crab. On Gansevoort Street, men in bloody aprons slung carcasses from trucks onto loading docks. One afternoon, she stood at the window of a pharmacy, transfixed by the glass eyes on display along with the kidney-shaped bowls the nurses had slipped underneath her when she'd been in the hospital. As she stared at these strange and familiar things, she realized that no one standing where she stood would see in these objects exactly what she saw. The uniqueness of her vision was at once obvious and astonishing. No one saw what she did when she looked at the garbage floating in the East River, the torn boxes and bird feathers spinning lazily in the current as if they were vacationers at Maxwell Place Beach lolling in the shallows. No one saw how a seabird diving toward the water paralleled exactly the harplike cables of the Brooklyn Bridge. For the first time, her singularity, the fact that she felt different from every person she knew, made sense to her, and she realized that no matter where she went in the world, she would have a point of view that no one else could possibly have. Her mother's pathetic euphemism to explain her husband's abandonment: *He's gone away.* Now Vera began to imagine places she knew only by name: Singapore. Chicago. Rome. She had never before considered that *away* could be a place, a possible destination for a person like her father or like her. She saw herself on the streets of exotic cities, an emptiness in the shape of a girl.

The following day, as Vera hung the new prints to dry, she heard a familiar slide of boots and then felt his hands around her waist. All the exhaustion and resentment she had built up over the last few weeks of Everett's absence, all the pretense of being fine with the terms of her marriage to a man who required solitude and distance for his work and whose idea of family was just that: an idea—all of this dissolved. He was back. He smelled of saddle leather and dust and pine.

"To what do I owe this pleasure?" she said, not turning to greet him, unwilling to betray her need and give him her full attention quite yet.

"I wasn't working well. I thought there might be some other work I could do better." He stood behind her and lifted his hands until they cupped her breasts.

"Ah," she said. "So I'm supposed to stop my work, which is going well, by the way, because your work is not?"

"Who is that thing?" he said, leaning forward to get a closer look at the prints.

"That thing is Eleanor Cunningham, who says she met you."

"Don't remember."

"She says her daddy's a big admirer."

"Hmm. Maybe I ought to try to remember the ones whose daddies admire me."

"Especially if they have money."

"Funny eyes," he said, unbuttoning Vera's shirt.

"She wants a man to brush her hair," she said.

14

E leanor Cunningham was the first. Or the first Vera knew about, anyway. Vera learned about the affair from whispers at parties, saw the news in people's glances whenever Everett's name came up. Finally, one of her clients told her that she'd seen Everett with a young lady, the daughter of the brass man, and, oh, wasn't that the same girl? The one in the photograph hanging in Vera's studio? Vera pretended not to be bothered, suggesting that the relationship was merely the natural outgrowth of Everett's business dealings with the father—Walter Cunningham was a big supporter of Everett's, she'd explain. Wasn't that wonderful? All the while she kept up this inane patter, something disintegrated inside her.

She found out that there had been others: a young acolyte whom he professed to have taught life drawing, a Mexican painter, a woman notorious for her affairs with well-known married men. Vera knew that if she said anything to him about his infidelities there would be no argument, no begging for forgiveness. He would simply leave. The marriage was based on the condition of his coming and going, which she now understood was not simply a matter of geography. He still made love to her, still called her his "city lass," but his affection made his deceit even more distressing. There were weeks when he was around the house so much and was so attentive to her and the boys that she could almost convince herself that all that she'd heard was ungrounded gossip. But then, when he climbed on top of her in bed, she would smell something foreign on his skin.

T he boys are too cooped up in this city," she announced one day, when Everett informed her of his decision to spend the autumn months in Taos. "We ought to go with you. They need to run around."

"You won't get any arguments from me," he said, surprising her. She watched him warily as he took the boys on his lap, spread out a map, and showed them the route they would take across the country. To their overlapping and excited questions he answered yes, they could ride a horse and no, they could not shoot a bear, but if they were very, very good he would let them hold a real gun. The aspects of his character that drew Vera to him—his remote self-sufficiency, his unapologetic maleness—were the same ones that had hurt her, and yet she could not stop herself from believing that he wanted his family with him. He wanted her with him.

The drive to New Mexico was tedious. The boys fought. Everett drove with one hand and reached behind him with the other to swat whomever he could reach. The resulting silence would last only until Miller crossed the imaginary line Philip had declared as the boundary between their separate backseat kingdoms, and the fighting would begin again. Vera spent most of the trip turned around in her seat, singing "Tea for Two" or playing slap-hand with one boy and then the other. When she drove, Everett slept, untroubled by the boys' complaints. Often she wanted to wake him and tell him to entertain the children with a cowboy story. But then he would demand to drive and he was a terrible driver, as distracted at the wheel as he was in marriage, his mind on somewhere or someone else.

She was happy during the early autumn months in Taos. San Francisco had become a mean accompaniment to her marital stress. Businesses were shuttered; people were losing jobs. All anyone talked about was the economy, and those conversations inevitably ended in leaden silences followed by nervous denial. And putting distance between herself and her clients, those high-class newsmongers with their meaningful stares, was a relief. In Taos, she and Everett were out of their element and so had to rely on each other. They felt like a couple in a way they hadn't in a long time, not since they roamed the streets of San Francisco during their courtship, the physical eccentricity of their union and their manner of dress, and Everett's belief in his artistic greatness, making them feel that they had been chosen for a special future.

Everett had been invited to stay and work in Taos by a wealthy Boston woman who fancied herself an artists' patron and who made a habit of bringing painters and musicians and writers to her ranch so that they could create, untroubled by worldly concerns. While in Taos, Adele Peabody went native, decorating her home with an abundance of kachina dolls and woven baskets. She had a husband back East but kept an Indian lover who worked around the ranch, repairing fences and cars. He provided entertainment for the guests at dinner when he would sing his nasal, plaintive songs while slowly beating a cowhide drum. The mood was unconditionally festive and gay at the Peabody ranch. There was always an opportunity for an impromptu play or a musicale. Each evening, dinner at the main house was one of drunk hilarity and it was an unwritten rule that no one was to introduce topics about politics or the economic disaster that had by now spread throughout the country but that, like some biblical plague, had passed over this ranch set in the remote wilderness of New Mexico. Vera and Everett were given a small adobe on the property for the duration of their stay, as well as a studio for Everett to paint in, although he preferred to work out-of-doors. Vera was enchanted by the mud-colored house. She loved the smooth curves of the walls, the way the fireplace was built into the clay as if a hand had sculpted the whole enterprise with a single swift gesture.

She was also intoxicated by the smoky, cooked-meat smell of the piñon wood fires that burned each night in Mrs. Peabody's huge stone hearth. She and Everett were often invited to dinner at the big house, and the little boys stayed home under the care of an old Tewa woman named Millie. Mrs. Peabody addressed Vera as "Mrs. Makin," and Vera, who had continued to use her maiden name for her work, did not correct her because the name tied her to Everett in the woman's mind and hopefully in the minds of her female guests. No one asked Vera about herself on these evenings. No one knew that she ran her own studio and made half the living of her family and these days more than half. The evenings were devoted to a tacitly agreed upon adulation of the visiting artists who would drink and expound and tell stories all intended to satisfy Mrs. Peabody's notion that she had surrounded herself with a fast and fascinating crowd of significant people.

During the days, while Everett was at work, Vera and the boys took long walks in the sedge meadows, stopping to inspect the few late-season wildflowers that had somehow survived a hot, dry summer—the bell-shaped penstemon and the bright orange Indian paintbrush whose name delighted Miller so much that she cut a few of the buds so that he could dip them into his father's watercolors and make designs on paper. Some days, she took the car and drove toward the Sangre de Cristo Mountains whose foothills were covered with juniper and ponderosa pine. She played with the boys in the creek, helped them search for trilobites and fossil clams, showed them how to crack open an aloe leaf and use the sap on their cut fingers. They grew drunk with exhaustion from their games and their arguments but refused to give up the day to the fading light. On the nights when she and Everett did not dine at the main house, they lay outside with the boys underneath blankets and waited for shooting stars while coyotes and hyenas barked.

After the newness of the place wore off, the long hours of the day moved slowly. There were times when, reading aloud to the children in an effort to collapse an afternoon, Vera's mind wandered to concerns about having closed up her studio back in California. Her clients said they would remain loyal, but with the holidays coming, she imagined some of them would not wait for her return and would find other photographers to take their Christmas portraits. She worried about why Everett came home so late on the evenings when she did not accompany him to the main house because one or another of the boys was down with a cough or because she was frankly bored with the insipid conversation of Mrs. Peabody and her guests. The boys never complained about their father's absences. They were more used to him being gone than having him home, and his triumphant returns from a trip or even simply from a day of work, when he would regale them with stories about a drifter he'd come across or surprise them by digging into his pocket and pulling out a piece of rose quartz or feldspar, had become the expected rhythm of their lives. He was the entertainer. She was the cook, the cleaner, the henpecking wife who, just that morning, unleashed shrill hysterics about the Newport whore who had captured Everett's attention with her wide-open vowels and her décolletage. Everett received her outburst with a bored calm, as if her demand for fidelity were something quaint.

"What does that mean?" Philip said, his head heavy on her shoulder.

She had been reading but she had no idea what was happening in the book. She looked at her children, their dirty legs splayed on the couch on either side of her. Miller's hand carelessly fingered his penis beneath his pants. Philip picked at the yellow crust that lined the edges of his nose.

"I don't know," she said.

"Why don't you know?" Philip said sleepily.

"Because I don't know everything."

"You don't?"

It hadn't occurred to her before to take pictures while they were in New Mexico. She did not think of her work as anything but commerce, and there was no money to be made photographing a prickly pear cactus. In San Francisco, she had befriended photographers who thought of their work as fine art. She'd admired the soft-focus pictures they took of girls posing as nymphs by garden fountains or green

peppers photographed in such a way that they looked like naked bodies, but she found it embarrassing to think of her own work as personal
expression. She photographed rich ladies. She made a living. She did a
job of work. *Verrichte einfach einen guten Tag Arbeit*, her mother would
say. *Go do some work.* She had brought her camera and an enlarger to
Taos thinking that she might drum up some business with Mrs. Peabody's rich friends, but the equipment had sat untouched until now.

The boys, excited about having an important job to do and energized by her renewed sense of adventure, wrestled heroically with her
tripod while she carried the bulky Graflex, leading them into the desert beyond the house. This was Everett's landscape, and experiencing
it now not as a playground for her children but as a potential subject,
she saw what drew him to it. The land was frankly sensual. The dry
thirst suggested unslakable want. The bald earth between the sparse
growths was almost risqué. The plants, crabbed and spiked to ward
off predators, seemed to her to be all the Eleanor Cunninghams of the
world combined, their impenetrable exteriors a shrewd provocation.
There had been a time when she couldn't imagine how Everett found
inspiration during those months spent in such a raw and relentless
landscape, not to mention physical comfort. But of course he had.

The boys were tired. They complained about the tripod's weight
and finally refused to continue. She kept going. Her eyes fell on a
rock banded by a ferrous red stripe. A lizard scurried past, trailing its
S-shaped tail. She tried to find a way to see the ruddy succulents
around her as pure geometries, to find them beautiful or stark or even
startling, to rid them of their association with her husband and see
them for herself. She studied the lucent green leaves of a corn lily,
which covered the poison of the plant. She called for the boys to

bring her the tripod, and after much whining they did. She set up her camera and went to work.

That evening, when she and Everett went to dine at the main house, she told Mrs. Peabody that she needed a space to make into a darkroom.

"But why, dear?" Mrs. Peabody said, the wattle beneath her chin shaking merrily.

"Because I am a photographer."

"Oh, but we have a photographer coming quite soon!" She mentioned the name of a man so well-known that Vera immediately felt embarrassed for implying that she might be his professional colleague. Still, the following day, Mrs. Peabody sent her Indian man to Vera's house to tell her that he had cleared out a shed for her use. Vera enlisted the boys in helping her to wash and clean the developing trays and to hang a blanket over the places in the shed where light splintered through the planked walls.

She ended her first session in the new darkroom disheartened. The images she'd made in the desert were unconvincing. The beauty she'd seen with her eyes was inert, the forms taking the shapes of platitudes, generic postcard images that travelers would buy and send home to prove they had been to a place. Her close-up pictures of a cactus flower, the shed skin of a black-tailed rattlesnake, and the sun-scorched bones of a dead cow were rank imitations: flat, unyielding, without resonance, as though her mind was already made up about what she was looking at before she lifted the camera to her eye. The pictures were evidence of her dulled imagination.

15

In late October, she began to notice a car making its way along the road outside the adobe. It passed at precisely eight o'clock each morning and returned at sundown. The driver wore a trilby and sat erect at the wheel as if he were pantomiming a driver. When she was next at the main house, she asked about this stranger and learned that he was the photographer Mrs. Peabody had mentioned. He had come to Taos to make a study of the mesas. He did not eat with the rest of the guests, Mrs. Peabody said in a hushed, important tone, as though his rejection of her company was a mark of his superiority.

The regularity of the man's comings and goings, and the fact of his unwillingness to bend to the demands of Mrs. Peabody's social agenda, indicated a purpose and an independence that stirred Vera. Her days took on the shape of this stranger's habits, as if his passages were a signal he was giving her, although she had not yet decoded it. She waited each morning for the crunching noise of his car as it passed close to her house. At the end of a day, when she was feeding the boys their dinner or giving them a warm bath and feeling exhausted by their high-pitched bickering, she would hear the sound of the engine and stop whatever she was doing in order to stand in her open doorway and watch the car drive by. Her excitement reminded her of the thrill she once felt when she heard Everett's boots shuffle across the floorboards outside her studio. But her feelings did not have to do with the man in particular or any notions of romance. They were related to ideas that had been taking vague shape in her mind. Despite the disappointing outings with her camera, she had begun to sense that, with her studio work, she had put herself on a train—a smooth and reliable train—and that this train was taking her to a destination where she didn't want to go. It was a place where Everett was the artist and her life's purpose was to serve his particular vision. Her job was to ply her pedestrian craft no differently than if she were sewing dress sleeves in a sweatshop, to raise the children, and to collude in the lie of their marriage. She felt the same frustration she'd experienced on those nights of her false labor with Miller: she had the urge to make, to create, but that urge was thwarted each day when she photographed plants and rocks but produced nothing worthwhile. But here was this man, this photographer, coming and going each day, taking pictures of the mesas because he was compelled to do so. Why? Did it have to do with their flat-topped configuration? With the way afternoon light fell on their slopes? Vera couldn't answer that question. What she did know was that something in him, in that man in particular, was moved to put a frame around those mounds in order to answer the question for himself. And what about Vera? If she had all the freedom in the world, what question would she ask?

N ovember brought winter with a fierce immediacy that caught everyone by surprise. Each colder day was increasingly filled with the boys' runny noses and coughs and their restlessness at being trapped inside the adobe. Vera asked Everett about going back to San Francisco, but Mrs. Peabody had given them the house until Christmas, and he still had work to do.

"Why?" she said. "No one buys art anymore. No one has money."

"But now I have the low winter light!" he said, as if this should put an end to tiresome discussions of finance.

She tried to bundle up the children and take them with her as she searched for a subject to photograph, but they were miserable in the cold, and she was forced to abandon any hope of work. Hours moved by sluggishly as she tried to involve herself in their games. She imagined there were other, better mothers who delighted in buying imaginary fruit from an imaginary store and paying for it with imaginary money. Miller was currently on a jag where he wanted to make a picnic out of sticks and leaves and rocks, put everything in a basket and take a long hike—which meant parades through the house's three small rooms—until he found the right spot, which was always in front of the fireplace, where they would lay out a tablecloth, unpack their lunch, and pretend to eat.

"No more," she said one day, after the third round of the game.

"Please, Mama," Miller begged, yanking her arm.

"Let go of me!" she said sharply.

Miller wept. Philip called him a crybaby. Wailing now, Miller pushed his face into her stomach and held her hips.

She heard the sound of the man's car making his afternoon journey back to the main house. "Stop it! Stop it right now!" she said. She pushed Miller away from her and rushed to the window, catching just a glimpse of the taillights as the car disappeared into the dusk. At that moment, more than anything, she wanted to be driving that car, coming back from an entire day of single-minded focus that did not include pretend picnics and crying children, and waiting for Everett or worrying over some pretty thing who had caught his eye at the main house, or having to endure the condescending Mrs. Peabody who seemed intent on making Vera aware of what her life was and what it was not.

She spun around to face her children. "See what you've done?" she shouted.

Miller's cry scraped her eardrums.

"He wet his pants!" Philip exclaimed triumphantly.

She walked across the room and slapped Miller on the cheek. He held his hand to his face and looked at her with animal incomprehension. Horrified by what she had done, she quickly helped him change out of his wet clothes, murmuring apologies, then she went to her room and lay down. The boys followed. They stood by her bedside, staring down at her worriedly. Philip stroked her cheek.

"I didn't mean to do it," Miller said in a small voice.

She reached for his hand and pulled him down to her, wrapping him in her arms. "It's not your fault. It's Mama's fault. Mama did a terrible thing. Please forgive me. Do you forgive me?"

"Yes."

When Everett arrived that evening, she met him at the door. "We need to leave," she said.

"Three more weeks," he said.

"We need to go now."

He washed the paint off his hands, changed his clothes, and left for dinner at the main house. He did not come home that night. There was a girl just arrived from New Haven, the daughter of someone or the niece of someone—Vera had not bothered to find out. She'd seen the girl's soft mouth and didn't need to know anything more to understand what would happen.

When he returned the following morning, she was dragging suitcases across the snow and putting them in the trunk of the car.

"It stormed all night, Vera. We will freeze to death if we leave now," he said, following her back inside the house.

"We will freeze to death in this godforsaken mud hut," she shot back.

"That is ridiculous, and you know it."

She turned on him. "What is your plan, Everett?" she said.

"My plan is to finish my work," he said evenly.

"Is it your paintings you are referring to or another sort of work you have yet to complete?"

She did not wait for his answer. She dressed the boys in their coats and hats, lifted Miller onto her hip, and led Philip by his hand to the car. Once they had settled into the back, she tucked a blanket around them. She sat in the driver's seat and waited. Twenty minutes later, Everett finally emerged from the house and got into the car. They stopped at the main house, where he left instructions to have his paintings sent to San Francisco. As soon as he was back in the car, Vera bore down on the steering wheel, cutting new tracks through the virgin snow.

As they drove down from Taos, the boys regained their buoy-
ancy, excited to be leaving and dazzled by the way their ears popped
as they reached lower elevations. But while they laughed and asked
why this was so and how long it would take to get to California and
if they could stop for ice-cream sodas, Vera and Everett fell silent.
The road was crowded with cars loaded with entire households'
worth of furniture. Single men walked along the berm carrying suitcases or loose bundles. A girl stared at Vera through the back window
of the car ahead of theirs. The palm of her hand lay against the glass.
She was pressing so hard that her flesh was colorless. Vera could not
tell if the girl was waving or if she was testing the boundaries of her
new and reduced life.

16

San Francisco, California, 1932

It was New Year's Day. Vera stood at the window of her studio, watching the street below. Unlike most New Year's Days she remembered, when the city was quiet and people were enjoying a bedridden hangover and the last hours of their holiday before the year of work began, the streets were filled with jobless men, moving sullenly along the sidewalk. It was raining, but only a few of them raised umbrellas. The rest simply hunched their shoulders and lowered their heads to take the brunt of the weather's blows.

In the year since their return from Taos, Everett had not sold a single painting. The entire body of work that he had made during that terrible autumn was stacked up against the walls of his studio. Vera's clients had finally begun to feel the economy and were no longer calling as frequently. When they did, they asked her to come to their homes—a time-consuming effort now that she and Everett had sold the car. The wealthy ladies of the city did not want to travel to her studio where their chauffeurs would have to escort them through the throng of unemployed people to reach Vera's door.

Vera and Everett were living apart now. They could no longer afford the house on Russian Hill. If they gave up their studios there was no possibility of income, so they each moved into their own separate workspace where there were no kitchens and only communal bathrooms in the hallway. They had sent Philip and Miller to live out with a woman in Oakland who had opened her home to children whose parents could not afford to keep them. Vera could not bear to think of Miller's and Philip's faces when she and Everett took them to Mrs. Wilson's house. They had made the ferry crossing on a bright and clear day. The boys gripped the rusted railings of the boat and stared down at the churning water. The gulls touching down and riding the tides would have once incited their playfulness, but now they were blank-faced, as if these patterns of nature were as inscrutable as the future that awaited them across the bay. Vera had kept up an enthusiastic conversation about the Wilsons' backyard with its tree house and the Wilson children, who, yes, were younger and, all right, they were girls, but wouldn't they be fun to play with anyway? And who knew what other children would be there? Philip and Miller would make new best friends! When they finally reached the Wilson home, Vera and Everett knelt on the lawn and once again explained to the boys that there were many children just like them who were going on adventures while their parents worked hard so that they could bring them back home. The boys nodded solemnly, but Vera knew there was no agreement, only acceptance, because it was their fate to be at the mercy of adults, and now there was something else called the "times," or "these goddamn times," or sometimes, from their father, "these fucking times," and a new realization that even though their parents had control over mealtimes and bedtimes and times to wash hands and brush teeth, there was this other kind of time that their parents had no power over.

"They are smart boys," Everett said on the ferry ride back to the city, when Vera broke down. She nodded as he reminded her that at least they were not leaving the boys in one of the state's orphanages that were swelling daily, that at least their boys were in a proper home. "They understand what has to be done," he said. But right before Vera had left Mrs. Wilson's, Miller asked her whether they could leave now and go roller skating in Golden Gate Park. He did not understand. And why should he? Why should a child understand why his parents leave him? It had been horrible to watch the boys disappear into the house with Mrs. Wilson. The woman had left their small suitcases outside on the porch. Vera worried aloud about this all the way back home. What if it rained and everything she had packed for them—their favorite books and pajamas and Miller's stuffed bunny—got soaked and ruined? Everett snapped at her and told her that he didn't raise his boys to need fancy pajamas and dolls. For the rest of the ferry ride, Vera and Everett stood apart from each other. When they walked off the pier, they went their separate ways without saying good-bye. The marriage was over.

Were the boys having a happy New Year's Day? She hoped Mrs. Wilson remembered to have them open the cards Vera had brought with her two days earlier, when she'd gone to visit. She'd put candy in the envelopes—toffees for Philip and lemon drops for Miller.

The rain trickled to a halt. On the street, people lowered umbrellas, shook out hats, pulled their suitcases from the alcoves where they had stashed them during the downpour. Vera noticed that the slant of warm yellow sunlight did not act on the pedestrians as it might have in another time when sun glittering through the last sprinkles of rain was a renewal and people quickened their step as if infused with fresh energy. There was no reason to walk swiftly. There was nowhere to go. Nowhere to lug those packed suitcases filled with everything a person owned. She thought of her boys' red suitcases left abandoned on that porch. The whole world had been abandoned. Vera saw that now, saw the strange, sad dance of people moving here and there or not moving at all. A man sat on an upturned apple box waiting for . . . just waiting. Another man pushed a wheelbarrow filled with bags, a dog riding aloft, a scruffy figurehead. Four men leaned against a wall, their faces in deep shadow. Each had one leg crossed casually over the other as if he was simply passing the time, and of course that was exactly what each was doing: waiting for this awful time, this god-damn, this fucking time to pass. The sun struck the wet pavement making it look like a sheet of mica.

She had to go down into the street with her camera and take pictures of those men leaning against that wall. The idea struck her cleanly and precisely, a knife slicing through the muddle of her thoughts. She was certain that this was what she needed to do.

Negotiating the streets with the heavy Graflex was difficult. The crowd was denser than it had appeared when she was standing in her studio, looking at it from above. The frustration and squelched energy was palpable and frightening. It occurred to her that someone might try to steal her camera, and that she could easily get hurt. For a moment, she considered going back to the safety of her studio and waiting for a call from a lady in silk who would rattle on about her summer home or her father's boat while Vera took her picture, but she kept going. There were women on the street, but mostly there were men: men in rags and men in suits. Before reaching the group she'd seen by the wall, she noticed a crowd gathered in a breadline. Once a line had been a symbol of a peaceable conformity, a social contract that had been struck among civilized people who knew that if they waited their turn, they would get the good things life had to offer. Now a line was a sign of futility, and as if in recognition of this, the breadline was no line at all but an amorphous cluster of bodies hemmed in by a wooden fence on one side and a building on the other. She readied her camera, trying to find a good angle. Her awkwardness and effort sundered any idea she had about trying to be inconspicuous. Adrenaline made her hands shake. Someone bumped into her from behind, and she turned, half expecting to be warned off and told to go back where she came from. What right did she have to take photographs of strangers? But she knew these faces. Even if she had never seen a single one of these people before, something deep inside her recognized them. These people had been made to feel inadequate, abnormal. Their lives were disfigured by circumstance. She had to take their pictures because what she saw, what *she* saw, marked her as much as a limp or the fact that she was the only gentile in a school filled with Jews or that her father did not love her enough to stay.

A man in a crushed and dirty fedora leaned against the wooden railing, his arms protectively shielding a dented metal cup. He looked up at her from under the brim of his hat. She waited for him to tell her to leave, but, after staring at her for a long while, he simply looked down at the ground. She framed him. The pattern of hats and other men's dark coats were his background. She adjusted the focus. She took a picture.

Mary

17.

Porter, California, 1935

She'd seen him before, driving his truck through the groves. She wouldn't have noticed him except that the truck had the name of the grower painted on it, and, when pickers saw that truck driving past, they hissed warnings at their kids to stop fooling around, worked a little faster, climbed the ladders to get at the high oranges, and disappeared in the leaves. Mary did not appreciate being stalked and threatened, and she looked straight at the driver to let him know it.

James and Ray played nearby. Ellie, Trevor, June, and Della spent the day at school, which was just a three-sided shed set up next to the outhouses at the camp. There were days when the heat created a stench so terrible Mary told her kids to stay home rather than risk whatever sickness might be spread by the smell of the waste. Ray was old enough for learning but he was a troublemaker and too jumpy to sit still. Mary hoped he would calm down soon. He was difficult to keep with her. He would follow a butterfly or a sound, and often, when she climbed down from a ladder with a full basket, he would be gone. Once she'd found him hanging off a high branch of a tree. If she hadn't seen his feet poking out he would have fallen and broken a leg or worse. James was a worry in a different way. He rarely spoke. He was content to play alone for hours, and if she tried to entice him out of his quietness with the promise of a sucker on payday, the bribe didn't seem to matter to him. At the drugstore in town, the other children would press their noses against the glass candy case and loudly debate flavors, but when she asked James if he wanted cherry or root beer, he would simply nod and she would have to decide for him. Women looked at him with pity because they thought he was slow, but Mary knew his problem was something else. When Toby died, James had been too young to understand and too old to forget the sorrow she carried around that made her smile come a second too late and made her ears grow dull so that her children would have to call her three or four times before they could get her attention.

Ray said something to James and then punched him in the arm when James didn't respond. As she scolded Ray, Mary noticed that the company truck was parked twenty feet away. She shouldn't have looked that driver in the eye. Now she'd been marked as someone to watch. She cursed herself for her bad attitude, warned Ray to stop bothering his brother or else, then went back to work so that she wouldn't be accused of agitation. A group of pickers had set out demands for better pay and conditions. The next day, those same men and their families were gone, replaced by people who were so grateful for the work that it would be a while before they would cause trouble.

The driver got out of his truck. He wore clean slacks and a shirt that still bore the creases of pressing. The cleanliness set him apart. That and the skin on the back of his neck, which was so pale it seemed to reflect the sun. He gestured with unscarred hands as he spoke to the field manager. Mary's fingers looked like carrots just yanked from the ground. The dirt was so deeply encrusted in the lines that scored her palms that a fortune-teller would have had no trouble seeing whether her life was lucky or not. After years in the fields, her skin was beginning to darken, as if her mother's Cherokee had finally surfaced to offer its protection. A few months earlier, Mary had gotten word that Doris had died of pneumonia. She had lost the farm in Tahlequah, and Mary's brothers had taken her with them when they moved to the western part of the state. Just in time for all that dust that made it impossible to go from the house to the privy without tying a rope to your waist so you didn't get lost. A life of throwing water on a dirt floor and beating sheets with a broom twice a week, and it was dust that got Doris in the end. *There's nothing I can do about that, either.*

The man took off his hat and ran his hand over his blond hair, which fell just below his ears, a length that would have been a tease to the lice that made women in the camp take razors to their children's scalps. There were days when Mary thought her kids were of a race of bald, alien creatures from the funny pages who had landed on a citrus farm in California. The sun picked up the golden hairs on the man's forearm, reminding her of the wheat fields back home, and then of Toby. It had been four years since his death, but she could still summon the feeling of his hand on her calf when she climbed the ladder to unload her sack of cotton onto the bed of the truck. Her skin had been a magnet to his fingers no matter how tired and sore and sick he was. But when she tried to summon his face, she could see him only as he was at the end, his lips nearly black, his eyes sunken in their bruised sockets. It was painful to see untouched beauty in the form of this golden man.

One afternoon, she walked some distance from the camp to find a place to go to the bathroom, leaving Ellie and Trevor in charge of the others. She knew it was vain to crave privacy, but it irked her that the things in life that should belong solely to an individual—what a man and woman got up to at night or what a body had no more use for— became the day's news to strangers. She heard a voice behind her. "Excuse me, ma'am." It was no more than a hoarse whisper. She'd heard of women being raped by desperate men and quickened her pace, but his footsteps trailed hers. She knew she would not be able to outrun him if it came to that. She spun around, screamed, and clawed at his face. He cursed and jumped back. With horror, she realized she'd attacked the man from the truck. He would fire her for certain. She would not be able to collect for the work done so far that week, since the agreement was for six days' work or no pay at the end of the day on Saturday. She would pack up before dinner. The children would complain; they were hungry all the time now and they waited for her to feed them the way her old farm dog used to wait by his bowl with a craven look in his eyes. She would be hard-pressed to find another camp before nightfall, but the kids were used to sleeping in the car. How much gas was in the Hudson? She had been planning to fill up on payday. Her fingernails had scratched the man's cheek. Would he have her arrested?

"You oughtn't to sneak up on someone that way," she said, her adrenaline making her unaccountably brave.

"I didn't expect to be attacked."

"If I'd really attacked you, you would be bleeding."

"I've seen you," he said.

"And now you see me again."

"My name is Charles Dodge. Charlie . . ."

Dodge Farms, she thought. "Good for you."

"I don't know who you are."

"My name is Mary Coin, and if you're going to fire me, just let me know it. I got kids back there who don't need me to linger with strangers."

"I'm not a stranger. We've just now exchanged introductions."

"Knowing the name of a man doesn't count as familiar."

He had a careful smile, as if he were waiting for someone to ask him what there was to be happy about. Maybe he would let her work through the end of the week.

"Do you mind if I walk with you?" he said.

"You want to escort me while I take care of my needs?"

His face colored. "I'm sorry that you don't have more privacy at the camp."

"Are you going to do anything about it?"

"I don't see how it's possible," he said apologetically.

"Then don't be sorry. Except about your bad timing."

She turned and walked on. She found some high bushes, lifted her skirt around her waist, pulled down her underwear, and squatted. Suddenly, the situation struck her as funny and she started laughing. Her urine spluttered in fits and jerks, which seemed still more amusing as it brought to mind James standing with his pants pulled down, his sweet, dimpled bottom so carelessly exposed while he concentrated hard on his pee.

When she headed back toward camp, the man was still by the side of the road, staring into the brambles as if he was studying something important there.

"I was just . . ." he said, but he had obviously not thought up a reasonable excuse.

"Some people would think it a queer thing to wait on a woman when she's doing her business," she said.

"Do you always say what you mean?"

"I'm not clever enough to make things up." She started walking toward the camp, and he walked alongside her.

"I envy you," he said.

She stopped and looked at him. "You know what? If you're going to insist on talking to me, you cannot say things like that."

"I don't understand."

"When you say that you envy me, you're putting me down."

"But I'm not."

"You think I haven't read my Bible? Blessed are the meek? There's nothing blessed about having to empty yourself in the bushes."

"I just wanted to talk to you," he said quietly.

"You won't get what you came for."

His expression fell. "You think so little of yourself?"

"The opposite," she said. They had reached the edge of the camp, and she walked away from him quickly in order to put distance between herself and gossip.

He was in the grove again the next day. She felt his eyes on her as she climbed up and down the ladder, knew that he could see the sweat stain that ran down the back of her blouse and the dark half-moons of wetness underneath her arms. She refused to meet his gaze. She felt enraged that he had so easily taken control of her thoughts, as if she were simply part of the land over which he had rights. But at night she found herself restless and irksome, each child doing or saying something that annoyed her. She could not sleep and spent hours outside the tent pacing here and there and nowhere, just walking to stop her body from feeling itself. The next time she saw him in the field, she looked right at him and did not turn away. When she walked out of the camp that evening, he was there.

When they were finished, he stayed on top of her. His spent weight anchored her in a way she liked. She never stopped moving from one farm to the next, and when she reached a new place, she had to set up the tent and get the children settled and prepare food and keep them as clean as she could, and get them to go to school if there was a school nearby, and then she went to work and picked and pulled and climbed up and down ladders. Except for her few hours of restless sleep each night, there seemed to be hardly any time when she wasn't in motion. Now came the relief of his body making it impossible for her to move, this solitary moment of not having to make a decision. But she immediately distrusted the feeling realizing it was a figment of loneliness and knowing, too, that there was nothing to be gotten from this more than what she had already received—a little warmth and that blessed moment afterward when her thoughts were caught in the space between seconds and she just hung there, momentarily free until it passed. She pushed him off her, lifted her hips, and tugged down her dress.

"You're beautiful," he said.

"I know what I am." She stood up, straightened herself out, and walked away.

They met each evening for two weeks. When she started to bleed she did not come to him. During those days she could feel his eyes on her but she didn't look up. If she passed him at the weighing truck she struck up a conversation with another woman so that he would not try to talk to her. When her week was over, she felt the familiar agitation in her breasts and thighs and, the next time she saw him, she made sure to catch his eye.

"I thought you'd given up on me," he said when she met him on the road that evening.

"I never counted on you to begin with."

"You always do that?"

"Always do what?"

"Decide what a thing is before it's happened?"

"I don't have the luxury of chance, mister."

"Don't call me mister, like I'm some man you bumped into on the street."

"But that's who you are. Exactly that man."

He stood close enough to her so that she could feel his breath on her face. She felt self-conscious, ill-equipped for what was happening. "I haven't washed," she said quietly. "I stink of dirt. Of your dirt."

"I don't care."

"Of course you don't."

"Please, Mary," he said. "Please."

He wanted to know things about her. Where was she from? Who were her parents? He was intrigued that she was a half-breed, and he studied her face, looking for the Indian in her. He never asked about the man who gave her six children, and she was relieved not to speak Toby's name. The omission allowed her to pretend that what she was doing was separate from her real life, and that the comfort and excitement she felt were in her control. She could walk away at any time. It would be as if these tussles in the weeds had never happened, as if this man were just a character from a dream.

"How many brothers and sisters do you have?" he asked one night. He was lying on top of her and he gently blew strands of hair off her forehead.

"What do you want to know all these things for?" she asked.

"I want to know you."

"Why?"

He laughed. "What do you think we're doing here?"

"Fucking."

He rolled off her and lay on his back.

"What?" she said. "Are you courting me? Are you going to marry me?"

"You have a hard heart, do you know that?"

"Look at me," she said.

He stood up, buttoning his shirt, adjusting his trousers.

"I said, look at me." Her dress was open, her chest exposed. "You know what I think when I see myself, when I see these?" She slapped her hand over her breasts. "I don't think of you kissing them. I think, I wish I still had milk coming and that one of my kids was young enough to drink it, 'cause then it would be one less hungry child at dinnertime."

"Sometimes I don't understand you at all," he said.

She stood up, buttoning her dress. "I don't need you to know what my favorite flower is or the name of my first dog. That doesn't do me any good."

"You want me to pay you?" he said angrily. "Is that what you're after?" He reached into the back pocket of his pants and took out his wallet. He tossed some bills on the ground between them.

"I'm pregnant," she said.

She could tell by his reaction that although he was curious about the particulars of her past, he would not be interested in her future.

18.

Bakersfield, California, 1935

Earl said "These kids of yours" when they were making too much noise in the back of the car or when a virus of giggles ran from one to the other inside the tent when they should have been bedding down for the night. Still, he smiled when Della put her head on his shoulder during a long car ride, and he loved to make a penny disappear in his sleeve just to elicit Ray's awed surprise.

"You don't have to tell me they're mine," Mary said, to let him know that she had no expectations of him.

She met him in December, a month after the baby was born. Driving as far from the Dodge groves as her gas would allow, she found day work picking beans and cabbage. The jobs were scarce. The roads were filled with trucks and cars. Families with no cars walked on foot. Some people simply sat by the side of the road as if they'd finally decided to remain in one place and see if the hard times would pass by like bad weather. In Bakersfield, she left Ellie in charge of the others and joined a hiring line. When she reached the front, the foreman looked her over, judged her wizened frame and her bone-thin arms, then pushed the air with his hand as if the wind he created would be enough to blow her away.

The car was nearly out of gas. Her kids hadn't eaten anything to speak of in two days. "Sign me up," she said.

"We need to get this harvest pulled before the cold weather comes in."

"I know what the work is."

"Move on, ma'am."

"You're paying thirty-five cents an hour and you're turning me down? Bet you won't let me work for free, neither."

A man behind her laughed.

"We don't need troublemakers," the foreman said. "I'm telling you to move on."

Two goons stood behind the foreman, cradling rifles. She wasn't surprised. She'd seen a man leap across a table and try to strangle a bursar on payday because he didn't think he was getting his due. Armed men patrolled the fields now, watching who was talking to whom.

"Move on where?" Mary said. "To the not-hiring farm down the road? Or the one after that?"

"Lady . . ."

"I've got seven kids and no gas in my car."

"You know how many times I hear that story every day?"

"Well, it's no story. It's my life. If I say I'll do a job, I'll do it just as good as anyone."

The goons shifted their guns, but she would not back down. She couldn't. Finally, the man held out his pen and she signed. When she walked away she did not sense her victory. Since giving birth, something had weakened in her, and not only in her body. It was a faltering of her spirit. Each day it was harder for her to pretend that somehow life would turn out all right despite illness and hardly any food, and the grinding noise that came from underneath the car hood, and the sores on Trevor's lips, and the baby's angry diaper rash, and having to camp in ditch banks where the water was too dirty to drink. Even Della and June, those two silly girls who could sit in a half-broke Hudson and pretend they were Cinderellas going to the ball to meet their Prince Charmings, had lately grown somber. Mary hid the fact that she didn't eat most nights, claiming that she needed to wait until the heat of the day wore off to find her appetite. Her tongue would grow thick with longing as she watched her children chew and swallow. They hadn't seen the inside of a schoolroom in months. Ellie and Trevor worked in the fields with her now. June brought the baby when he needed feeding, which left Della in charge of James and Ray. Mary might as well have poured gasoline on a fire.

"He's right, you know," a man said to her as she headed back to the car. He was tall and broad-shouldered and he would have filled out his clothes in another time. He had a wide face, and when he smiled, his cheeks creased in dimples, and lines spoked out from the corners of his eyes.

"Right about what?"

"You look like you could break in two."

"Think what you want. I don't have time for conversation."

"Can I at least thank you for giving me a good laugh back there?"

"You can thank me for whatever you want as long as it doesn't cost me."

"Saying you're welcome don't cost."

"You'd be surprised," she said.

She reached the car. Ellie and June were changing the baby on the front seat.

"He stinks, Mama!" Ray shouted.

Mary studied the thin yellow liquid in the diaper.

"He's got the runs," Ellie said. "I already changed him twice since you been gone."

Mary finished pinning the fresh diaper. "He needs to drink more." She sat down on the runner and opened her shirt.

"You want me to fill the water bottle, Mama?" Trevor said.

"That's ditch water," Mary said. "He'll have to make due with what I've got for now."

The man was still lingering nearby.

"This is not a peep show, mister," Mary called out to him. She took her breast in her hand and squeezed.

"I've got some good water," the man said.

"I don't have any money," she said. The baby cried. She looked at his eyes. He was too dried out for tears.

"Water's free," the man said. "One free thing there is."

"And air," June said. "Air is free."

The man smiled. "You're right about that."

"And dirt!" Trevor said.

"And stars!" Della said.

"But you can't own stars, anyway," June said. "So that don't count."

"Doesn't," Mary corrected distractedly.

"It counts. It counts!" Della said.

"She don't know anything," June said.

"I know you're a dummy," Della said.

"Enough!" Mary said.

The children stood by their mother, studying the stranger.

"Words are free," Ellie said quietly.

The man looked at her appraisingly. "That's a smart thing to say."

Ellie beamed. She was nearly fifteen now and had turned inward in a way Mary remembered from her own girlhood, when her dreams were more compelling than the reality of helping her mother keep house. As they traveled from farm to farm, Ellie sat in silence, holding the baby, lost in thoughts about a boy she saw at a filling station or about the movie stars she read about in the magazines that sometimes circulated through the camps, their pages nearly transparent from so many eager hands. More than once, Mary had caught Ellie twisting her limp hair around her fingers, trying to force a curl so that she would look like those glamorous women. Mary told her to quit it or her hair would fall out. Even if Mary had money for indulgences, she would not have let Ellie waste it at a beauty parlor. It made a girl weak to imagine that things would be given to her simply because she had the advantage of a popular hairdo. Mary often told her kids stories about her childhood in Tahlequah—the way Doris tied strips of cloth soaked in kerosene around her children's legs in order to do battle with the endless barrage of flies and caterpillars and spiders that shared the house with them, about the long winter when they had eaten squirrel. Mary didn't want her children to think they were singled out for hardship.

"So, what do you think?" the man said to Mary. "How about some free water?"

Earl had been working the fields, traveling from one to the next by foot. Before that, he'd spent time unloading the ships in the port of San Diego and had worked in a slaughterhouse in Los Angeles. He told the boys stories about getting into scuffles with rough sailors and he told the girls that he had seen Clark Gable walking down a street called Sunset Boulevard. Although Mary was sure that most of what Earl said was at least half a lie, she couldn't help but feel grateful when the children begged him for another story. Earl knew to let James be by himself and he didn't remark the way other people often did when the boy did not respond to questions. "I like a boy who keeps his thoughts private," he said.

"I never know what he's thinking," Mary said.

"One day he'll start talking and there will be no stopping him."

"You don't know that," she said.

"I don't know that the sun is going to come up tomorrow, either. But I believe it will."

She was unaccustomed to talking freely about her children. Her relationships at the camps were cautious. She kept her family close, sometimes not letting the children play with strangers. Every week it was harder to keep up, and she didn't need a nosy neighbor making judgments. She turned socks inside out one day and then right side out the next, washed hands and faces before each meal but bodies only once a week. She went through the motions of housekeeping in her tent, but her effort was so futile that sometimes she felt like a fool for hanging on to the habits her mother had taught her.

Despite circumstances, Earl always had an air of bemused calm, and his playful manner gave her a little unreasonable hope. Sometimes he would come by the tent, tell a joke to one or another of the children, and then leave without so much as saying hello to her. Other times, if she had to stop work in the fields to nurse, he might walk by and casually drop a few heads of cauliflower into her bushel basket to make up for her lost time. Earl shared everything he had with her and the children and said nothing about it. If they were in town on a Sunday and passed a soda shop, he'd start patting his pants and jumping up and down, claiming that something was burning a hole in his pocket. The younger children would laugh and say they knew how to save him if only he would take out his money and buy them a Nehi. Even Ellie was not immune to his charm though she would often roll her eyes if one of his jokes was particularly bad. Trevor openly idolized him after Earl revealed that he had once witnessed Babe Ruth score a home run.

His lighthearted nature was only dimmed by the growing unrest among the pickers. People gathered in the evenings outside the camps to listen to young men from San Francisco talk about strikes and unions. Earl joined these meetings, but Mary refused. She had seen what happened to agitators in other camps, how they had barely enough time to gather their children and their belongings before the goons chased them out. Most harvests were out of the ground by now, and she could not risk even a pitiful wage for whatever work she could find. She kept working while others shook their fists and shouted above the roar of the grower's trucks about a sick child or dirty water. One afternoon, as a truck drove from the field to the road, pickers ran alongside it, shouting, *"Thief! Slave driver! Murderer!"* Men picked up sticks from the ground and began waving them in the air. A rock hit the side of the truck, and then another, and then it seemed like every picker had a rock in his or her hand and was denting metal and breaking windows. Someone torched the grower's sign at the entrance to the camp. Ellie was among a group of older children throwing dry leaves and grasses onto the blaze to egg it on.

Mary grabbed Ellie by the arm and pulled her from the crowd. "You keep out of this or I'll lose my job," she said.

"You already lost your job," Ellie said. "Didn't you hear? They fired everyone." She was crying now. "They fired *everyone*, Mama. They don't care about us. They don't care about anybody."

"Who are they going to get to work?" Mary said, but the answer was obvious. There were always more people. Mary and Ellie ran back to the tent. She shouted orders for the kids to pack up. Every single person in the camp was going to be on the road soon and looking for a job. She was determined that her family would be the first to find one.

Just as she settled into the driver's seat, Earl appeared with his rucksack and a cardboard traveling case.

"Thought I'd come with you," he said.

"You have a particular interest in a widow with seven children?"

"I have a particular interest in your car. And I don't mind who's in it, either."

19.

Nipomo, California, 1936

They had been traveling together for two months. During that time, they had worked only fourteen days between them. After a spate of unemployment, something would turn inside Earl and he would grow restless and disappear, sometimes for a few days. When the children asked after him, she would make up excuses that he had gone looking for work or that he had a sick relative living nearby he needed to visit. The relief she felt when he returned scared her. One of these times he would be gone for good, and she needed to remain strong in the belief that she could do this thing on her own. For the first time in her life, she was careful at night, making sure that he was outside her before he let go. She wanted no possibility between them.

The Hudson had broken down the night before outside Nipomo, near a pea field. The baby had a chesty cough. It would not do to have him sleep out-of-doors in the tent, so everyone slept cramped inside the car. When Mary woke, the windows were fogged, and she wiped her sleeve on the windshield. The hood of the car was up, and Earl was bent over the engine. She put her lips to the baby's forehead. He was warm. His eyes were glassy. She opened the car door and stepped outside, tucking him beneath her coat. Her shoes broke through a thin layer of frost. A cold wind carried voices from the clutter of shacks in the pickers' camp. She would find out if someone there had medicine they were willing to give her. She could ask about jobs, too. There was no hiring sign, but it was cold and people could be sick. There might be at least a day or two of work for Earl.

"The radiator is busted," he said.

"You wouldn't happen to know how to fix it?" she said.

His look was his answer. Ellie came out of the car, pulling on her coat.

"Come with me," Mary said to her daughter. "Let's see the new people."

Ellie shrugged and followed slowly, her eyes scanning the ground. Mary had taught Trevor and Ellie how to judge the smell of dead birds to determine their freshness. The birds were keeping them going now. Birds and whatever winter produce fell off trucks. Ellie was listless; all of Mary's children were. They were down to one hot meal a day, but she knew the dullness signified a worse kind of vacancy.

At the camp, people dismantled tents and roped mattresses to the tops of cars. Others hoisted their bundles and suitcases and walked toward the road.

"That's not right," Mary said.

"What's not right?" Ellie said.

The fields were empty. Mary spoke to a woman and learned that an overnight frost had killed off the peas. All of the workers had been let go.

The baby coughed and then moaned. His cheeks were splotchy and red, and Mary could feel the heat coming off him. No one she asked had medicine, or if they did they were not willing to give it to a stranger. She and Ellie returned to the car.

"He's burning up," Mary said to Earl. "We've got to get somewhere warm."

"I guess I'll go, then," he said.

And there it was: what she had been waiting for. Even though she had steeled herself to the eventuality of his permanent departure, she could sense that it would undo her.

"Trevor, how's your energy holding up?" Earl said.

"Don't you dare do that," she said sharply.

"Do what?"

"He's just thirteen years old. He can't take the load of this family himself. I always have and I always will. With or without you. Go if you're going and leave my boy alone."

He stared at her. She wished he would just gather his rucksack and his suitcase and leave. She was tired of pretending that she could make a family for her kids. She was tired of sex, tired of need.

"I thought he could help me take this radiator into town so we could get it fixed," Earl said quietly.

She knew she had hurt him. But she could not ignore that it felt good to release all her exhaustion and worry on him, to stab him with his weakness. She said nothing as he and Trevor lifted the radiator and started down the road. Ray and June ran after them, but Mary was too tired to call them back.

She figured it would take Earl and the kids a good hour to walk to Nipomo. Once in town, there was no telling how long it would be before they found someone to fix the radiator for the little money Earl had on him. Ellie wanted to hunt for dead birds, but Mary told her to stay close. There were still people in the camp—unhappy, hungry people who had no work. It was not a place for a girl to go wandering off by herself. And Mary wanted Ellie near. She felt exposed by the side of the road with no means of leaving if that collective misery should turn into anger. Della held the baby in the front seat of the car while Ellie and Mary staked the two knobby poles into the ground and set up the tent. Ellie untied the rocking chair and the stool from the roof of the car. Mary pulled the stool underneath the tarp to get out of the cold, then called for Della to bring her the baby. His fever had risen. James and Della had both started coughing, too. Mary thought about making a fire and setting water to boil. The children could sip hot water. But she'd have to send Ellie to look for ditch water and she didn't know if Della and James would be able to find wood dry enough to hold a flame. A car passed, moving up the highway from the south at a speed that suggested the driver was so eager to get someplace that he didn't care that driving fast used up more gas than driving slowly. Mary tried to think back to a time when she'd been eager to reach a place. Those first few trips to new mill towns had been filled with anticipation, knowing she'd have a company cabin to make into a home, that there'd be a school for the kids, that Toby's brothers and their wives would be with her. But the last time she could really recall pure, uncompromised excitement about getting somewhere was when she ran across her mother's farm and through the gum trees to meet Toby, already imagining his hands on her, his greedy, sloppy enthusiasm, his stunned pleasure.

She knew the baby needed to drink if his fever was going to go down, but he refused her breast. She held the back of his head and pushed her nipple at his lips. He started crying and she snapped at him and then she regretted those words. She knew Toby was right, and that a child understood no matter how small he was. James and Della played with the swag of rope tied around the tent pole. Ellie sat in the rocker, braiding her hair. The baby was so hot. Mary loosened the blanket around him but then worried that he would catch a chill.

A car passed from the north. Mary recognized it as the same one that had driven by not five minutes before. This time she saw that it was a woman at the wheel. She wore a funny hat that tilted on her head like a Necco Wafer, the candy June was so fond of even though the other children said it tasted like dust. The car slowed as the woman steered it off the road, pulling up and parking right alongside the Hudson. She stepped out of the driver's seat adjusting the hat on her head. She went around to the trunk, opened it, and took out a camera. She limped when she walked. A little woman with a funny hat and a limp. Mary would tell the story to the others when they returned.

"My name is Vera Dare," she said.

"All right," Mary said.

"Do you mind if I take your picture?"

"What for?"

"I work for the government—"

"I'm not with any strikers, if that's what you think. I don't want problems."

"No, that's not it. I take pictures to show the government how things are so that they will help people like you."

People like you. Mary did not have the energy to speak. Della and James stood near her, wary of the stranger. Ellie stayed in the rocker, playing with her hair.

"Would it be all right, then?" the woman asked.

The baby let out a cry. Mary shifted him around in her lap. Maybe he'd take the other nipple. "I guess," she said, hardly paying attention. All she could think about was her baby and getting liquid into him so that he didn't dry up. "I've got to feed this baby."

"Go ahead," the woman said.

Mary was coaxing her nipple into his mouth when she heard the click of the camera. She looked up, surprised. What was it about some things happening that made it seem almost unbelievable that they had happened at all? It was like when she watched Ray tearing off at such a speed that she knew he would trip and fall. And then when he did fall, she would have to convince herself that this small accident had, in fact, occurred and that she had not invented it. She wanted to tell the lady to stop what she was doing, but it was already done. And what was the difference, anyway? Mary felt the baby's lips go flaccid around her skin. She shook him a little bit to try to get him to focus, but she knew it would do no good. The woman stepped forward and took another picture.

"How old are you, if I may ask?" she said.

"Thirty-two," Mary said. She licked her finger and rubbed it over the baby's dry lips.

The woman moved forward and took another picture. "How many children do you have?" she said.

You never knew what a stranger's questions really meant. "How many kids do you have?" could mean "How much food do you have with you, and if I send my kids by at suppertime, will you feed them?" "Where is your man?" might mean "Is there anybody to protect you, or would you be easy to rob?"

"Seven," Mary said. Why had she answered?

The woman squinted at Mary as if she was trying to see something particular, the way Mary did when she searched for a nit in her children's hair. The woman held the camera at her chest and peered down into the eyepiece. She seemed dissatisfied. She moved to the right. Mary felt self-conscious, as if she was failing at something she hadn't even known she was trying to achieve. *She doesn't have an authentic look.* Wasn't that what the photographer had said so long ago when Mary had stood shivering in the town square in that shred of doeskin?

"Where are the others?" the woman said as she focused her camera.

Don't answer. "Radiator's busted. They went into town to get it fixed." What was it about this woman and her camera that made it seem like she had the right to know everything about Mary's life? As the woman repositioned herself one foot, then two feet closer, Mary felt trapped. So dug in there was no way out.

"Food is scarce?" the woman said.

"That's right."

"What do you live on?"

"Killed birds and frozen vegetables."

"You have much work lately?"

"Not lately."

"That's the story I hear everywhere I go," the woman said, distracted by some mechanical problem with her camera.

The story, Mary thought. A poor woman holding a sick baby. Two sniveling children and a girl wishing she had movie-star hair. What story should she tell this woman? *I have a man who will leave one day.*

I have a girl who likes Necco Wafers. The baby let out a miserable cry. She wished she'd asked Earl to pick up some medicine in town. But she'd been flustered when she'd wrongly accused him of wanting to abandon her and she hadn't thought clearly. And how would he have enough money to pay for the car and the medicine? She should have told him to forget about the radiator, that the baby was more important. But without a car there was no chance of work, and with no work there was no way to pay for the fever-reducing syrup this baby needed. There was all this useless thinking *what if,* as if there were some other choice to make when there were no more choices. There was only whatever was going to happen.

"Maybe I can get the little ones to turn around," the lady said. "That's right. Just turn right around so you're not looking at me. One of you on each side of your mama. Just like that."

Della and James did as they were told and faced away from the camera. James leaned into Mary's shoulder to let her know he was there. Her protector. Her silent guardian. The baby made small mewling sounds. Mary put her hand to her chin and worried the tiny scar that remained from when her mother had held four quarters in her hand and cut her across the jaw. She looked away.

The woman took a photograph. "Thank you," she said. "I've got what I need." She turned and limped back to her car.

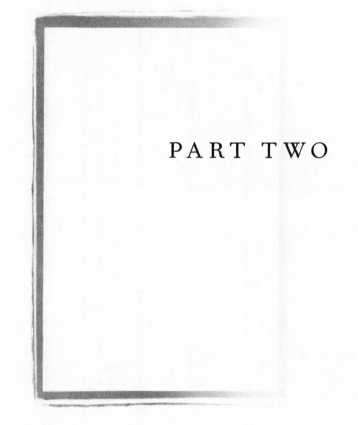

PART TWO

Vera

20.

Steep Ravine, California, 1965

She had a plan. One final project. She would photograph her family. She'd photographed all over the world, in Ireland and Egypt and Venezuela. In California and Arizona and Utah and Oregon. In Syria and Texas and Ceylon. She'd taken thousands of pictures of strangers in strange places. But she had never photographed the people closest to her. A snap here and there, of course. But she'd never taken them on as a real subject. She would photograph them at home, at this simple cabin sitting on a cliff above the sea. Here, on the edge of the continent, where the walls shook when a powerful wave crashed below. At this place that was so redolent with life that it was the only place she could imagine dying.

Dying turned out to be a concerted activity, something that required effort and a kind of specific contemplation. It was not unlike the state she'd been in when she'd made the best of her photographs and had experienced a transcendent focus, a sense of being removed from time as if her whole existence was narrowed down to one precise instant on the continuum, a second made infinite. This was what death would be, too, she imagined: a moment that would happen once and then recur each time it was encountered in memory, just as a photograph was new each time it caught someone's fresh gaze. All those egregious euphemisms for death—slipping away, passing on—they suggested an attenuation, which was not at all what dying felt like. It was seizing the right moment that would tell the whole story. She had to be ready.

"You and Miller bring little Teddy here this weekend," she said, summoning the image of her youngest grandson, all wheeling arms and legs and energy as if he were put on earth simply to keep molecules of air in motion. "Call Philip and tell him I want little Maggie and Benjamin here, too. I want everybody here."

"Let's see if you're up to it, Vera." Miller's wife, Melanie, came into the living room with a plate of food. She had such a good, strong face, Mellie did. Those quick blue eyes always searching for oncoming hurt. A husband like Miller couldn't be easy. He was a man so remote that he must require a woman to study his every lip quiver and barely perceptible shift in expression in order to try to understand him. Just like his father. Everett had been so frustratingly independent. Although not really, she supposed. He needed all those women, didn't he?

If Vera had the energy right now she'd take a photo of Melanie. But she had not eaten much in the last few days and she felt weak. It had become harder to swallow as her esophagus constricted, the cancer a literal lump in the throat. Mellie was always optimistic, cutting the cheese and bread into ever smaller morsels, patiently offering them to Vera with a fork one at a time as if she were feeding a doll at a child's tea party. Vera had not asked Mellie to drive out from the city each day, or to ferry her to doctor's appointments, or sit with her while she received her treatments when there had been any point to them, and she wondered whether her dedication was just an overflow of unspent care. Vera imagined that the young woman's natural exuberance and her disturbing tendency toward organization were so thwarted by a taciturn husband and a dutiful child that she found purpose in managing a dying woman. In her bright yellow shift that stopped above her sturdy, thick knees, with her blond hair pulled back from her forehead by a wide pink headband printed with daisies, Mellie was a flutter of words and make-work, the kind of person who thought life needed more life in it all the time.

"I want my grandchildren here," Vera repeated. She was embarrassed by the petulance in her voice, the whine of childhood making a repeat and final performance along with the need for cut-up food and twice-a-day naps and the humiliation of occasional wet sheets. *I will cook*, she thought. *A three-bean soup. There will be hot chocolate and marshmallows to chase the afternoon chill. I will take my final photographs and with any luck, after they leave, I will die.*

Mellie sat down next to Vera and began to shuffle through the day's mail. "Bill, bill, junk, junk," she said. "Something from a college in Kentucky, something from *Look*. Do you want me to open these?"

"I'll do it," Vera said. She alternated between feeling grateful for Mellie's attention and being irked by the notion that everyone assumed she could do nothing for herself. Mellie, good at sensing Vera's moods, now claimed the impossible—that the kitchen had gone to hell—and left her alone.

The college was mounting a Vera Dare symposium the following winter and they would be honored by her presence, all expenses paid. Well, that was out of the question, of course. She would be dead by next winter. She found a pencil and scribbled "send regrets" on the letter so that Mellie would know how to respond. It was a relief not

to have to take part in one more of these vaguely embarrassing pub-
lic rituals where she had to manufacture a requisite amount of self-
regard in order to justify other people's decision to celebrate her.
Adulation had the converse effect of making her feel like a fraud. No
one knew what it had taken to do the work she did. No one knew
what it had cost.

The letter from *Look* was nothing but a typed note on magazine
letterhead. *Please forward enclosed to Miss Dare.* Stapled to that page
was another letter written by hand on a sheet of flowered stationery:

Two Years ago it was called to My attention that This Photo
appeared in Look Magazine and in U.S. Camera. Since I have not
been consulted, I request you Recall all the un-Sold Magazines.
You would do Vera Dare a great Favor by Sending me her address
That I may Inform her that should the picture appear in Any magazine again I and my children shall be Forced to Protect our rights.
Trusting that it will not be necessary to use Drastic Means to force
you to Remove the magazine from Circulation Without Due Permission to Use my Picture in your Publication I remain

Respectfully,

Mary Coin

Some ghostly feeling took possession of Vera, as if her body had
been replaced by something vaporous and uncertain. She felt everything at once: cold, feverish, heavy, light. Was this it, then? Was she
dying? "Drastic Means," she said out loud.

"What's that, Vera?" Mellie called from the kitchen.

Mary Coin. Vera's inhale came with an alarming sound, and Mellie rushed in looking concerned. The oxygen tank stood in the corner. Vera refused it because the mask was uncomfortable and because the idea of walking around with a green canister trailing behind her like a woeful dog was unseemly.

Mellie took the letter from Vera's hand and read it. "What picture is she talking about?"

"It's nothing. Not important," Vera said, unwilling to mention the picture that no longer existed as a photograph for her but had become something else in its ubiquity, a loud gong that seemed to drown out everything else she had ever done in her life.

"What do you want to do about this?" Mellie said, waving the letter lightly back and forth.

"Get rid of it."

Patrick's car crunched over the dirt drive. Vera listened for the ease and hiss as he turned off the ignition. Even after all these years, her heart quickened when he came back from wherever he went during the day—to the office the university still kept for him, where he puttered among his reports and talked to his acolytes, to the pharmacy to collect whatever new drug her doctors prescribed. Drug upon drug upon drug until it was impossible to know which of her complaints were authentic and which were the result of this chemical laboratory she had become. She suspected that sometimes Patrick had nowhere to go but that he needed to get away from her and her eagerness for death. Such a solid man who peered intently through his round wire-rimmed glasses in order to look at difficult things, and yet, in this most irrefutable aspect of life he wished to dwell in obfuscation. "You look fine, Vera," he said each morning when he turned his gentle, still boyish face to look at her in their bed, even though her complexion was crushed and sallow and she was growing more frail by the day. It was the same thing he'd said to her on the morning of their wedding in '35 when she'd arrived at the county clerk's office in what was essentially a clean version of her work outfit—brown slacks, a white camp shirt, her beret. She'd considered something more festive, but dressing up in a new frock for serious-minded Patrick McClure seemed a silly and frivolous expenditure at that time. When she'd married Everett, she'd worn a getup that could only be described as Edwardian circus. The whole event in her studio had felt like a performance they were putting on for each other, which, in the end, was what their marriage had turned out to be. Her marriage to Patrick was earthbound and frank. A formal outfit would have been useless, as well, for they were in the middle of a job in the Imperial Valley and would be going straight into the fields after the ceremony, he to gather more information about the conditions at the workers' camps, she to take photographs in order to put faces to his statistics.

He was such a terribly awkward man. When he first observed how easily she approached strangers and gained their trust, he told her she seemed kind. He said this with the somber intensity she had not yet gotten used to, and she thought he was chastising her for her lack of scientific rigor. She had just been hired to work with him, and she wanted to be taken seriously as a documenter of the truth and not as a dilettante intent on making the poor out to be quaint or picturesque. "If you knew me any better you would not call me that," she'd said. When she noticed his hurt expression, she realized that he had been flirting. This was the first moment when she'd felt that unexpected—what was it, a chill? A rearrangement of particles in the air mimicked by an alteration in her cells? She was taken by surprise; she was a mother of small boys, still married to Everett, although only because it cost money to divorce—they barely spoke anymore and saw the children separately. Later, after she and Patrick had begun their affair, it amused her to think that this professor of economics who was so bent on exactitude had used such an inaccurate word to describe her. *Kind.* She knew she was curious and demanding. She had more than once been accused of being hard, which she attributed to her mannish face, a certain crease between her eyes that had deepened over the years, and the fact that she looked at a person until she saw him, which sometimes took an unnervingly long time. She knew she could sniff out a lie and that she could tell when she was being cheated out of money. All of these skills had ensured her survival when she came West and made herself up out of nothing, and again when she had muscled her way into this government job documenting migrant farmers. But kind?

When she and Patrick arrived at a new farm, he would stride into the field in his chino slacks and oxford cloth shirt as if he were a civilian walking through the field of active battle, too intent on his mission to notice that he was unarmed. He would not rest until his numbers—of bushels and pay scales and water breaks and outhouses—were absolutely correct. Meanwhile, she would wander into the campsite. She recognized the way women standing outside their shacks and tents studied her suspiciously. She would tell people her name. She would talk about the heat or the cold. If there were little boys she would mention her boys, the games Philip liked to play, the way Miller referred to daydreaming as "wandering around in my brain." If a little girl was interested in her beret, she would take it off and let her try it on. A mother might smile, seeing her daughter preen and remembering, perhaps, when she had stood in front of a mirror in easier times admiring a particular shawl or her wedding dress. Vera knew photographers who tried to capture pictures on the sly without asking for permission. But these were proud people working hard against all odds, and Vera believed they deserved her acknowledgment. She explained that the images would be used to encourage the politicians to build proper worker housing, schools for the children, to provide doctors at the camps. She was honest. But was she kind?

Would Miller and Philip call her kind when they said their speeches over her grave?

Patrick came into the house carrying a grocery bag in each arm. He had always loved to do the marketing, but now it had become an obsession. Each day he announced that he had seen some marvelous tomatoes at a roadside stand near Stinson Beach, or that the zucchinis in Marin were as big as torpedoes. The inverse relationship between his desire to fill the house with food and her inability to eat it made her sometimes angry, often sad, occasionally as delighted as a young woman being given yet another unnecessary bauble by a lover.

"How's my girl?" he said, setting the bags on the coffee table.

"Your girl is a bit so-so today," she said.

He rubbed her back lightly.

"Listen, dear," she said. "I've invited everyone here for the weekend."

"Everyone?"

"Philip and Miller and their broods. The whole lot of them. It's warm. The little ones can sleep outside. I'll set up the teepee."

"That's a job of work for one woman," he said knowingly.

"You know what I mean." In this marriage, she was allowed to be impulsive and even, on occasion, pettily tyrannical. He was steady and indulgent and charmed.

"I want a campfire and marshmallows and ghost stories. I want swimming and games and lots of food," she said. "I want it to be perfect."

After Mellie left for the day and while Patrick was busy in the kitchen, Vera retrieved the letter from the trash. She was not a habitual archivist, and Patrick had a way of going through the waste-paper basket, certain that she was throwing away important information. She complained that when he did this she had to go through the process of discarding things all over again. "I don't want to die asphyxiated by all this *stuff*!" she'd complain, although her heart would catch when she'd see him wince. She knew that it was not the bits of papers or orphaned earrings he was trying to salvage. She would hide the letter in a cigar box where she kept all the birthday notes he'd given her over the years. Each one was a simple sentiment written in his crabbed, left-handed scrawl—*I love you always,* or *You are my true love.* She'd traded in a marriage to a capricious philanderer for one to a loyal realist, but after all these years, she could finally take a man at his word.

She smoothed out Mary Coin's letter and reread it.

She was certain no one at *Look* had responded. The woman had no rights over the image. None of those people did, the farmers and bosses and little children and unemployed mothers and fathers leading their families down empty roads. The camera did that—it asserted your significance and robbed you of it at the same time. It looked at you and then turned away. At any rate, the photograph belonged to the government. If Vera had received a dollar for every time that picture had been reprinted she'd be a rich woman, but she'd made nothing more than the minimal salary she'd been paid. It would be easy enough to clear up this misunderstanding. She would draft a response and send it to the woman. It was the right thing to do.

But even as she made this decision she was unsettled. The letter's intent went beyond anything as simple as the desire for compensation.

I and my children shall be Forced to Protect our rights.

There was something disconcerting about the curious capitalizations. Just as a photograph was a series of symbols extracted from a tapestry of visual information, these emphasized words seemed implicative to Vera, their value foregrounded. There was urgency in those capitalizations. The words were freighted with—what? Vera could almost hear the emotional shake of the woman's voice. She had agreed to be photographed, but of course no one really knew what it meant to have one's picture taken. Everyone thought they did. But no one did.

The letter was an accusation. Vera hadn't known she had been waiting for it.

21

S hhh, shhh." It was Patrick, leaning over her.

"What? What is it?" Vera said, struggling to focus.

"You were screaming. You must have had a bad dream."

"Bad dream," she repeated. But it was no dream. It was life, as true as it had been so many years ago when she was a little girl lying in the hospital bed, and that nurse—what was her name? *For sure you'll be lame, so.* A damning sentence uttered as lightly as a nursery rhyme. She must have been dangling in some area of consciousness that came before dreaming, or maybe it was a deeper kind of dream that circled back toward reality, a place of clear, tactile recollection.

"Peg," she said.

"What, darling?"

"Nurse Peg."

Patrick fitted the oxygen mask over her nose and mouth and turned the knob. A sibilant white noise filled the room, which quickly lulled him back to sleep. She removed the mask and sat up. It took her a few moments to gather the strength to stand. As she crossed the room, she steadied herself first on the dresser, then the chair, then the door frame. The floorboards were cold beneath her feet. But it was good to feel cold wood. It was good to be awake in the night with the soles of your feet pressing against the floor, to feel the watery, chimerical sense of being conscious while the rest of the world slept. She wondered whether the pains and deprivations of illness were a way for a person to feel most alive before the end, to sense every nerve and cell and muscle to their utmost so that there would be no mistaking that one had lived.

She searched for the photo. She never liked to display her work around the house. There was something unseemly about doing such a thing, like leaving your drying brassiere hanging on the shower rod for guests to see. She finally found it in the living room among a group of framed pictures stacked upright against a wall. As she brushed the dust off the glass with the sleeve of her nightgown, she remembered how excited Miller and Philip became whenever she or Everett pulled into a filling station on the long trips to and from Taos. The boys stopped fighting while they watched the attendant scrape away road dust and bird droppings from the windshield with his rubber-edged tool. She could still picture their amazed expressions, as they saw a more sharply brilliant world reveal itself through the windshield. That was the thing about looking through frames: you saw something you had seen before, maybe hundreds of times, but you noticed it differently. She set the picture against the wall and sat opposite it. The photograph embarrassed her. It was not that she didn't think it was a good image; it was. She had made plenty of poor ones in her career and she knew the difference. She'd found the right distance between herself and her subject this time. She'd gotten just close enough to the woman and her children so that she had not forced a point of view by being too aggressive in angle or by including ironic juxtapositions. The picture had been effective because every single person who looked at it had to decide whose side he was on. But over time it had been so reproduced, so co-opted, so burdened with the obligation to represent an entire era, that it had become something both more and less than the image she had taken that day. It reminded her of an overdecorated soldier who looks less like a hero and more like a little boy playing dress-up. Sometimes, when she came across the image in a book or an article, she averted her eyes.

Like the woman in the picture. Why did she suddenly, at that last moment, turn her gaze away from the camera? Often, people Vera photographed asked her how she wanted them to look or stand—should they comb their hair or put on another dress? She told them they should do whatever made them feel comfortable. As much as she liked a photo that captured some unconscious moment, she also appreciated the formality of the pose. Maybe this was the effect of all her years working in the studio. People talked about the truth as being something you had to steal when the subject was unaware. The phrase was, after all, "taking a picture." But the truth was as much in the way a woman arranged her hair or rubbed a stain off her child's chin before allowing the picture to be taken. The truth was often a performance of an idea of truth.

Why did the woman look away? The question was vexing. Maybe she had lost her nerve and this turning away was a willful disappearance, the way a child covers his eyes and believes no one can see him. Perhaps she thought Vera pitied her. Vera hoped that wasn't the case. Pity was a horrible thing.

Where was the father? Oh, yes. She remembered. He was gone,

repairing the car. She wondered if she would have photographed the family had he been there. Maybe it had been his absence that attracted her. A family minus a father was an unbalanced proposition that the eye always wanted to correct. Perhaps she had been drawn to the fact of their waiting because she knew so well that aching experience where time stretched and slowed, where your sense of purpose dissolved and everything was directed toward *When will he return? What if he doesn't return?*

She told the woman what she was about, and the woman agreed to have her picture taken. Vera started at a distance, maybe thirty feet from the tent. The older girl sat at an angle in the rocking chair, leaning against its back, her head resting in her arms. She looked as if she was daydreaming, and maybe she was. It was a lovely pose, charged with some idea the girl had of herself that was so touching to Vera. Which was probably why she had framed the girl out of the following shots. It was her instinct to move away from easy sentiment. The mother sat inside the tent with the baby and the two small children. Vera took a picture of the woman as she nursed her child. The skin of her breast. The stretch of it, like a pale rise in the landscape. Vera took a few more shots. Then she asked the two little ones to stand on either side of their mother and turn around. Why had she done that? It was not her habit to arrange people. Something about their faces had bothered her. So many children she photographed were uncannily wise, their youthful whimsy snuffed out by hard knowledge. But these two were still openhearted. And they were so attached to their mother, so certain she would protect them from this stranger with a camera. Their smooth, thoughtful expressions, their mussed hair. Those children made Vera think of her boys when they woke from sleep, their wayward locks, their expressions still distracted by dreams. She was abruptly gripped by the certainty that she needed to see Miller and Philip as soon as possible. The feeling descended on her with the full force of an emergency, as if her boys were in distress and she had to get to them immediately.

"That's right. Just turn around," she encouraged when the children were slow to respond to her request.

But even when they faced away, she could still see their innocent expressions. She took the final photograph, packed up the Graflex, and left.

On the long drive home, it began to rain. Her leg ached. It was always worse in the rain. There were times when she regarded her body as nothing more than a machine that eased and swelled depending on the weather. The windshield wipers were worn down, and she leaned over the steering wheel in order to see between streaks of water. She was frustrated that the weather was slowing her progress, and that it would take her that much longer to get to the boys. It was only Thursday and she was not expected until Friday, but she would get them from the Wilsons' and bring them to Berkeley. She'd treat them to a day off from school. Mrs. Wilson would frown in her disapproving way, but Vera didn't care. Nothing was learned in school; *she'd* learned nothing there, in any case. She considered stopping to make a phone call to alert Mrs. Wilson to the change of plans, but it would be better to surprise the boys. On Fridays, Miller might stand outside the Wilsons' house for two hours before her arrival as if the force of his vigilance could cut time in half and bring Vera to him more quickly. Mrs. Wilson said this was a testament to his love for his mother, but her faint praise was laced with accusation. The notion that her children experienced her comings as a kind of salvation made Vera feel all the more guilty for continuing to board them during the week. Once she and Patrick had married, she'd given up her costly studio and moved into his two-room apartment, which was hardly large enough for a couple, never mind adding two growing boys into the mix. And, Vera reminded herself, she had to work, and her work required her to be on the road most weeks. That was the nature of the job, and this government contract was a godsend. Everett was broke and contributed to the children's welfare only sporadically. Working as hard as she did was her best chance of getting a larger place so that she could bring Miller and Philip back home for good. And Patrick always reminded her that the work was necessary and that it was a different form of selfishness to put her family above those who were impoverished and whose numbers grew daily.

When Miller was six, he had taken to carrying a rucksack on his back all day long, even during school hours when he was sitting at his desk. And what was in the pack? Rocks. Certain rocks he had found and imbued with particular personalities or meanings. Happy rocks. Sad rocks. Angry rocks. Rocks for killing bad guys. If the exact rocks were not there when he looked in his pack each morning—if Philip had stolen one, or if Mrs. Wilson had unloaded the pack to shake out the dirt and neglected to replace them—Miller would burst into tears and refuse to go to school. As Vera drove, she thought of her boy with that bag of rocks bouncing on his back as he played a game of stickball and she sat forward in her seat as if this would get her to him faster.

That girl on the rocking chair. Vera was angry at herself for not taking her portrait. When she had moved closer with her camera, iso-lating the woman and the smaller children, the girl had wandered off. Hers was such a tender age when the slightest gesture could be per-ceived as insult. Vera hoped she hadn't hurt the girl's feelings. But the arrangement of the smaller ones around their mother had been right. When she had told them to turn around—that had been right, too. Their slim necks like the trunks of young trees.

She had forgotten to write down what the woman told her! Vera pulled the car over to the side of the road and took her notepad from her bag. What had the woman said? Did she give her age as thirty-two? Did she say she had six children or seven? Her husband was a native Californian. No, she hadn't called him her husband. She'd said "my man." Vera had been so tired. She had not wanted to turn back. When she had first noticed the sign for pea pickers, she had driven past. She had enough pictures for the week. There would be nothing that would prove the point any more than all the other photo-graphs she'd taken: the situation was dire, more than dire. People were starving. They were living like animals, barely holding on to their dignity. But an insistent voice inside her head told her to go back. It was a compulsion, an itch she had to scratch, because she knew that despite the commonality of the conditions, the farmers were not a monolithic group. There were no two people the same, and there was always the possibility that she would see more or differ-ently, that she would take a photograph that would make the story that much more sharply true. And there had been people by the side of the road. She'd seen that as she'd driven past, hadn't she? A woman and children? Every human face was a mystery.

It was not her custom to ask so little, to spend such a meager amount of time with people. Words were so important to the project. Often she submitted pages of text to Washington to go along with her photographs, descriptions of a place, or of what people were eating, or the cost of food at a camp store. People said such remarkable things. She was careful to write down their exact words. She flipped back through her notebook and read some of the entries.

I've wrote back that we're well and such as that, but I never have wrote that we live in a tent.

A piece of meat in the house would like to scare these children of mine to death.

When you gits down to your last bean, your backbone and your navel shakes dice to see which gits it.

It's the same old dirty story wherever you go.

Vera couldn't remember what else the woman had told her. She had been so impatient to leave, to get away from those children who crowded around their mother, wanting to touch her, to make sure of her and make sure that Vera knew that they belonged only to her.

M rs. Wilson looked annoyed when she opened the door to the soggy mother of her charges. "You can't just show up," she hissed. Vera, too exhausted to be polite, said, "They'll need their jackets. It's raining out."

Her surprise appearance made Philip laugh but Miller look worried, as if she had come to announce terrible news. She reminded herself that Miller was a worrier by nature. A doorbell would ring announcing the postman and Miller would look up with a start as if the house were being robbed. If Vera used a certain tone of voice when she called his name, he would know he was in trouble for tracking mud through the house instead of leaving his shoes by the front door as she asked. He would slowly shuffle over to her, his eyes already brimming, his lips soft and pulpy. She would have to hold herself back from excusing him because a child had to know what was expected. She had learned that lesson from her mother. Mediocrity was unacceptable.

The boys were talkative on the short drive from Oakland to Berkeley. Philip had made a papier-mâché Zeus holding a thunderbolt for his science project on electricity. Mr. Wilson had helped him rig wires and a battery to tiny Christmas lights. When Philip pressed a button, the thunderbolt flashed. Miller had finished reading *The Count of Monte Cristo*. He also reported that Mrs. Wilson had made an apple brown Betty, and both boys traded silly jokes they had invented at the expense of the dessert's ridiculous name.

It rained all that weekend, which made the apartment feel even more cramped than it already was. The children played rounds of Parcheesi. Miller sulked when he did not win, and Philip teased him about being a sore loser, and then they bickered until Vera separated them and suggested they all go for a walk and sail paper boats down the rain-filled gutters. Philip complained that this was a babyish thing to do, but after winning his race against Miller's boat, he crowed in triumph. She cooked a pot of beef stew and made biscuits that ended up looking like large clots of wet tissue, which gave Philip the idea of soaking sheets of toilet paper and then throwing them up to the ceiling where they stuck until they dried and, to the children's delight, plopped down on the kitchen floor as if a giant bird were defecating. The apartment smelled of cooking meat and the indiscriminate bodily odors of boys. She fed and arbitrated and cleaned. She tried to keep up a football conversation with Philip and listened to the exaggerated stories the children told about how horrible the Wilson daughters were, or she half listened because she was already thinking about Monday, when she would be able to go to the basement of the building, where the landlord had allowed her to set up a makeshift darkroom, and develop the pictures she had taken of that woman and her children. For most of the weekend, Patrick sat in his favorite chair writing up his reports, ignoring the clamor that surrounded him. It never crossed his mind that it should be otherwise. But of course they weren't his boys, and he had more pressing things to do than listen to them jabbering about episodes of *The Green Hornet* they'd heard on the Wilsons' radio.

My throat hurts. He took my baseball glove. I'm hungry. But I'm still hungry. I'm thirsty. I'm so bored. But Vera loved them so! They would bake oatmeal cookies. That would pass the hour until bedtime. And the children didn't fight when they helped her in the kitchen as long as she gave each one a spoon to lick. And, oh! Miller! You broke the flower vase! Oh, it's all right. I didn't mean to be mean. Yes, Philip, it is funny. Mean to be mean. It was a special vase, yes. But it doesn't matter, does it? (Yes, it did. Everett had brought it back from Kayenta. She was no longer his wife, but there were pleasing emotions that could still be roused by a vase or one of the carved canes Philip kept by his bedside at the Wilson home.

Bedtime!

Monday morning finally arrived. She rose early and drove the boys back to Oakland. Mrs. Wilson patted their heads as they filed past her, as if counting them to make sure Vera returned all that she had taken out.

"I'm a little bit jealous of you, you know," Mrs. Wilson said as Vera was leaving. "You do whatever you want."

"I do what the government tells me to do."

"You talk to people. You talk to strangers, for heaven's sake!"

Vera had once overheard Mrs. Wilson tell her husband that Vera was not very attractive in her slacks and sturdy shoes and with her hair cut as short as a boy's.

"I don't talk to anybody," Mrs. Wilson said wistfully. Suddenly she brightened. "Hey now, did Miller show you his painting?"

"What painting?"

"The one he made at school. I told him he takes after his father." She turned and called back into the house. "Miller! Miller?"

Miller came to the door, his face expectant. It was cruel of Mrs. Wilson to call him back, to make him think that maybe Vera would take him again.

"Show your mother the picture you made!"

In a moment, Miller reappeared with a sheet of heavy paper on which he'd drawn a woman wearing a cocked cap and slacks. The woman held a camera to her face. He had a sure hand and his rendering of the camera was particularly detailed. The lens stared out from the housing like an eye.

"That's lovely, Miller," Vera said. "You are a very good artist."

"It's a picture of you holding up your camera!" Mrs. Wilson mimed holding a camera in front of her. "I said why don't you draw your mama's face? She has such a pretty smile. And do you know what he said?"

"No."

"He said, 'I don't know what she looks like.'"

"That's ridiculous. Miller knows what I look like. Don't you?" She felt ashamed to display her insecurity in the form of this question. "Don't you, Miller?"

"Yes," he said quietly.

"What color is my hair?"

"Brown."

"And my eyes?"

"Brown."

"Well, they're hazel actually. So next time you can draw a picture of my face. Now go and get ready for school."

"I thought it was such a funny thing for him to say!" Mrs. Wilson said, after Miller had disappeared into the house.

"I'm sure you did," Vera said. When the woman did not catch her sarcasm, she felt a mild victory, but she was still unsettled. "My children know what their mother looks like."

"I didn't mean anything by it," Mrs. Wilson said, nervously patting her apron pockets as if she could already feel their emptiness should Vera decide to find a new placement for the boys.

Vera drove home and went directly to the darkroom. She was right about the picture. Of the six exposures, the one that she had felt at the time, felt in her gut as if there had been a sudden synchronizing of all the heartbeats in the world—that was the one. She sent it to Washington that afternoon and sent another copy to the *News*. She was not in the habit of submitting photographs to the papers, but the woman and those children—she couldn't explain it. She had seen worse—children covered with sores, pregnant women who looked too weak to make it through the ordeal of birth—but this woman and her children, that baby in her arms—there was no time to wait for the people in Washington, there was just no more time.

The picture was published the following week. Not long after, a shipment of supplies was delivered to the pea pickers' camp near Nipomo.

"It doesn't do that woman and her children any good," Vera said. She and Patrick were lying side by side in bed at a tourist cabin outside San Bernardino. "I'm sure she's long gone from that place by now."

"It's for the greater good," Patrick said.

"Oh, what does that even mean?" she muttered.

"It means that—" he began in his patient, teacher's voice.

"I know what it means, for God's sake."

Vera reached for the water glass on her bedside table. It was smudged with the imprint of someone else's lips. Well, they'd stayed in worse places. She drank, then wiped her mouth with her sleeve. It would be two weeks before she saw her children again.

They were safe, she reminded herself. They were well cared for, even if that Wilson woman was insufferable. Patrick leaned over and kissed her neck. She had argued that they ought to drive to Berkeley for the weekend, but Patrick was right: they could not afford to waste that kind of money on gas. And they had already told the children what the schedule would be, and it might be confusing to them in the future if plans were not fixed. And, he'd argued, it would be good for the two of them to have a weekend alone even if they had to spend it in a dirty room. He had a way of separating everything in his mind so that one concern did not affect another. The work was separate from the children. The issues in the marriage were separate from the inevitable tensions that arose when they worked together. But to her these considerations clustered in an unyielding knot that sat in her stomach and never loosened unless she was absorbed in taking pictures or ensconced in the quiet of her darkroom focusing on making good negatives. So the work was an antidote to the guilt, which arose because of the work. And around and around.

"She said they ate dead birds," she said.

"Who?" His voice was muffled by her skin. She looked down and saw his erection pressing against the material of his pajamas.

"That woman in the photo. She said her daughter was good at killing birds."

He leaned back against the thin pillow and sighed.

"Philip is relentless with Miller," she said. "Always picking on him. He puts that knife in and twists. What does Miller have that he's got to be jealous of? Philip is older, he's stronger."

"It's the way of brothers," Patrick said.

She exhaled heavily. Patrick had a habit of ending a discussion he was not interested in with these sorts of meaningless platitudes.

"When Miller was little, just learning to talk, he'd look at something, a window, say, and he'd call it 'that rectangle that you look through,'" she said. "And Philip, no matter where he was in the house, would hear it and say, 'The word is *window*.' I swear, that boy can hear his brother make a mistake a mile away, but try to get his attention when you're standing right in front of him."

They were quiet for a while.

"I always liked the way Miller described it, though," she said. "A single word reduces a thing, don't you think? A window is nothing. But a rectangle that you see through . . . that's something, isn't it?"

The ocean roar was so loud at night that even though the cabin sat high above the shore, Vera had the sense of the waves lapping at the walls. Sitting opposite the photograph, she felt small inside of time. A rectangle that you look through. The feeling of seeing an image emerge from a bath, the blacks and grays separating themselves from the not-quite-whites. It was like a birth. There you are, she'd said to each of her sons when they were born. There it was: a newly printed photograph. The thing suddenly real in her hands. And then it left her hands and went into the world and became this— She looked at the picture. At first she had been proud of the attention the photograph brought to the farmworkers. And she would be lying if she said she did not enjoy the recognition that came with its publication. It had given her a career. You could say you didn't care, that all that mattered was the work. But that was bunk. Everyone had an ego. But sometimes, when she was introduced at a party or a conference, she could see the faces of her new acquaintances adjust as they scrolled through all they knew or had heard about the photo and then related to her as if she were a set of assumptions.

A bird flew into the window of the cabin with a sharp clap of sound and dropped onto the deck. Vera walked over to the glass and saw the mark where the accident occurred. The bird lay in a pool of amber light thrown by the outdoor fixture, injured but still alive. It tried to rise to its feet. It flapped its tail feathers but could not manage any real movement. It opened and closed its beak, then spread its wings and began to rock from side to side in an attempt at liftoff. Stretching its neck at an odd angle to work against inertia, it managed nothing except small lateral movements across the deck.

"Come on. Come on," Vera whispered. But even as she urged the bird to life she knew it was useless. She should call Patrick. He could go outside and throw the bird into the air in the hope that, with a little help, it would find its wings. But she knew the bird would only fall back to the ground and undergo another devastating impact. It was too late for the bird. Its initial collision with the window had done it in, and anything she might try would only serve to salve her guilt, nothing more. She could not turn away, though. It would be a horrible thing for the bird to die alone. She would be its last witness. But a witness only looks. She had seen so much in her life, but she understood so little.

I and my children . . .

She gave the dying bird her gaze. That was all she knew how to do, and it wasn't enough, in the end. The bird folded its wings into itself and was gone. It had taken a terribly long time for it to die. A lifetime, it seemed to her.

"Vera?" It was Patrick, hair askew, his pajama bottoms twisted around his waist.

"A bird has died on the porch."

"I'll get it," he said, grabbing tongs from the fireplace.

"Leave it be," she said.

"We don't want a possum."

"Please, leave it be!"

"Vera?"

She was crying now. He put his arms around her and whispered into her hair. *Shhhh. Shhhh.* Why did people try to shush trouble away as if it were an unruly child? They didn't want the anger, the inconvenience, the ungainly mess. Patrick needed her to be docile. She would do that for him. He was so good. She let him lead her back to bed and lay passively while he tucked the sheets around her. He drew the blanket under her chin, smoothed her hair. He told her she looked fine.

22.

As requested, Miller and Philip brought their wives and children for the weekend. Vera took out her Nikon and cleaned the lenses. If she could muster the energy, she would begin her project. She decided that, in order to make photographs of any resonance, she would have to treat her children and grandchildren, at least photographically, as strangers. And, as she always did when she began to work, she would start by watching. She would see how they moved, how they grouped themselves, how the house and the ocean worked on them. People in places.

Walking toward the cliff's edge, her Nikon slung around her neck, she leaned heavily on her cane. She had resisted the cane— after all those years of masking a limp, a cane seemed a particular insult. But she had fallen twice in the last few months, and now Patrick insisted on it whenever she left the house. She felt the sea wind swoop up to greet her. Down below, the coastline was cut in such a way as to suggest that the ocean had taken a ravenous bite out of the land. The children scampered on the beach.

People in places. It was only when she had left her studio and had begun to photograph men and women in the context of their lives that she had known what to do with hers. She was surprised it had taken her so long to figure this out. She had spent her childhood in a city where, despite the tall buildings and bridges, the real monuments were human—the somber faces of men and women lost in their exhaustion as they trudged home, the stretched mouths of vendors hawking bok choy in Chinatown, the little boys with curled forelocks racing among the food carts on Delancey. She hadn't had a camera then, hadn't even thought about taking a photograph. And yet, when she looked back, she counted those images as her first pictures.

Her grandchildren chased the waves in and out, hoisted kites into the air, or threw glops of wet sand at one another. Their bodies were exuberant exclamation points, bent-over commas, crouched and contemplative periods.

"Don't you want a chair, Mother?"

It was Miller. She had not heard him come out of the house. Tall and lean, he had inherited Everett's stance in an almost chilling way. Her first husband's erect posture suggested the showman but masked a deep unease. When Everett sat, one leg bounced restlessly against the other. His long fingers whose passage across her skin she had once craved and whose travels across other bodies she had envied were always at play as though he was marking the seconds as they passed. Miller had adopted Everett's long-legged habit of kicking his feet out in front of him when he walked. Of course, it had occurred to Vera that he might have picked up his odd gait from her, the way a child takes on a parent's accent or an idiosyncratic gesture. Her limp, and the embarrassment and ambition it had created in her, were not the qualities she had wished to pass on to her younger son.

"Take me down to the beach," she said, motioning with the end of her cane.

"If you'd like, Mother."

He was so cordial. When she called him on the telephone and he was busy with something, he would say, "May I call you back?" *May I,* as if she were a business associate who required a particular formality. *I am your mother!* she always wanted to shout. But if you had to claim a thing it wasn't really yours. Philip was lighter of spirit. He didn't mind making a joke of hard times, teasing her about how lucky he was to have lived with the Wilsons all those years; otherwise, how would he have picked up Mr. Wilson's highly scatological vocabulary?

Miller grasped her arm and guided her carefully down the wooden steps.

"Tell me something," she said.

"What?"

"Anything. Tell me how you are."

"I'm fine, Mother."

"No one is fine. Fine is a placeholder."

"You always like to stir things up."

"I just like a plain answer."

"The plain answer is that I am fine."

"How is your work?"

"Busy."

"You chose the right place to be a geologist, I suppose. All those earthquakes."

"I'm not a seismologist, Mother. You know that."

She did know this, of course. He worked for an oil company. She had only been trying to make a feeble joke, but he was not one for small talk. In conversation, they were like people who had gotten lost on the way to somewhere but were both too stubborn to ask for directions. She stumbled over a rock, and he caught her.

"Are you all right, Mother?"

"Fine. I'm fine," she said, then laughed. "We're a pair, aren't we?"

"What do you mean?"

Sometimes she wanted to shake him. Mrs. Wilson had once said that Philip was easier to love. Vera had thought the woman cruel for saying it. "I love my boys equally," she responded, insinuating the woman's inferiority. But of course this was not true. She loved them differently; it was impossible not to. Philip, the playful extrovert, gave her confidence. Miller had been so quiet and hard to reach, so prone to tears. He had made her feel that nothing she said or did could make him happy.

Once on the beach, she walked away from him. She hoped she could manage the shifting terrain of the sand without making a fool of herself.

"Grandma! Grandma!"

She waved. The children continued their games. She padded along the scalloped line drawn by the tide, her sneakers and the tip of her cane making loosely formed indentations in the wet sand that were quickly filled by incoming water. She watched as the imprints disappeared. It was the opposite of a photograph coming to life. But that was not life, was it? Life was this sinking in, this evaporation, this dissolve until what was there might never have existed, its brief presence leaving no trace. Perhaps it had been a monumental self-delusion to imagine that her work had captured life. Hubris, really.

As if life could be stilled when it was always running, always moving, just like her grandchildren.

She reached the place where a serrated line of rocks prevented her from walking farther. She was overwhelmed with a profound lassitude. Her throat felt tight. Had she taken her medication? Was it possible that she was no longer able to walk a few feet of beach? Doors were closing one after the other and too fast. The children lay on their towels now, shivering probably; the water was so cold. Beyond them stood Miller, a black figure backlit by the sun. He had lifted his hand to his brow presumably to keep her in his sights, and a near perfect triangle of sky showed through the space created by his bent arm. Vera's eye immediately framed the image. Would she include the sea? That would be mawkish. And it would have nothing to do with Miller, right at this moment on this beach. Miller, her inscrutable son whose dutiful attentions could not be mistaken for love. She raised her camera to her eye, shifting him to the center of the frame. But she was too far away. It would be no good unless she could get closer.

Climbing back up to the house was difficult. The impatient children squeezed past with their towels and buckets and sandy thighs and ran ahead. She squeezed Miller's arm to let him know she needed to rest.

"I'll get Philip," Miller said. "We'll carry you the rest of the way."

"You'll do no such thing." Philip might make a joke of it. Queen Vera being borne by her loyal subjects—something like that. A quip that would have suggested their family history but in a way that gentled the past. For Miller it would be just one more instance of his mother's selfishness or whatever it was he told his wife, or probably didn't tell her.

After her nap, she sat at lunch, enduring the worried glances of her family. Despite having no appetite, she felt a renewed energy and was ready to begin her project. After the dishes were cleared away, she slung the Nikon around her neck, gathered the children, and proposed a safari. It was their favorite activity when they came for visits. Once they were outside, the little boys raced around finding sticks to serve as guns or arrows for bentwood bows although they knew that a safari with Grandma, even a make-believe one, was of a different sort, and that they would be hunting not with weapons but with their eyes.

"Be still!" she said, holding her cane out to stop their movement. A squirrel was perched on the tip of the Alphonso mango. "See there?" she said. The children crowded around her, following the line of her outstretched finger. Gasps of recognition and a whine from Maggie who could not see the squirrel and felt left out. "See the stripe on its back?" Vera said. "Tell me what else."

"It has a long tail," Benjamin said.

"Where is it? Where?" Maggie complained.

"What else?" Vera said.

"Fingers grabbing," Teddy whispered.

"Claws," she corrected. The children watched the squirrel. She took a picture of Ben wiping his nose on his shirtsleeve. Suddenly the squirrel sensed their presence and darted away. Maggie's expression crumpled into righteous anger as she realized she had missed the excitement. Vera took a picture of the moment before tears. She took another of Teddy crouched over something in the grass. Of Maggie, this time laughing. The satisfying click of the shutter. The feel of the cold metal against her eye. Blur to focus.

Teddy found a fallen branch split into the shape of the letter *Y*. Ben pointed out the way the angle of the roof cut a cloud perfectly in two. The children were getting good at seeing what was not obvious, and her praise was extravagant. She took more photographs. Teddy studying a mushroom. Ben leaping up in a vain attempt to capture a butterfly. Maggie with her expression of perpetual anxiety about being left behind by the bigger boys. Teddy, again, with his heart-breaking elbows. Ben, who had a tubby boy's waddle to his run and who seemed enviably at ease in the world.

"Grandma! Look! A snail!"

"Grandma! Come here! I found a dead bee!"

There was so much to look at. Still so many unframed worlds for her to capture. The sense of time slipping away, of these perfect children eluding her. Her throat closed. She needed her oxygen. *No.* She needed to sit down. Where was the chair? She could not get a breath. Her head was spinning. Not in front of the children. Not yet!

It was dark. She lay in her bed. The screen door leading from the kitchen to the yard squealed softly. The scrape of someone bumping into one of the dining room chairs. How had she gotten here? The last thing she remembered was being in the yard with the children. Patrick slept by her side. The sound must have been one of her sons, restless in the night just like his father. But when the bedroom door opened, she saw a small figure backlit by the soft glow from the outdoor lights.

"Grandma?"

"Come closer."

It was dear Teddy, standing by her bedside now, his wrists showing below the too-short sleeves of his pajama top.

She put out her hand to touch him. "What is it, darling?"

"You fell down at the safari."

"Yes, I did. I'm sorry."

"Did you die?"

"No. Not yet. Can't you sleep?"

"I heard something," he whispered.

"What?"

"I think it was a bear."

"There are no bears here."

"I think it was a bear, Grandma." His voice trembled.

"Do you want Grandpa to take you back to the teepee?"

"I don't want to sleep there anymore."

"Do you want to sleep with me?"

"Yes."

She lifted the corner of her blanket, and he slid in beside her. He laid his head against her chest and snaked his arm across her stomach. She prayed to a God she didn't believe in to keep her alive through at least this night.

When she woke in the morning, she was alone. She heard the sound of breakfast outside her bedroom, the clinks of cereal bowls, the hum of conversation. It took her a long time to sit up. Every muscle in her body hurt. Finally she managed to pull on her bathrobe. It took another five minutes to stand.

When she entered the kitchen, Teddy saw her and lowered his eyes.

"What do you have to say to your grandmother?" Miller said.

"I'm sorry," Teddy said.

"Sorry for what?" Vera said.

"For disturving you," Teddy said.

"Disturbing," Miller corrected.

"But it was no disturvance at all," Vera said, winking at her grandson.

"A boy his age should be able to sleep on his own," Miller said.

"It was just a nightmare," Vera said to Miller. "You had your fair share when you were his age, crawling into bed with me and your father at all hours."

"I don't remember that at all," Miller said stiffly.

"Well, of course you did. It got so that we talked about putting a lock on our bedroom door."

"Maybe you should have," Philip said, grinning. "You would have saved me some very traumatic experiences!"

"Well, Everett and I were in the habit of sleeping in the raw. And you boys surprised us a time or two."

She was immediately aware of her mistake. She and Everett had been in bed when they told the boys that they were separating, not long after that awful time in Taos. They had decided to avoid the funereal quality of a serious conversation—boys on the couch, parents standing before them to issue the news. They wanted things to feel normal, like any other morning when Philip and Miller would burst into the room, filled with energy and ready for their parents to tell them what adventures the day held. Had they actually thought that would be best? To lie in bed and tell their children they were no longer going to live as a family? What she wanted to say was that it

had been lovely to see Teddy's spectral presence in the night, that to
have him lie beside her had been such late and unexpected luck. But
she had queered the image.

By late morning, the adults were preparing to leave. Mellie and
Philip's wife, Nancy, looked here and there for lost toys and missing
socks. Philip and Ben tossed a football in the yard. Miller stood by the
cliff's edge. The wind filled the back of his shirt and blew his trousers
against his legs.

Vera put her camera around her neck and joined him. Together,
they studied the ocean. The waves were topped with whitecaps. Patrick was swimming with Teddy and Maggie.

"One last swim," she said, watching as Patrick hoisted Teddy
aloft and then dropped him into the water. The weekend had worn
her out. As soon as her family left, she would need to lie down.

"We can come back," Miller said. "Whenever you want to see the
children."

They were both quiet for a moment.

"You never really liked it here, even when you were younger," she
said. "I suppose it was a boring place to bring teenagers. Not much
action."

"It was fine."

He would never let her know what he felt. It was a decision he
seemed to have made long ago, one that he would keep to the end.

She lifted her camera and took his picture.

His anger flared in an instant. "What are you doing?"

She took another photo.

"Please don't."

"But I want to take your picture. I've never done it properly."

"It's too late, Mother."

"What are you talking about?" She took another shot. He turned away. She took another. There he was. Her boy with the rocks in his backpack. Her boy who sucked his fingers so that she had needed to put a special bitter-tasting polish on his nails in order to stop his teeth from bucking. Her lovely boy who looked at her with amazement when she taught him how to draw the sweet drop from a honeysuckle flower, who cried with her when Christopher Robin had to say good-bye to the Hundred Acre Wood, who had grown tall enough to one day lift his tiny mother into the air like a rag doll. She'd thought he meant to hug her, but he was simply moving her to the side so he could move through the hallway on his way out of the house. She took another photograph.

"Stop, Mother. Please. It's not necessary anymore."

She lowered the camera. He was right. There was no point in pretending. She had taken a handful of pictures over the weekend, but they were only the maudlin shots of a grandmother besotted with her grandchildren. All her life, she could come upon a nameless stranger and make some private aspect of his character instantly known to the hundreds or thousands who might see the photograph she made of him. But her family . . . she knew their names and yet she could not take a photograph that would reveal them, even to her.

It came to her then that she had never written down the names of the people she photographed. That had been a guideline of the project. It was a way of protecting people so that nothing they told Vera or Patrick would compromise them. Until she received Mary Coin's letter, Vera had never known the woman's name.

23

How could she explain herself?

Dear Mrs. Coin . . .

She would start from the beginning with the history. She could explain about William Henry Fox Talbot. *How charming it would be if it were possible to cause these natural images to imprint themselves durable and remain fixed upon the paper!* She could explain about daguerreotypes and salted paper prints and albumen prints and tintypes and photogravure. But none of this information would have anything to do with what happened when one person lifted a camera to her face and took a picture of another. It was more complicated than love. It was more complicated than sex, than children. Or maybe it was the exact expression of those complications, which included intimacy and distance, holding and turning away, lies and never the truth.

It had been two weeks since her family had visited. The house was empty now. The quiet had the hollow gnaw of hunger. Outside, rain fell in straight lines, a child's drawing of rain. She was grateful that the weather had held up for the weekend, that the children had been able to swim and play croquet.

Patrick was in the kitchen, mashing up a banana with milk, hoping that she would eat something. The days when Mellie didn't come for one reason or another—today Teddy had a slight fever—were difficult for him. He wore himself down trying to be helpful. One afternoon, after he had cooked food she would not eat and cleaned the oven she had no more use for and washed soiled sheets, she found him sitting naked in a drained bathtub, crying. The fact was that as Vera drew closer to death, Patrick became less essential. More and more, her days were a private conversation between herself and her body. She hoped there would not be many more of them. She looked at her hands. Her nails needed trimming. She stood up slowly and negotiated her way to the bathroom. Her nails were thick and yellowing and required a firm grip on the scissors. Her cutting hand shook, and the clippings scattered against the porcelain sink. She felt nauseated as she watched the water slosh around the drain, drawing the detritus of her body into the pipes. And then where would they go, these pieces of her? Into the ocean, she supposed. She looked at her face in the mirror. How should she compose the letter?

My Dear Mrs. Coin,—

Patrick peeked into the bathroom. "You okay?"

"Just grooming myself."

"Not on my account, I hope. I love you just the way you are."

"I know it, Patrick. I know you do." She wanted to reassure him that he had loved her precisely right. He would need to have that sense of a job well done. Reassurance. That was it.

Once Patrick left her alone in the bedroom, she sat at her desk and took out her stationery box.

To Mary Coin,

I would like to let you know that the photograph I took of you these many years ago was and is the property of the United States Government. As such, I have no control over how the photograph has been used. I want to reassure you, too, that I have never profited personally from the picture of you and your children.

A lie. Maybe not in direct dollars, but she had profited. She had the satisfaction of being known for her life's work. A man from New York City had asked if she'd like to have a retrospective at the Museum of Modern Art. He meant a posthumous exhibition, of course; these things took years to arrange. Odd to agree to that, but she had.

She took a fresh piece of paper from the box.

Dear Mary Coin,

The picture of which you speak has become synonymous with my name and my identity so much so that I sometimes think that when people hear the name Vera Dare they think of you and imagine that this is what I look like. To be honest, you are better looking than I am. Also, I have not been much of a mother to speak of, although my children have turned out all right, I suppose. But children turn out one way or another, don't they?

Suddenly she felt angry. She crossed out what she had written. How dare this woman accuse her of being a terrible mother? How dare she point out her ugliness and her limp and her choice to go out in the world and take what she saw into her camera because the children at school called her a dirty goy and she didn't want to sit in those classrooms where they were all so smart at reading and math while she knew nothing except what it was like to lie in bed for a year and what it was like to have mothers pull their children away from her so that they wouldn't get what was catching? How dare she accuse Vera of her ambition? It was true. Yes, it was true. She had been relieved when she'd come back to her studio after dropping the children at the Wilsons' for the first time. She was eager to be alone with that horrible, ugly, riveting desire that had been germinating inside her. She felt her ambition as a disfigurement, something deeply unfeminine and not worthy of a mother. She tried to hide it just as she hid her leg under long pants or skirts. In those early days, when she had just begun to take pictures of the world around her, she would walk down the street carrying a small sack of groceries, just enough to feed herself, and she felt women looking at her, their eyes hardened by disapproval, as if they could see her selfishness. Back then, people were mired in their own miseries, and if they were looking at her at all, it was because they wondered what food she had in her bag and where she had gotten the money to pay for it. Still, she could not help feeling that the things she wanted for herself were damnable.

Dear Mrs. Coin,

I don't believe that I have ever really been a Photographer in my life. What I have Done is approach the world with a camera in front of my face. I have pressed my finger down and turned the World into its Opposite. Then I have waited in a Dark Room for Light to come through the negative and for Halide crystals to turn into metallic silver on photographic paper, and for the World to turn back the Right way again. I have put that image in fixer solution so that it will not fade away. So you can call me a Fixer, which is the only Title I can claim and which is the only Crime I can be accused of.

She could not catch her breath. Her oxygen tank stood in the corner. Her hands began to sweat. She must have made a noise because Patrick came quickly and helped her to the bed, fixing the mask to her face, twisting the valve so that the gas began to flow. She winced as he pulled a strand of her hair from underneath the elastic head strap, and he apologized for hurting her. She motioned for him to bring her the stationery and a pen, but he did not understand. If she died now, that last version of the letter would become the end of her story, and this was not how she wanted the story to end.

24

W hat time is it?"

"Did you say something, Vera?"

"I don't know what time it is!" she said.

"Calm down, dear. Calm down."

She felt as if she were in an airplane that had suddenly lost its bearings. "Tell me!"

"Just half past four," he said. He sat down on the bed next to her and patted the spittle on her lips with a tissue. Was it time to lay more hot towels on her legs?

"Papa?"

"It's Patrick, my love. You're confused. You just had a nap."

"Will I be ugly all my life?"

"You're beautiful, Vera."

"Is that why you went away?"

"I'm right here."

"What time is it?"

"It's the afternoon. It's four-thirty in the afternoon."

Philip had been born at ten fifty-seven in the morning. Miller at three forty-nine in the afternoon. She'd made Everett look at his watch. Time mattered. A picture doesn't bring someone to life. A picture is a death of the moment when the picture is taken. Whenever you look at a picture, time dies again.

Papa drew the covers up to her chin. He told her to lie still so that it wouldn't hurt so much. He told her she looked fine.

Dead Man's Float. The picture could be taken from above if she stood on a stepladder. Or she could stand in the hallway and include the frame of the door and maybe only a bit of her side and her hand and a fraction of smooth sheet. But she could not take the picture. She was the picture. It was being taken of her. The light was too bright. She held up her hand to shield her face.

Walker

25.

Porter, California, 2010

The business of cleaning out his father's house has fallen to Walker. He is the obvious choice; sorting through all of George's belongings and determining what is of value is not that different, at least as far as his siblings are concerned, from what Walker does for a living. Of course, it is a massively dissimilar undertaking. His siblings' casual attitude about his work surprises him less than their emotional indifference to the shared history the house represents, but nostalgia may be Walker's particular affliction, his brother and sisters having inherited their father's unsentimental pragmatism. He has waited until the first-semester reading period to begin, much to the dissatisfaction of Evelyn and Rosalie who would have preferred to sell the house as soon as George died. The real estate market will not pick up until spring.

Walker spends the first hours inside the house paralyzed by the task. The rooms are filled with the collected stuff of a life that was largely withheld from him. The fact that he now has access, and that George is not there to rebuff his inquiry makes him feel like a criminal or a cheat. The sheer size of the job overwhelms him. He is deflated by the same hopelessness he felt when he decided to paint the baby's room on Elizabeth Street in anticipation of Alice's birth. With the first brushstroke of primer, the eight-by-ten chamber seemed to expand, revealing the Sisyphean nature of the task, and he sensed his defeat. Lisette stood at the door and monitored his infinitesimal progress, her blooming body like a ticking clock. Parenthood took on the same quality of temporal paradox. While Lisette managed with foresight and practicality—the next diaper size at the ready, preschool selected well in advance—he straggled, unable or maybe unwilling to grasp how utterly children pitched a person into his future.

In the late 1800s, when the house was first built, it was remote, set among what were originally wheat fields at a distance from the town. But after Theodore Dodge turned from dry crops to citrus, and a highway was built bisecting the family fields, the noises of trucks lumbering north and south, heavy with produce or cattle, became a constant accompaniment to the more pastoral music of farming. Walker remembers his mother urging his father to build a wall or plant a stand of tall trees around the house to block the sight and sound of traffic, but George rejected the idea. Much to her frustration, he also refused to buy something new when something old would do. The furniture is an unfashionable amalgamation of the decades— deco pieces from Grandfather Charles's time, tufted couches from the forties, Danish modern coffee tables Walker's mother bought when he was a boy to liven up the house that came with her marriage into the Dodge clan. There is a new television in the sitting room— Walker and his brother sent it when they realized George was watching more interference than actual news each evening on a thirteen-inch Sony—but the dishwasher door is held together by silver duct tape.

Some of the telephones in the house still have their rotary dials, and the house's original phone, the Western Electric dial stick with its earpiece attached to a cord, sits in the hallway nook as it did nearly a century ago when making a call was an important activity that, like confession, necessitated its own discrete location. Walker can spend hours trolling through junk shops and antiques stores to familiarize himself with just such anachronisms, but in his father's home he cannot view the bedside table with its broken drawer or the threadbare barn jacket from the 1960s hanging in the front hall closet as anything but the cost-saving measures of a man who owned one suit and who spent the Dodge money as if it didn't belong to him.

The house is stamped with the particular superstitions of his childhood. When Walker passes the laundry chute, he feels the never-chanced urge to slide down its dark tunnel and land in a bale of towels. Standing at the door of George's room, he still experiences the primal discomfort of the parental double bed. He gets waylaid in Grandfather's Library, as it was called when he was a boy, a room he was allowed to visit only when Charles was present. This seems to have been a rule that extended to George as well; Walker cannot remember ever seeing his father in this room. But that may have been the result of predilection: George, busy with rainfall charts and crop yields, had no time for books. All these years later, the room still harbors the aura of the illicit. It is a gentleman's library from an earlier time, filled with crackle-bound volumes about science and astronomy along with Aristotle and Shakespeare. Grandfather Charles was sent East to university, and when he returned to take up his place in the family business, these books must have been all that was left of a buried intellectual ambition. Walker doesn't know that this is true. He is doing what he does instinctively: imagining the stories that the objects around him tell. He was only three when his grandfather died and, although he knows it cannot be possible, he has distinct memories of the day. The family was gathered around the table for Thanksgiving. They were eating jellied consommé with filigreed spoons. Charles, complaining of indigestion, pushed his chair from the table and then walked upstairs, past the dark and somber oil portrait of Theodore Dodge, a painting that always frightened Walker because of the man's yellowed skin and penetrating gaze. Fifteen minutes later, when Grandmother Naomi went upstairs to check on him, Charles was already dead. Walker knows that his recollection must be made up of recounted stories, and that his image of his grandfather must be a construct derived largely from photographs. But the moment feels visceral to him as does his memory of standing in the doorway of this library after the death was announced. His mother sat on the wicker settee with Alma on one side and Beatriz on the other. The three women held hands and cried unabashedly. He had wanted to go to his mother but he could not cross the threshold into the forbidden room.

Walker knows his grandfather principally by the possessions that remained in the house for years after the man died. His field boots sat on the porch. His three-piece suits hung in a closet off the upstairs hallway, smelling of mothballs. When Walker opened the door—something that he liked to do to test his bravery—the slight wind made the wooden hangers shift and clack against one another, causing the dark suits to animate in a slow, ghostly fashion. At some point, Walker's mother had enough of the clutter and packed the suits and boots and walking sticks off to charity. Somehow, the books in the library escaped her efforts to clear the house of its past, or maybe she felt the library's inviolable aura, too.

Walker takes his time looking through the books. He will keep some, especially the early western novels and a few of the first editions. Others he will offer to the local library. What they pass up he will bring to a bookseller he knows in San Francisco who will appreciate the trove and be honest with Walker about its value. As he pages through certain books, he sees that some are home to the debris of his grandfather's life, an empty seed packet perhaps used as a bookmark, a prayer card from the church Walker attended as a boy where he perfected the art of hiding his own treasures inside hymnals—comics and paperback stories of sports heroes. Tucked between the pages of *Ramona* is a Christmas list from 1941. Uncle Edward was given a subscription to *Lone Scout* magazine. George received the prize of a Heathkit. Walker pulls a heavy book of collected poetry off a shelf and sits down on the wicker settee. The padded cover of the volume is embossed with gold and the pages are tissue-thin and fragile. Stuck between two of them is a yellowing piece of newsprint. The deckled edges nearly break off as Walker unfolds it.

He recognizes the photograph instantly. The image is so familiar that it seems like one excavated from personal memory, the way he can summon the exact contours of his favorite childhood Rock 'Em Sock 'Em Robots although he has not seen them in thirty years. The woman holding her baby. Those two backward-facing children. A splotch of ink mars the woman's forehead, a printing fault he often runs across in old newspapers. Even in this faded image it is still possible to see the dirt on the backs of the children's necks. Walker remembers the year Isaac wanted to dress as a hobo for Halloween.

The costume—Walker's oversized jacket and pants, streaks of Lisette's eyeliner on the boy's cheeks to mimic dirt—was an uncomfortable reminder of all the times Walker's father had castigated him for having a lazy and entitled character. "You could be one of them!" George would say, gesturing angrily toward a window as if a farmworker had miraculously appeared on the front lawn to remind Walker of his unearned luck.

Walker has occasionally used the photograph in his classes and he is familiar with the bare facts of the woman's story: the frozen harvest, the unsuccessful search for work. He remembers something about a broken-down car. Walker glances at the poem on the facing page called "The Highwayman," which is unfamiliar to him. He scans the first few stanzas. *He whistles a tune to the window, and who should be waiting there, But the landlord's black-eyed daughter, Bess, the landlord's daughter, Plaiting a dark red love-knot into her long black hair.* The murder ballad of dark nights and doomed love rolls rhythmically toward a grand, melodramatic finish. A lowbrow choice, Walker thinks, for a man who read Euripides, but a discovery that begins to add flesh to the cardboard notion he has of the grandfather he barely knew. Walker turns back to the article. He wonders if the Dodge camps were as awful as the one described, if the children wandered aimlessly during the days, unschooled and unattended by parents who were in the fields, if the smells of putrefaction carried from the unsanitary facilities caused people to cover their noses and mouths with kerchiefs, if there was always the threat of fire from open flames lit inside tents to ward off the nighttime cold. He is certain the answer is yes, although he is ashamed to realize that he has never spent any time studying the labor history of his own family. If Charles was any kind

of humanist—and to judge from the contents of his library, he was—
Walker can imagine the article pricking some free-floating guilt on
the man's part, which may account for why he saved it. Perhaps he
even took action based on some newfound sense of justice. But Walker
can equally imagine that Charles would have read the article, recognized his complicity, and then performed the moral calculus that made
it possible to convince himself that the Dodge camps were not as bad
as the one described. Walker knows what it takes to create a business
on the scale of the Dodge enterprise, and it is not a social conscience.
Maybe Charles was drawn to the strange combination of blunt truth
and ineffable mystery in the woman's gaze or by those two children
facing away as if they had no particular identity but were only two of
the thousands of children trapped by fate. Or maybe he was struck, as
Walker has always been, by the baby who knows nothing but the
warmth of his mother's skin and the smell of her milk and who does
not yet realize the circumstance it has been born into. Walker folds the
article and replaces it between the pages of the book. It is never simply
the particular discovery that piques his historian's curiosity. It is the
next question that matters: Out of all the millions of objects that were
tossed into the trash bin of time, why did this one survive?

A fter one day at his father's house mostly spent moving piles of
papers from one table to another, Walker asks for help. Angela
is between home-nursing jobs and welcomes the extra work. She
arrives with Beatriz who still has the zeal for organization that
Walker remembers from when she was his *niñera* and demanded that
he keep his toys in the boxes she had carefully marked: *camiones,*

bloques de construcción, soldados de juguete. Back then it was Beatriz's mother, Alma, George's *niñera*, still employed by the family as the majordomo, who looked on like an aged general seeing to it that a battle plan was well executed. Now Beatriz assumes the overseer's role, seated comfortably in an easy chair, her arms folded over her heavy chest. The sunlight angling in through a window catches her chin whiskers. Beatriz says she is glad Alma did not live to see her Jorgecito die. It would have killed her, she adds, and she and Angela and Walker laugh at the feeble joke. *Mi hijo* was what Alma had called George. My son, even when he was grown and had taken over the farm. Walker remembers his father's uncommon humility whenever Alma was near, how he would put on a jacket if she said it was cold outside or how he would stub out his cigarette in her presence because she thought that smoking was a dirty habit.

The three of them spend days sifting and organizing. The work is exhausting and unexpectedly emotional. Angela and Beatriz are practical about getting rid of useless fripperies like the plates with the unnerving big-eyed children Walker's mother collected, while at the same time they are mindful that items that strike Walker as valueless will be of interest to someone else. They seem to hold in their minds the exact layout of any number of their relatives' homes and know that a certain chair will fit perfectly in a cousin's kitchen or that a brother-in-law who is a fool for a game of dominoes will find a great use for an old folding card table. Beatriz reveals herself to be the quiet keeper of Dodge lore and she makes sure that Walker holds on to a certain hooked rug his mother made when she was pregnant with him, even though they all agree that the pattern of amoebic blobs is hideous. Beatriz demands that the set of iced-tea tumblers go to Walker's brother, whose young children will surely be delighted by the built-in glass straws just as Walker and his siblings were, and as George was before that. Each of the three is occasionally caught off guard by sorrow. When this happens, the other two pause in their zeal to toss and save until the moment passes.

During a lunch break, when they eat the gorditas Beatriz brought from home, she reminds them that she and George are milk siblings. Beatriz is only six months older than George, and her mother, Alma, nursed both of them for a time.

"This is why I am *tan pequeña*," Beatriz says, using the English-and-Spanish blend that she and Walker have communicated in since he was a child. "Your daddy, he steals all *la leche!*" She lets out a great, mirthful laugh.

"He was your first playmate," Walker says.

She waves a warning finger. *"Señora Naomi no permita que se."*

Walker shakes his head at his family's entrenched caste system, but Beatriz does not acknowledge the hypocrisy. A childhood of living among housekeepers and gardeners has made Walker familiar with the protective deflection of people who are privy to a family's intimacies but must play dumb as part of the contract of their employ.

As the days pass, Walker becomes weighed down by all the trivialities that make up a life—a dish filled with paper clips, a half-used tin of shoeshine, the bathroom drawer jammed with crusted tubes of ointments and the medicine-cabinet shelves imprinted with rust from cans of shaving cream. There are moments of poignancy—the worn-down toothbrush, the shot glass on his father's desk that contains a black Super Ball Walker remembers from his childhood, a special high bouncer that he played with incessantly, driving his father crazy with the arrhythmic noise. He wonders if his father felt sentimental about the ball. But Walker is projecting. The ball might have landed in that glass randomly and spent years untouched except by a maid's dutiful feather duster. George probably never noticed it.

There are other discoveries. The top shelf of a hallway closet holds a cache of broken mousetraps. Finding them, Walker is seized by frustration. What possible purpose could his father have had in keeping these things? What churlish parsimony would cause him to think that he could find some use for forty rectangular pieces of wood and coils of unsprung wire? In these moments Walker feels as he did when he was a boy and the sound of his father's drawling, slightly nasal voice or the sight of him cleaning the wax from his ear with the earpiece of his glasses would drive him wild with repulsion and shame.

"*¿Qué pasa con el sótano?*" Beatriz says when they have managed to pack up most of the first and second floors of the house.

"The basement," Angela says, translating the unfamiliar word. "She wants to know what you want to do about everything down there."

Walker remembers the basement as a cold, unfinished space that housed a clanking furnace and two industrial-sized and water-stained sinks. He was terrified by the mangle that lived there, and on laundry days, he would watch, mesmerized, as the wrinkled sheets were fed between the lips of the rollers only to come out the other side perfectly pressed. He lived in fear of Beatriz's warning that if he stood too close, the monster would grab his shirttail or a wisp of his hair and he would be sucked in and flattened.

"The appliances will be sold with the house," Walker says.

"No, no," Beatriz says, marching over to the basement door.

He helps her down the steps, and Angela follows. The temperature drops by at least ten degrees. He waves his hand in the air until he makes contact with the piece of string that hangs from the bare fixture. The yellow light illuminates a room filled with boxes.

"What is all this?" Walker says unhappily. He opens a box and pulls out a back issue of *California Farmer* from 1955. Once again, his anger wells up and he allows himself a petulant thought: perhaps his father saved all this useless junk simply to burden Walker with the problem of dealing with it, turning history into insult. He explains to Beatriz and Angela that he has to get back to his teaching and that he will return another time to deal with the contents of the basement.

"Mrs. Rosalie and Mrs. Evelyn," Beatriz says, insinuating that Walker's sisters will not be happy with the delay.

"I can't do this anymore," he says with more passion than he intended.

Beatriz puts a sympathetic hand on his cheek. *"Tranquilízate,"* she says as she did when he was young and he would retreat to the kitchen after a fight with his father. She would give him a glass of milk and a slice of cake and continue her work. Her calm would go a long way toward convincing him that the rage he felt would not ultimately destroy him.

Angela's husband arrives in his pickup and makes trips to and from the house, taking various items to the dump, the local thrift shop, and the homes of relatives. Walker rents a U-Haul to hitch to the back of his car so he can bring the boxes of books he's saved to San Francisco as well as the wicker settee, which is the one piece of furniture he has decided to keep. On Friday afternoon, the women hug him gently and then leave. He sits on the railing of the wraparound porch and drinks a beer, watching trucks and cars drive away from the groves carrying the last of the day's workers. The irrigation system goes to work now, and as the sun makes its final descent, the last glinting rays pick up the sprays of water for a brief moment before the trees become indistinct shapes against the dusk. When he was a boy, Walker imagined that the house *was* the Dodge farm and that the land was somehow ancillary to the beating heart where he lived and played and studied and fought. Now that the house is empty he cannot quite convince himself that these acres have a purpose without the anchor of the home. The land seems as weightless as a cloud that will float away on the next strong wind.

Back inside, he walks the empty rooms. He knows his father would not have been emotional about the house. He might even have been happy to know that it was finally being released from its oppressive familial duty. George had been ambivalent about carrying on the Dodge traditions. He insisted his children live up to this ambiguous set of values called "the Dodge name," which mostly had to do with never using their status to advantage. But he would not allow his shirts to be monogrammed in the family style and he refused to have his portrait painted so that it could stand in the town hall alongside the images of Charles and Theodore. Walker and his siblings spent their summers in the groves along with the migrants, picking oranges or driving the water truck. They were never paid. When Walker complained about working for free, George made him a deal: he would give Walker the wage his pickers earned, and in return Walker would pay for all the food he ate at the house, rent for his bedroom at fair market value, and a prorated portion of the gas and electricity. After a month, Walker was happy to relinquish his paycheck in favor of unlimited access to the refrigerator. But when Walker discovered *The Communist Manifesto* and *The Other America*, he regularly accused his father of everything from labor exploitation to noblesse oblige. "Why don't you just sleep with his daughter while you're at it?" Walker snarled one year, as his father left the house for his ritual day-after-Christmas meal with the family of his Mexican foreman. George did not respond but simply left Walker alone in the front hall, nursing his Pyrrhic victory: Walker's desire to disappoint his father had produced exactly that, and he spent the night ashamed not of his father but of his ineffectual self.

He should head back north before it is late, but he is too exhausted to make the drive. He takes out his computer, settles onto the floor of the empty living room and searches for information about the famous photograph. A number of related links appear. As he quickly peruses them, he recognizes the usual mix of the scholarly and amateur he finds whenever he searches the Web. Most teachers will warn their students away from the perils of unqualified sources. But Walker is always drawn to lay accounts. They can be wildly subjective and unreliable, but looked at another way, they are windows into eccentric curiosities that have their own value. He cross-references the links as best he can and discovers this: The woman's name was Mary Coin. She was born in 1904 or, according to some articles, 1905. She was either full Cherokee or mixed blood. She had six children or seven. An article compares the photograph to the *Pietà* both in its composition and in the way it serves as a ritual image. Someone has written about how the absent father in the photograph allows the viewer to take on the role of patriarchal savior. A feminist academic has written a dissertation about the photograph in terms of cultural theories and prejudices surrounding twentieth-century ideals of motherhood.

Walker finds a link to an article from a 1982 edition of the *San Jose Mercury News*. The headline reads: "An Appeal for a Face from the Depression." It is a direct request for money on the part of Mary Coin's family. The article describes how she is in a weakened condition after an ill-advised trip to San Francisco. Her children have vowed to give her the best care possible, but the cost of nursing and medication is prohibitive. "That picture's done a lot of good for a lot of people," a daughter, Ellie Velasquez, says. "And she never got anything from it. Not one dime. As far as I'm concerned, she's owed." A son, James Coin, remarks, "She never wanted anybody to know she was the one in the picture. I hope we're doing the right thing."

26

The basement is not insulated. It is so cold at night that Walker has to wear his jacket, and even then, his hands stiffen as he tries to figure out the best way to proceed. He knows it is foolish to start this job now when he is so tired and when he has to get back to the city, but he can't sleep, and the basement tantalizes. Mismatched file cabinets with rusted corners are lined up against one wall. Cardboard boxes are stacked five or six high. Some are so collapsed that the towers lean precariously and threaten to spill their contents over the concrete floor. A quick perusal of one of the most accessible boxes reveals years of tax statements. Another is filled with random brochures advertising agricultural products. In the far corner of the basement sit crates filled with plaques: 1960 Central Valley Businessman of the Year, 1962 Orange Growers Award, commendations from the YMCA and the Elks Club. Walker cannot deny the familiar tightening in his chest, the adrenaline he feels when he walks into a newspaper archive or someone's dusty junk-filled barn or when he finds a shoebox overflowing with photographs.

He is suddenly overcome by the feeling he gets each time he begins one of his projects, when he encounters an immediate sense of failure and questions why he has driven all the way to a town in Nebraska or Idaho to investigate some notion that any of his colleagues would find jejune. At these times, he feels certain that he will not discover a way to penetrate beneath the charm of a stiffly posed marriage portrait to find the particular character of a place and its people, to unearth the human experience of history. He reminds himself of what he always does in these moments of doubt: that what he seeks exists because everything does. The Dead Sea Scrolls, black holes, pharaonic tombs—all these things existed before men understood how to find them. It is the human fallacy to believe that we discover any single thing. It is only that we are slow to learn how to see what is in front of us.

After two hours, he feels that he has a sense of the general chronology of the boxes and he begins to dig in, starting with the earliest papers. He finds a land deed dating from 1902: *The State of California. Kern County. Know all Men by these Present that for and in consideration of Five Hundred Dollars in hand paid by Theodore Harris Dodge to the Southern Pacific Improvement Company the following described real estate, to wit: The South West Fourth of Section Five T 14 (south)—Range 12 west containing one hundred and sixty acres more or less.*

More or less. More now. Thousands of acres more.

He finds purchase orders for seed, for plows and horses. There is a bill from a farrier. A familiar ease settles over Walker. This is what he loves, this slow, careful excavation through time. He studies the elegantly slanted handwriting and carefully crafted signatures on the documents, takes pleasure in the arcane formality of the transactions. He discovers a roll of architect's drawings: the original schematics for the Queen Anne. A room marked "Child's Room" was his father's boyhood bedroom, then his own. His life, laid out before him here as a plan, an imagined future made manifest by the determination and luck of his forebears, moves him. He finds a notebook filled with arithmetic so faded that he can only make out that the numbers have to do with costs and profit. He imagines his great-grandfather Theodore's hand making these markings. He finds a payroll ledger that lists the farmworkers and their weekly take. In 1910, only twenty men were listed. Even adjusting for inflation, the pay is negligible. As Walker makes his way from box to box, from year to year, he finds many such ledgers. He studies the names and the human geography they represent. At first the surnames are mostly Chinese. But in ten years the rolls are filled with Japanese names, and ten years after that, with the signatures of East Indians. Soon, the workers are almost all Mexican or Filipino. By the 1930s, the farmworkers are predominantly white, the huge wave of Dust Bowl migrants having descended. He reads down the rolls. *Hubert Mills, Robert Worth, Renata Coleman* . . . The names are so evocative to him that he begins to recite them out loud, his voice echoing off the walls of the basement. Each represents a constellation of hope, wives and husbands and children relying on the dollar and twenty-eight cents that Mabel Fox made that week or the dollar and ninety-five cents William Streeter collected. These people are all dead now. But here are their names written by each of their hands, the same hands that pulled citrus off ornery branches. Each worker and each family so intimately connected with Walker's own, their meager earnings a stark reminder of the exploitation and moral ambiguity that lie at the heart of the Dodge fortune. *Victor Emerson, Willie Frank . . .*

It quickly becomes obvious to him that his great-grandfather and his grandfather, and even George, despite condemning Walker's chosen path, were inadvertent historians. Why else does someone save items that have no immediate use except that he recognizes the commemorative value of the moment even as it is lived? He knows that a simple bill for baling wire is as resonant an artifact as an ancient potsherd, and that within the transaction—money for wire—lies the story of a particular person and the time in which he lived. Walker used to think his father hid his identity behind his work. Now he sees that he had it backward, and that work itself might be the key to understanding George. He looks around for the boxes containing information from the year his father took over the farm. But then he decides to back up and start with the year of George's birth. He finds the box from 1935 and studies the contents. Despite the economy, the company bought two new Ford trucks . . . electric bills . . . water bills . . . He scans the payroll ledger for that year, reads the names of the workers. *Robert Mills, Eulalia Murphy, Curtis Sharp, Mary Coin.*

Walker feels an unnerving displacement, as if he has missed a tread on a stairway. It is the same sensation he felt many years ago, when he lost Isaac in the grocery-store aisles. He'd turned around, and in the space where Isaac was standing only seconds before there was emptiness. In that moment, Walker knew that life was a set of extravagantly enacted delusions to mask the fact that all the relied-upon verities were meaningless. *Mary Coin.* Her face comes to him immediately. He studies the ledger. Oddly, she has been paid more than anyone else on that particular payday—twice as much, in fact. It is hard to believe that the frail woman in the photograph could pick twice as many oranges as Robert Mills or Curtis Sharp, but there it is. He skips ahead in the ledger. Her name appears week after week. And then it is gone.

27

He is back in San Francisco, correcting papers at the university, when Lisette calls. Alice has been suspended from school.

"They found pills in her locker," she says.

"Pills? What are you talking about? What kind?"

"The bad kind, Walker. Vicodin. Oxy."

"Did you know?"

"Fuck you, Walker."

He takes a breath. "Where is she now?"

"Here. Grounded. For the rest of her life. Except for parent-escorted trips to rehab."

"Rehab?" Too much information is coming at him.

"Yes. Rehab. Every day. School rules, if she wants to be readmitted. If she wants to get a high school diploma and have a chance at a life."

He's still trying to bridge the distance between what he thought was happening in his life and what is actually occurring. "Isn't that a little extreme?"

"Wake up, Walker," she says, fighting with the emotions that are thickening in her throat. "Your daughter is popping pills."

He drives to Petaluma that evening. When Lisette answers the door, she looks shrunken. She seems to have exhausted all energy for facial expressions. She points up the stairs then disappears into the back of the house.

Walker tries to open Alice's door but finds it locked. He leans his forehead against the frame. "Let me in, honey," he says.

After a few moments, she opens the door. Without greeting him, she turns and goes back to her bed. She lies down and stares at the ceiling. He starts to summon the energy to be jolly and enthusiastic, to prove to her that his love will not diminish no matter what she has done, but he can't.

"You messed up," he says, sitting on the edge of her bed.

"Thank you for stating the obvious," she says.

"Why were you taking that stuff?"

"Really, Dad? Are you going to be like my therapist now?"

"I'm going to be like your father. What's going on with you?"

"I was stupid. I got caught."

"Getting caught is the least of your problems."

"I know that. Don't you think I know that? Do you think I'm an idiot?"

He tries to figure out what comes next. "Look," he says. "We'll get you help. You'll go to this rehab."

"I'm not a drug addict. I just took some pills."

I smoked but I didn't inhale. She is too young for the reference, and sarcasm will get him nowhere with her. "So what's your plan?" he says.

"I don't have a plan. I got kicked out of school. I guess I'll have a stimulating career in fast food."

Her attitude creates havoc in him. "You can be a snob about the people who work at Burger King, but the fact is most of them are high school graduates."

"Is this your idea of a pep talk?"

"I'm not here to give you a pep talk, Alice."

"Why are you here, then?"

They are both quiet.

"Can I ask you a question?" he says.

"Free country."

"What kind of person do you want to be?"

"What's that supposed to mean?"

"It means that at a certain point you have to decide who you want to be. You either want to be the person who is getting high all the time or you don't."

"Well, I guess I want to be the person who gets high all the time."

"I don't think that's true."

"You don't know anything about me."

"So tell me."

"Tell you what?"

"Tell me some things about you. Tell me who you are."

Alice sits up. She is crying. "How am I supposed to know that?" she says. "You act like it's so easy. Like pick one from column A and one from column B and then, presto chango, you are this perfect person who everybody loves and who is pretty and smart and is going to go to a good college and have this perfect life . . ."

"Oh, Alice." He reaches for her, but she pulls back.

"I fucked up, okay? I fucked up. Tell me how bad I am. Tell me how I have disappointed you and Mom. Tell me whatever the fuck you want to tell me and then *please* get the fuck out of my room."

He spends the night on the couch in Lisette and Harry's living room. He turns on the television, muting the sound so that he doesn't bother anyone. A late-night talk show is playing. He has no idea who the celebrity is, but she laughs and preens and waves and yanks down her too-short dress as the host teases and cajoles and pretends to flirt, or really flirts. The condition of watching the talk show is that you must accept that what is false is real and that what is real is false. Either Alice is a drug addict or Alice is not a drug addict, but the condition of being her parent is that he must accept that he can never be sure what is truth and what is the opposite of truth. All that he is certain of is that he has not provided her with whatever she needs. What is she missing? Security? Love? Or is it that he has not adequately shared himself with her and so denied her the firm foundation of history that anyone needs in order to say, "This is who I am"?

It is not so different for him. His history is lopsided. He can trace the Dodge lineage back, but what about the missing quarter of his heritage? The story has always been that George's mother died in childbirth. Either this is true or it is not. And if it is false, then it is also true, since the woman was erased from the family history as if she never existed. Not in a name, not in a piece of heirloom jewelry, not in a photograph of happier days. Mary Coin's face comes to him. Her skin baked and etched by the sun. Her thin lips gripped against—what? Eyes looking off toward—what? *You know, that picture of the woman and her children in the Depression.* It's all you have to say and people's faces open in recognition. They nod, a hundred suppositions falling into place about a woman they think they know.

You look but you don't see. It's what he's told his students hundreds of times over the years. You have to see past looking.

Isaac comes downstairs, barefoot but otherwise fully dressed.

"Do you sleep in your clothes now?"

Isaac smiles, sweetly embarrassed. "It's faster in the morning."

"You're ready to make a clean getaway." Walker is joking but he realizes that there might be some truth to this. He pats the couch beside him, and Isaac sits down.

"What will happen to Alice?" Isaac says.

"We'll figure things out."

"How will you figure things out?"

Walker looks at his son's earnest expression and comes clean. "I don't know."

"Maybe it's my fault," Isaac says.

"You didn't put the pills in her locker."

"She says things, and I get upset, and then Mom yells at her for saying mean things to me, and then Alice goes and does shit—I mean stuff. Sorry."

Walker puts his arm around Isaac. "It's not your fault."

"I just wish . . ." Isaac says, but he doesn't finish.

"What do you wish?"

"I don't know."

They watch the silent hilarity on the television. Isaac hunches, his shoulders turning in as if he wants to fold up. His sense of his insignificance is palpable. The storm of his sister rages around him, and there is nothing he can do to stop it or flee its path.

"Hey," Walker says. "What new apps have you invented lately?"

"Do you even know what an app is, Dad?"

"Yes I know what an app is. What do you take me for?"

"A Luddite."

"Good word. Although it sounds like an insult coming from you."

Isaac smiles down at his lap, shy and proud.

"I could use your help with all this computer stuff, actually," Walker says.

"How?"

"Do you think you can find anybody online?"

"Sure."

"Even if they're not famous?"

"You can find anybody," Isaac says, the devilish gleam of a proto-hacker in his eye. "You just have to know where to look."

28

Empire, California. Another town. When Walker arrives in a new place, he knows without ever having been there how it will be laid out. Historically, certain areas, often the north or the west sides, were typically the wealthiest, and if any remnants of architectural grandeur remain, this is where they will be. Whether there are actual train tracks or not, there is always the other side of something—a river, a gully, a dump—some division that allows a town to organize itself along class lines so that people know where they belong. Things are less insidious now than they were fifty or a hundred years ago, but the psychic territories remain.

Although there is sometimes a modestly refurbished old hotel in towns such as this one—a Mission Inn or a Pacific Arms—Walker always chooses whatever version of a Motel 6 lies off the highway. He likes the practical sterility of these places, the way the rooms seem to float in and out of time, bare stages on which scenes appear and then evaporate daily. It is June now, and the heat of the Central Valley has settled in for the duration of the summer. His room is dark. He forgoes the overhead fluorescents and turns on the bedside lamp.

Somehow, the stucco-ceilinged room looks more correct in a tawdry weak light, as if shadows and obscurity are the natural characteristics that allow for what takes place in motel rooms. He phones the rest home, learns that visiting hours begin at four o'clock.

He reminds himself that a newspaper article and a name on a payroll do not add up to much and certainly not a fanciful notion that he has allowed to blossom into a full-fledged idea just shy of fact: that somehow Mary Coin's connection to his family is intimate, that an article secreted between the pages of a poetry book signifies a buried emotion and that Walker's father's ambivalence about his position at the head of the Dodge clan, and his final wish to be burned, all add up to the answer to a question that was never allowed to be asked. Isaac's computer searches turned up the names of Mary Coin's children, all but one of whom are dead.

The nursing home is a beige, single-story building that, to judge from the small figure-eight planter that still bears the iron structure of a nonexistent diving board, must have once been a motel. Despite the season, the lobby is heated; the smells of industrial cleaners and food hang in the viscid air.

"I don't have you down for a visit," the woman behind the front desk says. She wears a scrub top printed with teddy bears. Her fingernails are long and elaborately lacquered with flowers. The manicure alone suggests the nature of the place. There is no medical heavy lifting here. This is where people wait for the end.

"I was put through to Mr. Coin a couple of times, but he hung up."

She laughs. "James is not a big talker."

"I'd really like to have a chance to meet him."

She looks skeptical. "We don't like to upset our clients."

"I think Mr. Coin's family and mine might be connected in some way."

"He's got Medi-Cal," she says suspiciously.

"It's not like that. I'm not after money."

She looks down at her desk and shuffles some papers, signaling that she is done with the conversation.

"When is the last time he had a visitor?" Walker says.

She makes a show of looking through the appointment book, then gives up the charade. "You're the first."

James Coin is wheeled into the common room by a tattooed orderly whose shaved head shines. He bends over the chair and speaks softly to James, then hands him a small object that looks like a garage door opener. "You press this if you need me, Mr. James. I'll come for you fast."

James is thin. More than thin. His clothes hang limply as if there is no actual body beneath them. The angular contours of his knee bones press against the material of his slacks. His skin is waxy and liver-spotted, his fingers curl against his palms. Surprisingly, he has a full head of hair, the leached color blond goes to with age. He does not look at Walker but instead stares at the blank wall opposite, and Walker cannot be sure the old man is aware of him.

He is not certain how to begin. In his work his conversation is strictly with the dead. Someone turns up the television and then quickly adjusts the volume. Walker reacts to the sound, but the old man does not. Maybe he is deaf, Walker thinks, but then remembers that the orderly spoke to him.

"My name is Walker Dodge," he begins, speaking too loudly. He looks for a sign of recognition, sees none. Of course, James would have been a little boy when his mother worked the oranges and he would no more recognize the name than those of the many other farms where she must have found employment during that time. Walker realizes, too, that if the name does register with the old man, it would certainly not elicit the heart-quickening reaction that Walker felt sitting in that chilled basement among his family records. Rather, the connection between James's family and his own would stir troubling memories. James moves his mouth as if he is about to say something but he is just worrying his gums. Walker reaches into his briefcase and takes out the photograph he's printed off the Internet. He touches James's shoulder lightly. James looks at him, and then his gaze falls on the picture. This is the first indication of interest he has shown, but Walker cannot tell what the man feels. When James looks away, Walker senses he has done something terribly aggressive, as if the photograph were one of maimed bodies rather than this man's mother and his siblings. He turns the picture over and lets it rest on his lap. He explains his story, tells James about the article in the poetry book, about the coincidence of finding Mary Coin's name in the work rolls, about the tiny suspicion that he knows is absurd but that he cannot banish: that Mary Coin was important to his grandfather in some particular way. The man's silence makes Walker feel as if he is on a disastrous first date and he says more than he intends. He talks about his difficult experience with his father, about George's death. Occasionally he stops talking, waiting to see if James will give him some sign that any of this information registers. James says nothing. Still, there is something about the man's silence that feels attentive, as if the quiet is a manner of being and not the result of a deteriorating mind. And for reasons Walker cannot explain, he feels drawn to James, who looks to be only a few years older than Walker's father was. The two men grew up experiencing the same history but from opposite sides of fate.

Walker glances around the room. A few plastic tables and chairs. Generic floral paintings hanging on the walls. A box of toys for visiting grandchildren. When George became ill, Walker's sisters wanted to move him to an assisted-living facility. They chose one and sent Walker the brochure. The home was a mock-Georgian manor sitting on acres of land. Welcoming outdoor furniture and games were set up on the evenly cut grass as if the residents were in the habit of taking afternoon strolls and challenging one another to games of lawn bowling. George took one look at the brochure and refused to waste the money.

"My father never knew his mother," Walker says. He thinks of his children, of Alice. "It's a terrible thing not to know your parent."

The orderly appears. Walker realizes James has signaled that he wants to be taken back to his room or some other safe place where he will not be attacked by the past or by a deranged college professor who has invented a false history to fill some maw in his life.

"I'm sorry," Walker says to the orderly. "Maybe I tired him out."

The orderly puts a hand on the old man's back. "We'll take a rest now, Mr. James." He unlocks the wheels of the chair, turns it around, and rolls James out of the room.

Walker drives back to his motel, feeling disconsolate. He was optimistic when he thought he might stay the night, that James Coin might have important things to share and that Walker would speak with him a second time, maybe even make arrangements for further visits. He gathers his bag and goes to the front desk to check out. Upset about the bungled meeting and the possible harm that he inflicted on a sick old man, he takes a sheet of university stationery out of his briefcase and writes James a thank-you and an apology. He has no way of knowing if tomorrow, when James receives this letter, he will remember who Walker is.

Mary

29.

Santa Clarita, California, 1982

Mary sat on the examining table, wearing a flimsy piece of paper that was supposed to be a robe, listening to the doctor explain things to Ellie and Trevor as if Mary would not understand. The doctor's fists were balled up in her lab coat pockets as if someone had told her that she moved her hands too much when she talked.

"But her numbers were down," Ellie said in the tone she used with difficult customers at the Pharma-Save she managed or with wrestling coaches who didn't play her twin seventeen-year-old boys to her satisfaction. She had recently tortured her hair into a permanent, and her curls jumped around like little girls desperate to go to the bathroom. Mary felt a sadness open up inside her not on account of the foolish disease that was making a repeat appearance but because of how dearly Ellie wanted those curls when she was a girl. It was strange how you knew from the very beginning what would happen in the end. Toby had the seeds of his death in him from the get-go. Ellie was a girl determined to get what she wanted even if she had to wait fifty years to do it. The problem was that no one wanted to admit that the story was already written. Well, she supposed that was what they called foolish hope.

"There are studies that link a good attitude to a positive result in certain circumstances," the doctor said, "but this is all anecdotal. Stomach cancer is particularly intractable at this stage."

"English, please," Ellie said. She was as smart as they came and she could knock someone down a notch by playing Okie and pretending she couldn't understand what they were talking about. She'd turn their assumptions about her ignorance right back on them like a boomerang and end up getting what she wanted. If Della or June were here they would act as if the doctor's words had the authority of God. Those two would travel from their homes in Bakersfield as soon as Mary called for them, but she had not told them about the new round of illness; she was not ready for their fuss. James was driving a long haul to Michigan. He was always a solace to her, and although she didn't like him driving an eighteen-wheeler all those hours with no one to keep him company, she was glad he wasn't here now. He was never comfortable around people, and the hustle of a hospital where nurses checked your most private areas without even introducing themselves would make him miserable. And she did not want to contend with that wife of Ray's who had a habit of turning someone else's tragedy into her own for the sake of attention. For now, she wanted Ellie and Trevor near her: Ellie, because she was a fighter and Mary didn't have a lot of fight left in her; Trevor, because Mary never wanted him to be alone with bad news. She would never forget the day he ran back through the camp where they had stopped after the car was fixed, waving a newspaper in the air, screaming, "Mama's been shot! Mama's dead!" The improbability of seeing his mother in the paper had made him lose all reason and it took a while before he realized that the big black spot on her forehead in the picture was just ink. Once he'd calmed down, she'd told him he had better give that paper back to whomever he got it from because she didn't have five cents to pay for it.

That was the first time she'd ever seen herself in a photograph. It was a queer feeling to study the face of a woman who looked like a stranger and have to remind herself that the stranger was her. It made no sense, as if her features were just shapes on a face that did not add up to the person who was in her mind's eye when she thought about herself. And what did a face have to do with it? A person was just feelings that came and went like clouds drifting across the sky and decisions that sometimes ended up to be good and sometimes bad. But this woman in the picture was someone who looked a certain way and would never change. Like a table or a shoe. Back in those days, Mary had stopped considering her looks and hadn't seen herself in a mirror for months. She'd felt angry at the woman in the picture for being so thin, and ashamed that her children were dirty, and, oh, all right, a little bit excited because now her kids were jumping up and down, yelling about how their mama was in the newspaper, and other women from the camp came to see what the noise was about. But later, when she was alone, she felt something else that made fear and shame and pride a lie: she felt jealous. She was envious of the woman in the picture because that woman had not had to suffer the future that began the moment the photographer got into her car and drove away.

Ellie wrote notes on a pad that had one of those infernal happy faces on its bright yellow cover. Mary wondered how she had lived long enough to end up in a world where people thought a cartoon drawing of a smile could make your problems go away. As Ellie peppered the doctor with the questions on her list, Mary thought about how her daughter liked things to be orderly. Ellie's house was too tidy as far as Mary was concerned. It was the kind of clean that shook a finger at you when you sat in a plumped-up chair or put your hand on a freshly waxed table, warning you not to leave any evidence of yourself. The Wrestlers—which is what Mary called the twins— skulked through the rooms like cat burglars, careful not to unsettle things. Ellie's husband, Valerio, worked nights on highway construction, so his presence was noticeable only as clues, his dusty work gloves in the utility sink, a bowl rinsed clean on the drying rack—he knew who he was married to. Mary took a deep breath and let it out slowly. Soon she would be living in that house. It would be the first time in sixty years that she would have to submit to another woman's rules.

Trevor stood behind Ellie, bowing his head as the doctor spoke. He was a big man used to hunching and stepping back so others could see. As the doctor delivered the bad news, he covered his eyes the way men did when they wanted people to think they were simply tired, but Mary saw his shoulders shake. She would have given anything to be able to hop off the examining table and wrap her arms around him, but she didn't have that kind of agility anymore, and her robe would certainly fall off, which would do Trevor more harm than good. He didn't question what the doctor said; he didn't have the imagination to expect more than what was in front of him. It was her fault, Mary thought. You can't raise children the way she did and tell them that they can be the president of the United States if they just work hard enough. She'd always told her children the truth. The sharp and dissatisfied ones like Ellie and Ray shut their ears to her and wanted what they wanted. The quiet ones like Trevor and James listened closely and believed what Mary told them more than she wished they had. Trevor was a good son and a loyal man, a quality that had kept him with women who loaded all their unhappiness onto his broad back like he was a mule and then left without collecting their baggage. There were times when it would have done him good to be more defiant like Ellie because it took a little bit of ill humor to make yourself up out of nothing. And Ellie was a good daughter in her way, which was the way of making decisions about the right route to take to get from here to there or where a person ought to live out the end of her life.

Well, there was nothing Mary could do about that, either.

Doris also said that Mary would not know who she was until she lost the things in her life. Mary thought it was not something a girl should have to hear on her wedding day. And now, sitting in this examining room, she knew her mother had been wrong. The hard bargain was that you lost and you lost and still you didn't know.

Ellie kept asking questions, trying to find some loophole in the doctor's logic, as if it were purely a grammar mistake that stood between Mary's life and her oncoming death. The doctor's answers were all versions of the same information: Mary's best, her only hope, was further treatment. Further treatment. Mary shut her eyes as if to block out the idea. She'd had enough of the sucking tiredness and the vomiting and tingling hands and not being able to stand cold and then not being able to stand heat and her tongue feeling like an eel inside her mouth. She'd had enough of her scalp hurting. And where would the money come from? It cost too much to keep her alive, and for what? A few more months? If there was one thing Mary could say for herself it was that she knew what was worth a dollar and what was not. When Ray was a boy, he used to tell her she could split a penny into four parts. He didn't say this with admiration because he wanted things—a toy truck he saw in the store window or second helpings when there was hardly enough to go around the first time. When she denied him, anger took over his body, and he would hold his breath until he turned blue, and she'd have to smack him on his back.

"But I don't *feel* sick," Mary said suddenly.

Everyone in the room turned to her as if they had forgotten she was there.

"You're sick if you feel sick," she continued, "and I'm feeling as good as I did yesterday and the day before. So we can stop all this and go home."

"Mrs. Coin," the doctor said. "The tests show—"

"The tests are one side of the story."

"I'm afraid that they are, unfortunately, the truth," the doctor said.

"Aw, honey," Mary said, suddenly feeling sorry for the doctor. "The truth isn't the unfortunate one in this room."

"Mother, now you're just being mean," Ellie said.

"Give me my clothes," Mary said. "I'm going home."

30.

People always talked about the body betraying a person in illness, but Mary did not believe the body had intentions. It was just a thing that worked until it broke down. People were the fickle ones. This is what she thought as she watched Ellie unload the trunk of her Tercel. Collapsed boxes that had once held aspirin and latex gloves destined for drugstore shelves were now going to be filled with everything that Mary had ever owned.

When she had woken up that morning in her trailer, made her bed and turned on her coffeemaker, Mary had been aware of everything as if she were watching another woman perform these tasks. There's that dying woman brushing her teeth. There she goes lifting the blinds. There she is cleaning the grease off the stove because it is rude to leave a place dirtier than you found it.

Ellie came inside, set down her awkward load, wiped her forehead with the back of her arm and started to reassemble the boxes with packing tape. She wore her blue smock from the drugstore. "There's no shortage of boxes in this world. Everything comes in a box, if you stop to think about it," she said.

"I don't think that's strictly true," Mary said.

Ellie looked at her mother. "Don't fight me on this, Mama," she said.

"Who's fighting?"

"You can't stay here anymore. You probably shouldn't have been living on your own for as long as you have. That's my fault, I guess."

"If you give in to a little cough you give in to everything," Mary said. Of course, this hadn't been the case with Toby or Betsy, or, in the end, with Doris herself. But some things were right even though they were wrong.

"Valerio and I want you to live with us," Ellie said. "The boys have already cleared out a room. They're excited to bunk together just like when they were little."

"Those boys are too big to fit in one room."

"It doesn't do for you to be alone now."

Now, Mary thought. Time was always being split between then and now. *Then* she had been a child in Tahlequah. *Now* she was a mother in California learning how to care for babies. *Then* Toby had been alive, *now* he was dead and she'd had to bury him and accept other men into her bed for reasons besides love. *Then* she had seven children. *Now* she had six. Except this separation of time was a false one. Because you never stopped being one thing when you became the other.

"So," Ellie said, "where would you like to start, Mama? I thought we'd start with the kitchen cabinets. You sit down and don't do a thing."

It went on like that all day. Ellie asked what Mary wanted to do about the cookbooks and then in the same breath mentioned how out-of-date those dog-eared books were and how no one in her right

mind should be cooking with that much butter anyway and no wonder half of America suffered heart attacks and weren't people just getting fatter and fatter? Or she pretended to consider where, in her
living room, Mary's green Naugahyde recliner would look best when
Mary knew there was no amount of money in the world that would
convince Ellie to let that chair in her house. It had belonged to Mary's
third husband. She'd divorced Tom Ducette, a drinker she'd had to
get rid of after he laid an angry hand on James, and met Nelson Hen-
dricks when she worked at an industrial laundry. He loved to bet on
the horses and he loved his awful cigars, but otherwise he was a
decent enough man to keep company with, and he could make her
laugh. On the weekends he sat in the recliner, holding his radio to his
ear and listening to the races, bouncing in his seat as if he were the
winning jockey. And then one day he stopped bouncing. She buried
him and decided that she was done with husbands.

"Maybe we ought to see if Trevor wants that chair," Ellie said.

"If you'd rather me die on one of your nice sofas, I won't argue
with you," Mary said.

Ellie clicked her tongue against the inside of her teeth the way
she did when she won an argument she knew she'd really lost. Then
she got back to work. She kept up her chatter as she packed the
boxes, laughing at the ancient eggbeater Mary had brought from
Tahlequah.

"You don't throw out anything, do you?" Ellie said, holding up an
iron with a frayed cord.

"Why should I throw that away?"

"It's cheaper to buy something new than get it fixed. With my
discount I can get you a new iron for twenty dollars."

"It works fine."

"This cord will kill you."

"The cord isn't what's going to kill me, honey."

Ellie's eyes filled. Suddenly, Mary saw her little girl standing before her, willing herself not to cry when Mary criticized her for not helping to put up the tent, or when she had to wear Trevor's shoes. Ellie tried to gather herself, wondering out loud whether she had cinnamon at home or if they should take Mary's jar even though it was probably ten years old, and how long did Mary think spices stayed fresh, anyway? Mary said there was something called advertising and that sell-by dates just made you buy more of whatever you already had enough of. Ellie said Mary was a paranoid old lady and Ellie wasn't going to kill her kids on account of ten-year-old cinnamon. By then she was crying.

"Come over here," Mary said.

Ellie didn't move.

"Sit right down," Mary said, patting her knees.

"Oh, Mama."

"Do what I say."

Ellie shook her head, but Mary insisted, and Ellie sat down on her lap. Mary felt a hard twisting in her belly and stifled a groan. She had lied to the doctor about the pain.

"I can't remember the last time I sat like this," Ellie said.

"Getting you to cuddle up was like trying to trap a fly."

"I didn't want to be a baby."

"I know that."

"I'm sorry about all this, Mama."

"I know that, too."

Trevor came by after his day at the garage, still wearing his coveralls. Mary liked seeing her children in their uniforms. She had raised them not to be afraid of hard work, and each one of them had a solid job. Not every mother could say that. Trevor stood in the bedroom doorway watching as Ellie packed Mary's clothes, while Mary sat on the stripped bed, worrying a mattress button. It was a good bed, and she'd grown accustomed to its particular contours, but it would have to go to the dump. Goodwill wouldn't take mattresses for fear of bedbugs or worse.

"Looks like you two got everything squared away," Trevor said. He had a habit of reminding people that he was of no use to them. He'd had one wife who left him and another who was about to do the same. He was aware that it was going to happen but didn't do anything to stop it because he knew that, big as he was, he couldn't stand in the way of his life.

"Those dresses. They can go to Goodwill," Mary said, eyeing the contents of her closet. "All of them."

"You ought to keep some," Ellie said. "What if we go out to a nice dinner? What if my boys manage to graduate high school?"

"They'll graduate just the same whether I'm wearing a dress or not."

"I can't believe you still have these!" Ellie said, holding up the white patent-leather shoes Mary had worn to Ellie's wedding. The pumps had made Mary's heels blister, and she'd finally taken them off and walked out of the church in her stocking feet, upsetting Valerio's family who weren't happy about their son marrying a white girl to begin with.

"Those can go, too," Mary said.

"Will you look at this?" Ellie said, holding up a felt hat with plastic fruit glued to the band. "Where on earth . . . ?"

Mary could still picture Doris's embarrassment when Mr. Winkler saw her staring at the red velvet hat in the window of his store in Tahlequah. He crooked his finger like he meant to pull her inside with an invisible hook. Mary was surprised when Doris let him have his way. She had never once in her life seen her mother submit to vanity, and the idea that Doris might consider the purchase struck Mary as so irregular that she felt frightened. Doris bowed her head when Mr. Winkler placed the hat on her as if she were receiving his blessing. He adjusted the brim, saying a *bissel* this way and a *bissel* that way and how *ele-kant* she looked even though Doris told him that if he didn't stop lying to her she wouldn't buy anything at his store ever again and she had girls who would need wedding clothes. She stared at herself in the oval-shaped mirror that stood on the counter. She tilted her head in a way that was unfamiliar to Mary and that made her realize that Doris had once been someone besides her mother. Doris's cheeks worked like she was having an argument with herself, knowing how much money the hat cost on the one hand and feeling the pull of a shameful and impractical yearning. Finally, she glared at Mr. Winkler and slapped her money on his counter as if she blamed him for her foolishness.

Mary had no idea what had become of that particular hat, but when she saw the one in Ellie's hand at a yard sale years ago, she bought it, put it in a box and stored it on a shelf in her closet. Now, watching Ellie place the hat on her head and pose, hands on hips in an unconscious mockery of Doris, Mary began to understand what it would mean to live under her daughter's roof. There were certain stories she would never tell her children, parts of her history she would not give away. How could she explain that the original hat sat untouched in its box beneath her mother's bed because to have worn it would have been a personal pleasure Doris would have considered weak? How could she make them understand that a person needed to know that desire was still alive even when there was no reason for it to flourish?

"Give it away," she said, waving her hand dismissively toward the hat.

When they finished in the bedroom, Trevor went outside to smoke a cigarette and wait for the Goodwill truck to arrive. Ellie sat at the small table in the trailer's main room and filled a box with the items Mary had chosen to keep, wrapping picture frames in newspaper. Mary sat on the recliner, her eyes closed, depleted.

"Will you look at this?" Ellie said.

"Whatever it is, I don't want it," Mary said.

"It just never ends," Ellie said.

Mary opened her eyes. Ellie was holding out a newspaper, and Mary took it from her. There was the photo, now as part of an advertisement for a museum exhibit in San Francisco. *Vera Dare: Framing the Truth*.

"Doesn't it just make you mad?" Ellie said.

"Oh, I don't know, honey." Mary could not tell her daughter what she felt. Over the years, she had listened to her children fret about the picture, complaining that it made it seem like Mary never stopped living in a tent and eating dead birds when she was living in a nice trailer in a decent trailer park and each and every one of her kids had a high school diploma. Ray and June had two years of JC, and Della would have, too, if she hadn't gotten pregnant so early, but you could never regret children no matter when they came. Once Ellie had even convinced Mary to write a letter to a magazine to tell them to stop publishing the picture. Mary pretended to care because it seemed important to Ellie, but payment or the lack of it was not what she thought about when the subject of the picture came up. She never talked about the baby, and her children knew never to ask.

The cranking gears were so loud that Mary thought the Goodwill truck was going to plow right through the wall of the trailer. She let Ellie help her out of the chair and they walked outside where the activity had drawn some of the neighbor children away from their street games. Mary knew it was exciting to watch people move away. She remembered this from the camps. People moved because they were either on their way up or on their way down, and watching a family lash rolled mattresses to running boards made a person feel lucky or left out.

The Goodwill men carried furniture and boxes from the house to the truck. They nodded politely at Mary but betrayed nothing in their expressions. She was sure they were used to all sorts of situations— clearing out the houses of the dead or the divorced or of people who had reached the point where giving up their favorite set of dishes or their television console was worth it for the negligible tax break. One way or another, these men's work came at the end of hard times, and she imagined they had perfected transparent expressions to avoid hurt feelings.

When the men finished loading the truck and Ellie was signing their papers, Mary walked back into her empty home. The sun had slipped away without her realizing it, and the main room lay in shadows. She started for the light switch but changed her mind. This was no longer her home. It was four walls wrapped around nothing. She looked out a window. Ellie and Trevor were loading up their cars with her suitcases. The porch lights from other trailers glowed. She felt a chill. She remembered nights of slicing cold, her kids tucked up into every nook and cranny of her. They breathed one another's exhalations. Sometimes, tired as she was, she would untangle herself from them and slip outside. She would listen to the cicadas scratch, to the sound of a night bird. She could sense the blood pulsing in her veins. At night she had been most certain that she would survive.

The truck pulled away. The curious children scattered. Trevor turned and gave Mary a wave and climbed into his pickup for the drive to Ellie's house.

"You ready, Mama?" Ellie said, standing at the trailer door.

Mary dreaded being swept up into a future she had no control over. She remembered storms from her childhood, when the lightning seized the sky and she would stare out the window, waiting for the following thunder. If it did not come, she was left with a feeling that she'd asked a question that never got answered.

31

She was due to start again on the treatments the following week. As if her children sensed the worst, they began to visit. Ray's girls were sweet but shy around their grandmother. They had been kept apart from the family by Ray's wife, who considered the Coins too low-rent for her aspirations. The woman read copies of *Ladies' Home Journal* and looked impatient to leave, but Mary said nothing because Ray's life was his own. June and Della were tearful, and it had been good to hug them. She was happiest when James returned from the road, but it quickly became evident that his siblings had left him with the dirtiest job.

"Sell my car?" she said. He had taken her to breakfast at a diner where she'd ordered coffee and toast. She didn't want her children to spend money on her.

"I don't like to think of you driving," he said.

"Don't think of it," she said.

"You know what I see out there, Mama? Kids with open bottles, high as a kite. I pass an accident nearly every day."

"Maybe I'm the one who should be worried about you."

"Come on, Mama."

"Do you know what would have happened to us all those years ago if we didn't have a car? We would have died. A car saved our lives."

"You saved our lives, Mama."

"How will I get around with no car?" she said quietly.

"Ellie can take you places after she's finished work. Valerio is home Mondays. And those boys can drive you wherever you need to go if Ellie doesn't need her car."

"You want me to be driven around by a couple of ignorant teenagers? They don't even remember to brush their teeth unless you remind them."

He smiled sadly. There was probably no one in the world who understood her more than James.

"All right," she said.

The day before she was due for her first treatment at the clinic, she stood by the window, watching Ellie yell at the boys about being late for school. Mary had given away her home and now her car. It was only a matter of time before she would give away her life. Valerio had already returned from his shift and was asleep. The television in his and Ellie's bedroom was turned up the way he needed it to be so that the buzzers and bells of game shows would block out human sounds that might wake him. After Ellie and the boys drove away, Mary ate a bowl of corn flakes. Then she got her purse and a sweater and left the house. The pain in her stomach was bearable if she sucked in her gut and walked slowly. She waited at the corner bus stop. When the bus arrived, she told the driver she had incurable cancer, and even though it was not a scheduled stop, he let her off directly in front of the Goodwill. The store didn't open for another hour, and the parking lot was empty. Green garbage bags filled with donations sagged against the double glass doors like people hunkering against the early-morning chill. One of the bags had burst open, as if someone had thrown it there carelessly. Mary thought about what she must look like to the commuters driving down the boulevard: an old woman standing outside the Goodwill next to this spill of yellow and pink and overwashed red, as if she was just another cast-off.

At nine o'clock, a girl with fiercely lined magenta lips unlocked the glass doors and allowed Mary inside. The only other person in the store was a man busily arranging clothing on a circular rack. Mary wandered up and down the aisles. There were so many things on display that no one needed in the first place: garden gnomes and tricolored whirligigs from children's birthday parties, a fondue set and a heart-shaped waffle iron that were probably used only a handful of times by their owners. Goodwill was a place of once pressing and now useless desires in the form of salt and pepper shakers that looked like a copulating couple, and a Day-Glo lava lamp.

As if her eyes had a homing instinct, she began to notice her former possessions. There were her kitchen table and chairs. There was the lamp that stood by her bed, a price tag dangling from the cream-colored shade. It was a strange feeling to see these things that had once belonged to her, that she had touched and used and sat on. And now they felt no more hers than any of the other items lining the shelves of the store. She realized how silly the idea of owning was in the end. Even with children. The belief that they belonged to you was a lie you told yourself to make sure you would protect them until they were old enough to take care of themselves. But they were never really yours, and the very things you had done to keep them safe might have hurt them in the end.

She walked over to a clothing rack.

"Can I help you, lady?" The man she'd noticed was practically shouting, and Mary realized that he was wrong in some way. His mouth was loose and his words came out smeared.

"I gave some things to the Goodwill a few weeks ago," she said. "I thought I might find them."

"You can't have them back!" he said. "No Indian givers."

"You know, that's not really true what they say about Indians," she said. The man looked at her with alarm and went off in search of the girl with the red lips.

Mary sorted through the racks until she found one of her good dresses, the one she had worn to the christening of June's little boy. On a wrought-iron plant stand that served as a display rack for rows of creased and worn shoes, she found her white patent-leather pumps. The red hat sat nearby on the bald head of a mannequin. She bought that too.

32

When she woke, the Greyhound bus was well beyond Santa Clarita and heading toward San Francisco. She was exhausted. The expedition to the Goodwill and then the bus station had worn her down. She hoped she would have the strength to do what she had planned. She looked out her window. Rows of crops were covered with protective tarps. Others were exposed, their leaves green and ready. The pickers were small dots in the distance that didn't seem to be moving. But she knew those people were in constant motion. Pick, put it in the sack, move forward. Pick, put it in the sack, move forward.

The bus pulled off the freeway at a rest stop. Mary used the break to call Ellie at work, but the girl who answered the phone told her that Ellie had left early for an emergency. Mary called the house. When Ellie heard her mother's voice, she screamed so loudly that the person making a call at the pay phone next to Mary's looked over.

"We just spent four hours driving all over creation looking for you," Ellie said. "We were about to call the police and file a missing-persons report."

"I'm not missing," Mary said. "I'm right here."

"Where?"

"Don't be more clever than you are," Mary said.

"Mama," Ellie said, with the false calm she used when she was angry with her boys, "you cannot just run out on me like that."

"Honey, I'm not running out on anybody. I'm just taking a little vacation."

"I'm gonna come get you. I'm gonna call the others . . . I'm gonna . . ."

But Ellie would do nothing, because despite Mary's age and her health, the rules of the family had been laid down long ago when her children's lives depended on a mute submission to her sharp looks or warning words. When Ellie was finished exclaiming over all the things she was powerless to do to her mother, she let out a sigh of resignation.

"Oh, Mama. Why do you have to be like you are?"

But that was just it. Mary was the way she was. Her children relied on that. She wondered how they would manage after she was gone. When Doris had died so long ago, it was weeks before Mary could think clearly and remember what she was supposed to do the next minute and then the minute after that. Even though Doris had shown Mary how to get rid of the chiggers that burrowed under skin or how to add potatoes to bread to make it heavy so it would fill a stomach faster, she had never explained how she had survived the death of a husband and the loss of a child. Parents never told their real secrets. They never let you know how they lived in the spaces between working and cooking and running after children and counting dollars.

Mary had never told her children about the dread she felt each night while she waited to fall asleep. She had never told them how she survived each day after her last baby boy was gone, after she'd done the most terrible thing a person could do.

"But Mama," Ellie said, as if reading Mary's thoughts. "What are we supposed to do now?"

Mary said nothing, holding her secrets close. She told her daughter not to worry, hung up the phone, and boarded the bus.

It had been nearly twenty years since she'd read about the photographer's death. She had seen the obituary in the newspaper. Instead of Vera Dare's picture, the newspaper had printed the picture of Mary, and for a moment Mary thought she was reading her own death notice. She had felt the loss as if something had been taken away from her in particular, even though, according to the article, the woman had a husband and two sons and several grandchildren who were, no doubt, feeling a sharper kind of removal. Still, there were unhappy things that you lived with so long that you missed them when they were gone. She'd cried when that old Hudson had finally given out, even though it had been unreliable and filled with hard memories. She'd cried the night she'd slept in a real home for the first time after all those years of tents and shacks and backseats. She'd wept for the lock on the door, the key in her hand. She hoped Vera Dare had not suffered, although she knew that probably she had, because most people do. She'd died of cancer just like Mary would die of cancer. Probably Vera sat in hospital rooms and watched the slow drip of medicine move from the plastic pouch down the clear tube and into her body. Most likely she sucked on candies her children gave her not because she thought a ginger lozenge would do any good but because making her children feel useful was worth the lie.

Mary wondered if all the pictures Vera Dare took lived in the photographer's mind just the way a child does even when you've tried to banish thoughts of him, the way a face you've forgotten and haven't seen for so long can come to you when you least expect it. You're brushing your teeth and you see him looking back at you in the mirror. Your eyes are his eyes that stared up at you while he sucked, as if he was not only drawing milk from your breast but an idea of who he was. You hold a cool peach and feel his cheek in your palm.

As the bus continued its journey, she dozed again, and when she woke and looked out the window, it was as if someone had reached back and grabbed the past by the collar and dragged it forward. The bus sped by so quickly that she wondered, for a moment, whether she had been dreaming of the house with those tiers of oddly shaped windows and that wraparound porch. But when the bus passed the sign signaling that they were leaving Porter, she knew what she had seen. She pressed her face to the glass, watching the rows of orange trees bending at uniform angles in the stiff wind. She stared at the land where she had spent so much of herself. But land was ignorant. It had no notion of what had occurred on it a half century before. It was a sheet of paper on which the stories of thousands of small lives were written over time. And to think that what had happened to her was any more meaningful than what might have befallen another person, or a cow, or an ant—well, there were all sorts of ways people convinced themselves they were above the thick of life, and all of them were wrong. She had avoided Porter for years, tried never even to think of its name. She had convinced herself that if she didn't acknowledge it, then it would not exist and neither would her longing. But it had always been here. This dirt. Those trees. That house.

When the bus pulled into the Visalia station, she got off. She read the schedule and saw that there would be another one coming through in five hours. The woman behind the ticket counter gave her the number of a local taxi service.

"That'll be forty dollars," the cabdriver said, after Mary sat in the backseat and told him where she wanted to go.

"I'll give you twenty," she said.

The man looked at her in the rearview mirror. "It's not a negotiation, ma'am. We charge by the mile."

"Thirty for the round trip."

He was about to protest.

"If you've got other customers, go ahead and take them," she said, looking at the empty sidewalk outside the bus station. "But to my mind, thirty dollars is better than zero dollars."

Once they were back in Porter, she pointed out the house from the highway, and the driver found his way to the service road that ran past the property.

"You want me to pull into the drive?" he said.

"Just stop. Right here."

He parked the cab on the shoulder of the road. When she did not make a move to get out of the car, he turned around in his seat. "Do you need help, ma'am?"

"I just want to sit here for a minute, if you don't mind."

33.

Porter, California, 1935

She didn't question Charlie when he told her he'd arranged for the kind of doctor who would take care of things. The inequality in the relations between them suggested that she had no say in this matter, and she couldn't risk losing her job. And what would she do with another child? Her kids grew hungrier as they grew bigger. There were times when she'd stand next to Trevor, realize he'd grown another inch, and something would collapse inside her. Ellie was so thin that she hadn't yet gotten her period. Other women in the camp told Mary to be grateful that the girl wouldn't be able to make babies yet, but the unnaturalness was upsetting.

One Sunday, she left the little ones under the care of Ellie and Trevor. She walked out of the camp and down the road to the place where she and Charlie usually met. He did not look at her when she climbed into his shiny DeSoto. When she mentioned the fancy car, he admitted that his mother thought he was out driving with a girl named Naomi.

"This Naomi is going to be your wife?" Mary said.

He didn't answer.

"You do with her what you do with me?"

"No."

When they rounded a corner, she saw a grand home set back from the road. The house was painted a pristine white and trimmed the color of raspberries. It seemed that there were more windows in the house than there were walls. Some of them were round, some rectangular; the one at the top of a pointed turret was cut in the shape of a crescent moon. The roofline stopped here and rose up there, as if the house had been built in stages by someone dreaming a new dream.

"That's yours?" she said.

"It belongs to my father," he said. "But I live there."

"It's where you're going to bring your wife? This Naomi?"

"I suppose so."

She looked back at the house, which sat proudly on its tuft of lawn.

"She'll like that," Mary said. "Any girl would."

He drove through town, past the shops that were closed for the day, their awnings rolled back against their brick fronts, past the Huntington Hotel and the grand-looking Adelaide Theater and a billiard parlor whose sign was a ball that doubled as an orange. She saw a sign for a doctor's office hanging outside a detached building, but Charlie didn't stop his car. Instead, he drove past the end of the main street and out again into farmland. He turned the car down a bumpy road that ran through a grove of lemon trees and headed toward a plain clapboard house. Sheets and shirts and men's drawers hung on a line strung between two trees. A girl stood on top of a tire swing. She eyed the oncoming car as she lazily worked her hips to get up some momentum. Two small boys took turns kicking a ball into the air. Charlie parked the car a short distance from the house. They both sat in silence, listening to the ticks and groans of the spent engine.

"Just go on in there," he said finally.

"By myself?"

"I won't be of any use," he said.

"I don't have money."

"It's already paid for."

"You've got it all figured out, I guess."

The door of the house opened, and a woman appeared. She cleaned her hands on her apron. Mary's stomach turned at the thought of what the woman might be wiping away. Charlie stared at his lap.

"Say my name," Mary said.

"What?"

"Say my name."

"Mary," he said.

"Mary Coin. Say it."

"Mary Coin."

She got out of the car and walked quickly past the children. Mary felt certain the girl knew what she was there to do.

The woman led her to a room that was dominated by a table draped in a white cloth. Two chairs stood at the end of the table. A man in shirtsleeves stood over a sink, washing his hands.

"She's here," the woman said.

The doctor was young. His face was as unlined as a boy's, and Mary wondered if, in fact, he was a boy playing at doctoring the way Ray played at being a train conductor. He dried his hands with a dishcloth. His palms were pink.

"You've done this before?" he said.

"Have you?" she said, but her bravado fell flat. She had no power in this situation. Charlie had most likely found a doctor who had nothing to do with his family, someone who needed the job so badly he could be trusted, or maybe paid, not to talk. "No," she said quietly. "I've never done this before."

"Take off your drawers," the woman said.

"Right here?" Mary said.

The doctor rolled up his sleeves and tossed his tie over his shoulder. "Lay out the instruments, please," he said to the woman.

Mary started shivering. She turned her back to the others and stepped out of her underwear. There was nowhere to put them so she held them. When she turned around, the woman handed Mary a cup and instructed her to drink. Fumes shot straight up Mary's nose and she gasped. Then she drank the liquor down quickly, feeling it cut against her throat. Her chest widened out with the drink's heat. She watched as the woman placed strange-looking instruments on a tray—thin, sharp-tipped lengths of metal, a pair of bent scissors and something that looked like a shallow spoon.

"You can get up on the table now," the woman said.

Mary did as she was told. She was shaking convulsively.

"It will go easier for you if you calm down," the woman said, not unkindly. "Now, I need you to slide down to the edge." Once Mary did this, the woman took her legs and put one, then the other, on the top rung of each chair.

"There will be some pain," the doctor said. "But that whiskey will help." He picked up one of the instruments from the tray. "At least it will help you forget," he said.

"What if I don't want to forget," she said.

"This isn't something you want to remember."

A s she walked toward the car, she had no sense of her body. Something had happened to her in the middle of her screaming, and the doctor's confusion, and then the woman's anger as she told Mary to quiet down if she didn't want to get them all arrested. Something had happened when she pushed away the doctor's hand, upsetting his instrument tray so that it crashed to the floor. She reminded herself to move slowly so as not to arouse Charlie's suspicion. She made a few noises of discomfort when she sat down in the passenger seat. It was not hard to pretend; she could still feel the man's cold, pink fingers on her skin. She imagined Charlie had heard her cries, but he must have assumed things were going as planned.

"So, you're all right, then?" he said awkwardly as he drove back through the lemon trees.

"You got your money's worth," she said.

"Oh, Mary," he said.

She saw that something had changed in him, that he was deflated, as if in the administration of some kind of obligation to his stature he had discovered he was a fraud. Well, they both were now.

"Just take me back to my children," she said.

Once again, they passed through town, where people gathered by the open doors of a church. It struck her as an amazing fact of human nature that even while people lost jobs and money, they still clung to their habits, their Sunday strolls, their belief in a terrible God. This was endurance, she supposed, this stubborn repetition in the face of the world making no sense. As they passed Charlie's home once again, she imagined a child growing up there. If it was a boy, he would be taught to uphold some unexplained code of family honor, to ride through the groves in his truck as if on the back of a fine stallion. He would learn how to level a glare that would keep workers from taking too much water, and he would turn into a man who had no idea who he was, just like Charlie had no idea what kind of man he was. If it was a girl, well, she would be like that Naomi, ignorant of the lies that underpinned her life.

Before they came within sight of the camp, Charlie pulled the DeSoto to the side of the road.

"You can make it back okay," he said.

"Are you asking or telling?"

"I'll be leaving soon. We have another farm. My father needs me there."

"If you're running away from me, I'm not going to say anything to anyone."

"I'm not running away."

She opened the car door and stepped out onto the road. "Well, good-bye then, mister."

34.

Sickness spread through the camp. There was not a day when one of Mary's children didn't have a nose running yellow. Their dry coughs were terrible memories of Toby's last days, and she had to keep herself from being harsh with them when they complained of aches or pains, her fear congealing into anger. Mary paid a half-wit named Lucille to look after her kids when they were sick. She'd spend the day in the groves worrying that Lucille would not be smart enough to come find her if someone's fever rose. Despite being near her term, Mary had lost weight and she worked slowly. There were times when exhaustion came over her with such force that she had to stop what she was doing and rest. She carried this new one like she had carried all the others, and the swell of her stomach was unmistakable. She was sure that any day the foreman would give her job to someone else.

The five-o'clock whistle blew. Mary dragged her orange baskets to the end of the row. When the truck finally pulled up to collect the day's take, she was shocked to see Charlie at the wheel. He had been true to his word, and she hadn't seen him for months. But now here he was, stepping out of the truck, as clean and golden as she remembered him. Before she could figure out how to hide herself, he noticed her. At first, his face opened with uninhibited pleasure as if he was remembering the way he whispered into her ear while he moved on top of her, murmuring words and half sentences Mary was never able to make out. But as his eyes traveled the length of her body, his expression turned to one of disbelief. James came running over and stood by Mary. Charlie looked at the boy's dirty face and his dusty clothes that were too big, and Mary could tell that he would consider the child in her belly as just another wretched thing.

She knew he would be waiting on the road for her later that afternoon, so she was ready for him. She didn't care if he followed her or if he watched her go to the bathroom. Let him know what it was like for her to live and shit and clean herself.

"Is it mine?" he said.

"It's mine."

"I talked to that doctor."

"So why are you asking me what you already know?"

The shouts of camp children playing games of chase and skip-rope reached them. Why did the sound of a child's happiness make her sad?

"Why are you doing this?" he said.

"I told you I wouldn't say a thing about what happened, and I won't. Now walk away from me before someone sees you."

He hesitated.

"Do it," she said. "Go."

At the end of the week, she went to exchange her chits for cash.

The bursar told her to sign her name and then handed her double the amount she was owed.

"That's not right," she said.

"If you have a problem with the pay, there are other farms down the road."

"You made a mistake to my advantage," she said.

He looked at her like he was trying to search out her strategy.

"This is twice as much as I got last week for not nearly the same amount of baskets," she said.

He looked at his paperwork. "I don't know anything about last week. It says here this is what you're due."

"I don't know," she said uncertainly. She didn't want to be accused of stealing.

"If you don't want the money, give it to the next person in line," he said. "If my accounts don't balance at the end of the day, I got a bigger problem than a crazy lady doesn't want her pay."

She closed her hand around the money. She walked past the long, patient line, looking down to avoid the gazes of the other pickers, certain they would know she had been privileged and why.

The next time she saw him in the groves, he did not acknowledge her, and there was no way for her to tell him to stop what he was doing. And then the bigger she got, the harder it was to work at a decent pace, and she stopped thinking about the fact that she was taking his money for her silence. Her children's stomachs were full.

Three weeks later, as she climbed down the ladder and hoisted a full basket onto her hip, she felt a stabbing pain in her stomach. She dropped the basket and clutched herself. James looked up at her in confusion. His face was a blur. And then he and everything around him became black.

When she came to, she was on her back. There were shadows above her.

"She needs to get back to the camp before she drops this baby right here," a woman said.

"Some of 'em come so fast you don't even bother to stop what you're doing."

"We need to find a doctor."

"Not likely."

And then women were holding her upright, urging her to move. "Come on, now, honey," one said. "It's not too far."

She pitched forward, slipping out of the women's grasp. She tasted dirt and vomit.

S he woke in a rush of terror. Hands worked between her legs. "Don't kill my baby!" she screamed, to make that boy-doctor stop what he was doing with his cold instruments.

"Shh, señora." It was a girl, sixteen or seventeen. She smiled and nodded reassuringly. She removed a bloodstained towel from underneath Mary and then put a fresh one in its place. Her hands worked precisely as she adjusted the bedclothes.

"What's happening?" Mary said.

"Shhh, señora," the girl repeated.

"Where am I?" And then she remembered. They had laid her on the bed of a truck. Someone had carried her up a flight of stairs. There had been a man telling her not to push yet, and then to push, push!

And someone had held her hand the whole time. She remembered
that. Was it this girl who was tending to her? Who was helping her
recover from—

"My baby! Where is my baby?"

The girl smiled at her.

"My baby!" Her throat was raw. "Where is my baby?"

"*El bebé está durmiendo.*"

"Dead? Is my baby dead?"

An older woman came into the room. She leaned over Mary and
gently pushed her shoulders back onto the pillow. "*Tranquilízate,*"
she said.

But Mary kept screaming, her voice grating against her throat
until she could hardly make a sound. The young girl ran out of the
door, calling, *Señor. Señor!* After a few minutes, Charlie came into the
room and stood by her bed.

Mary reached out and clutched his wrist. "What did you do to my
baby?" she said.

"The baby is fine."

"I want to see my baby."

The young Mexican girl returned holding a bundle. "*Un niño,*"
she said, leaning over so that Mary could see the tiny face shrouded
by white cloth, a baby set into a dish of vanilla ice cream.

"A boy?" she asked.

"*Sí, muy pequeño.*"

Mary held out her hands. She was startled by the weight of him;
he felt barely heavier than the blanket he was wrapped in. His face
looked crushed; his brow pushed down on his eyes. The bones of his
hand reminded her of the skeleton of a baby field mouse that Della

had once found. It was completely intact, missing only its future. Mary looked up and, for the first time, took in her surroundings. Everything in the room was white. White bureau. White bedframe. White curtains billowed in the breeze. A small crystal chandelier swayed, and a rainbow refraction of the cut glass pieces fluttered across the wall.

"Where am I?" she said.

"You're in my home," Charlie said.

"I told you this wasn't any of your business anymore," she said.

"You could have died. The baby could have died."

"That didn't bother you some months ago."

"You're not well," he said. "You had a hard time of it."

"My kids! Where are my kids? Where are they?"

"They're fine," he said. "They're being looked after."

"By who?" she said. "You just let any stranger take care of them?"

"There was a woman in the camp. She says she watches your children while you work."

"That Lucille? I have to pay her or she won't care for them right. And how's she gonna feed them?"

"It's taken care of."

She looked down at herself. She was wearing a white nightgown. Her dark skin showed through a fretwork of lace at the neck. Her hands, still crusted with dirt from the field, had left smudges on the baby's wrapping.

"Why doesn't he cry?" she said.

"His lungs are weak."

"He's not going to make it."

"He's here," Charlie said. "He's not going anywhere."

The older woman took the baby from her.

"Where is she taking my baby?"

"Cecilia knows what to do," Charlie said, smiling. "She raised me."

She slept so heavily that when she next awoke she felt as if her mind had been erased, wiped clean of all memory. She stared at the white walls of the airy room and waited for her brain to piece itself back together. She'd had her baby. He was alive. Her children were at the camp. They were being fed. She was lying in a room in the big house with many windows.

The young girl was by her side. Mary's breasts ached; her milk had come in. She made it clear that she needed to see her baby, and the girl quickly left the room and returned with him. Mary opened her nightgown and put him to her. She felt his lips on her skin, but he did not drink. After a few moments, he began to whimper. She ran her finger along the roof of his mouth in order to get him to suck on it, and then quickly replaced her finger with her long, warm nipple. But he simply dandled the skin in his slack mouth until it fell out. When she squeezed to get the milk going, her eyes watered from the pain. She needed him to relieve her. She rubbed the liquid on his lips to tantalize him, but he just continued to make soft, pathetic sounds. Mary felt helpless and ashamed and insulted by this tiny infant, this little thing that mocked her and whose birth had weakened her so that she had to be cared for by a man who'd just as soon this baby had never existed and who had no more use for Mary than he did for a broken-down tractor.

"He won't take to me," she said in defeat.

The girl's expression was odd as if she, too, was embarrassed by Mary's failure. Then Mary noticed that two lakes of wetness had spread over the front of the girl's blouse. She remembered that from her other babies: how the cry of a stranger's child would cause her milk to come.

"You have a baby, too?" she said.

"*Lo siento, señora,*" the girl whispered.

And then Mary understood. "You're feeding my baby?" She began to yell, repeating the question over and over as if it would begin to make sense. The girl became frightened and made for the door, but when the baby let out a shriek, she turned back, her face opening in surprise.

"*Un buen grito,*" she said, patting her chest.

He howled again. Mary laughed. "I guess he's got lungs on him now." She held him out toward the girl. "Please," she said.

The girl sat at the foot of the bed and opened her shirt. The baby took her milk and quieted, his little sucks and moans punctuating the silence.

"Mary," Mary said, pointing to herself.

"Alma," the girl said. She lifted the baby from her breast, covered herself, and then handed him to Mary. Mary patted his back and jiggled him up and down. When the burp came, both women sighed.

She begged Charlie to bring her other children to her, and early the next evening the door opened, and there they were. Della, June, and Ray ran to the bed and flung themselves across it, their dirty clothes like rain clouds against the white sheets. Trevor stood quietly by her side. Ellie stayed in the doorway, holding James's hand. She looked like a young woman—protective and wary and fierce.

"The lady gave us iced tea in the kitchen," Della said.

"That was nice," Mary said.

"And the glasses have straws stuck right on them," Della said. "And there was leaves in the tea."

"That's mint."

"We could put in as much sugar as we wanted," June said. "The lady said so."

Alma appeared at the door with the baby. Mary held out her hands. "Here he is," she said. "Here's your new brother."

"Oh!" June cried, as if she had just been given a doll. "Oh, I love him!"

James pulled away from Ellie's grip and came to Mary's side. He put his hand on her shoulder and looked at the baby. Mary stared into James's dark, wet eyes, which were as mysterious to her as a horse's.

"Lucille told us you were going to live here now," Ellie said. "She said you got yourself a leg up in the world and that you were taking your chance."

"Lucille has half a brain."

"You told us never to talk mean about people who are slow," Trevor said.

"Lucille said you made your luck on your back," Ellie said.

Mary looked at Alma but could not tell if the girl understood. She turned back to Ellie. "Every one of you was made on my back and every one of you is my good luck. Do you hear me?"

"Yes, ma'am," Ellie mumbled.

"Say it out loud."

"Yes, ma'am!"

The following morning, when Mary woke up, Alma was in the room, cleaning.

"Will you get me my clothes?" Mary said.

Alma looked at her blankly.

Mary pointed to her nightgown. "My dress. I want my dress back."

"*No más vestido.*"

"I don't understand you. I want my clothes. I want to go home."

"*Es sucio,*" Alma said. She looked down at her apron and pointed to a stain.

"I don't care if it's dirty. I'm not gonna spend the rest of my life in this"—she grabbed her nightgown—"this useless thing." She struggled to get out of bed. "Bring me my baby. *El bebé.*"

Alma left the room, and a few minutes later Charlie appeared at the door. "What's this I hear about you leaving us?"

"I have to get back to my family. I have to get to work." She sat down on the bed, exhausted. "The baby and I don't belong here."

"He's plumping right up," Charlie said. "It seems this house is doing him good."

There was something in his voice that made her alert. "My children need me," she said.

"I just thought, well, that he could stay here for a while."

"A while?"

"Well . . . for however long he likes."

"He's a baby," she said. "He won't be telling you what he likes and what he doesn't like for some years yet."

"Think about it, Mary," he said, sitting on the bed beside her, taking her hand in his. "Think of his life here. What we could offer him."

"What does your family want with a bastard child?"

"He's a Dodge."

"Just 'cause you've got money you think you can do anything you want with a person. Hire them. Fire them. Fuck them. Take their babies. I'm not leaving my baby with strangers."

"I'm not a stranger," he said. "Neither is Alma. He took to her so fast."

She slapped him across the cheek. "That's a vicious thing to say."

"You have six other kids."

"You think I don't know what happens when I spread my legs? That I'm just some idiot woman who doesn't know how to stop having babies? I chose all *seven* of my children. I *chose* them."

"I'm sorry," he said quietly. "I'm sorry for everything."

"Well, that's the difference between us. I'm not sorry for one single thing."

An hour later, while the baby slept peacefully on the bed, Mary let Alma dress her. She raised her hands like a child, and Alma lifted the nightgown over her head. Mary stood naked and unembarrassed as Alma took a damp rag and washed Mary's arms and legs, her belly and her back. She helped Mary into a stranger's green dress. She knelt on the floor and tried to fit Mary's feet into a pair of heeled shoes, each one decorated with a small bow on the point of the toe. They were the most beautiful shoes Mary had ever seen.

"Maybe I could have yours?" Mary said, pointing to Alma's woven sandals.

"*Mis zapatos?*" Alma said, coloring with embarrassment.

"*Sí.*"

Mary slipped into the girl's sandals, feeling their warm dampness. Her feet settled into the depressions worn into the leather. Alma put on the heeled shoes, her face opening into a wide smile as she admired her feet. When Mary was finally ready, she picked up the baby and settled him into her arms. Alma reached into the pocket of her apron and brought out a glass bottle filled with her warm milk. She tucked the bottle into the folds of the blankets.

Charlie was waiting for her at the bottom of the stairs. "What will you name him?" he said, when she reached him.

"George," she said. "My father's name."

"Georgie," Charlie said.

"Just George," she said.

"Will you tell him about me?" Charlie said.

"I don't lie to my kids."

"What will you say?"

"I'll tell him the truth. I'll tell him you were a decent sort of man in your heart."

B ack at the camp, the children were quiet and careful, unsure of her. The girls admired her green dress, touching the fabric as if it were made of jewels. James stayed close as she boiled potatoes, never letting her more than an arm's length from him. When George began to cry, she opened the top of her dress and put him to her breast. He turned away.

"What's wrong with him, Mama?" Della said. "Why don't he want to eat?"

Mary unscrewed the cap of the bottle. She dipped her finger into Alma's milk and rubbed the liquid on her nipple. She put George to her breast again. He sucked briefly before he stopped. His cries grew more disconsolate.

"Just give him the bottle," Ellie said.

"He has to get used to me," Mary said. She dipped and rubbed her finger again, and again he rejected her. His cries became screams.

"Why don't he want you, Mama?" Trevor said.

Mary held back her tears. She had to get him to feed from her or her milk would dry up.

"What are you gonna do now, Mama?" June said.

What now? It was the question that ruled her life. *What will we do now, Mama? Where will we go now? How will we eat now, Mama?* Her children stared at her, waiting for her answer.

The night before, Mary had woken in that white room to find Charlie standing by her bed. She had no idea how long he had been watching her. He was gentle as he led her down the darkened stairway and through the rooms of the sleeping house.

First he showed her a sitting room decorated all in blue. His mother's favorite color, he said. Then he took her to a darker room outfitted in a manly style. A standing globe was next to the window. A set of leather chairs were directed toward one another, waiting, she imagined, for men to sit in them and say important things. He showed her the dining room, where a silver vase filled with blush-colored roses sat in the center of a long mahogany table that was polished to such a high gleam that Mary could see her face reflected in the surface. Each time they entered a new room, Charlie turned on a light as if he were illuminating a magical world. When he switched off the light, Mary had the impression of that world disappearing forever.

"This is my favorite room in the house," he said, when they entered a library lined with books. He walked along one of the shelves, his hand running over the bindings.

"Have you read all these?" she said.

"A lot of them. I read literature in college. Not my father's choice."

"What did he want you to do?"

"The sciences. Something a farmer could make use of."

He pulled a heavy book out from one of the shelves and opened it, turning the thin pages with the tip of his finger. He read aloud. "*'The wind was a torrent of darkness upon the gusty trees, The moon was a ghostly galleon tossed upon cloudy seas. The road was a ribbon of moonlight looping the purple moor, And the highwayman came riding—Riding—riding— The highwayman came riding, up to the old inn door.'*" He stopped and smiled to himself.

"What's that?"

"This was my favorite poem when I was a boy. I made my father read it to me every night until I could read it for myself."

"Well, keep going," she said.

"It's a long poem."

"I've got a long patience."

He continued, gaining speed until he was reading in a rhythm that reminded her of a horse galloping across a field, tossing its mane from side to side. He read about the landlord's daughter named Bess who loved a highwayman so much she saved his life by sacrificing her own. When he was finished, he closed the book and replaced it on the shelf, lining it up so that it was flush with the other bindings.

"I would not shoot myself to warn my lover," she said.

"You'd let him be killed by the redcoats, then?"

"He was a thief."

"But she loved him," he said.

"Well, it doesn't pay to love a dishonest man."

A re you all right, ma'am?"

"What?"

The taxi driver turned around in his seat and looked at Mary. "Do you want me to drive you back to the bus station now?"

"So soon?"

"We've been sitting here for a half hour."

"I'll pay you more. Whatever you think is fair. I just want to sit here a little bit longer."

The taxi driver looked out the window. "Not a lot of houses like this around anymore," he said.

"Yes," she said distractedly.

"I'm going to go stretch my legs."

"Go ahead."

"Can I trust you with my car?"

She saw his teasing smile.

"You'd better take your keys," she said.

She turned her attention back to the house. She had always

thought Charlie had taken her on that midnight tour in order to show her how much better a life he could offer their baby. Now, so many decades later, she wondered if she had been wrong, and if he had only been trying to show her something of himself and let her know that she had relieved his loneliness for a time, and that he was grateful.

The door of the big house opened. A teenage boy ran out. He collected a bicycle from where it lay on the lawn and swung his leg over the seat. A man appeared at the door just as the boy pushed off and pedaled down the driveway.

"Walker Dodge! Get back here right now!" the man called out.

The boy reached the end of the drive and raced away.

The taxi driver returned and got into the car, saying something about that boy needing to be careful, but Mary didn't hear him. Her heart was beating too fast, and the rush of blood made her deaf. The man stood by the house looking in the direction the boy had gone. His gaze then settled on the cab. He stood too far away for Mary to make out his face. He began to walk toward the car.

"Please," Mary said urgently to the driver. "Take me back. Take me back to—" But she had forgotten where she had come from. "Please!"

The driver put the car in gear and drove away.

35

The San Francisco bus station was nearly empty. A woman stood at the ticket counter. A man wrapped in layers of coats slept on a bench. A poster advertising a runaway hotline showed a glum teenager sitting on a garbage-strewn curb. Mary walked into the gray drizzle of the afternoon. She saw a hotel across the street, but the men lounging in the doorway told her what sort of place it was. She had wasted so much money on that taxi ride to the house and the extra bus ticket, but what use did she have for her money anymore? She got into a waiting cab and told the driver to take her someplace clean.

All night long she lay on her hotel bed, not bothering to remove the spread. She dozed on and off. Every time she woke, she did so with a start, as if she had missed something crucial. She listened to the sound of nighttime delivery trucks on the street, to the crunch and grind of the ice machine in the hallway. She did not think the word *sick* could describe what she was feeling. It was more the sensation of her body shrugging itself off like a coat. How much longer would she be able to perform the particular sleight of hand that convinced everyone and even herself that this body and these thoughts added up to a particular person named Mary Coin? That was what living was, after all. A trick played on fate for as long as you could pull it off. She was in a hotel for only the second time in her life, and for the second time she did not know who she was.

In the morning, she showered and put on her dress and her white shoes. She sat on the bed and opened her purse, taking out an envelope that was wrinkled and soft. She'd carried the letter with her for nearly twenty years.

Dear Mrs. Coin,

There is a sense you get when you have taken the right photograph. It is a feeling that you have lived that second of your life more completely than any other. The moment opens, and you realize how much larger your life is than you thought it was, how much closer to a kind of . . . is it happiness? I don't know.

I saw you and I recognized you the way you recognize people in your dreams even if you don't know who they are. That's all a photograph is, really. A recognition.

Very sincerely, and with great sadness for the end of things.

Forgive me,
Vera Dare

Mary tucked the letter into the envelope and put the envelope back in her purse. She washed out the bathroom sink and dried it with a bit of tissue then straightened the bedcover so it appeared as if no one had been there at all.

36

A t first she thought someone had released a flock of birds into the room. The museum gallery whispered with the sound of wings and flight, and she thought of the starlings wheeling through the flat Oklahoma sky, a solid flag of them waving in the currents of a wind. Was that sixty years ago? More? She knew her death was near because time had begun to fold like a fan so that the past and the present rubbed together in ways that made her feel supple and porous, as if time were moving through her body and not the other way around. She clutched her purse to her chest, her palm sweating against the leather. In her other hand she carried the wrinkled bag filled with her travel clothes and the red hat. Her feet ached in the pumps. The pain in her abdomen told her that she was not going to be able to outrun herself for much longer.

There were no birds, of course, only the hush of voices and the soft rustle of feet as museum visitors shuffled past the photographs. The gallery was crowded, and people jostled one another to get closer to the images. They crossed their arms over their chests as they studied the work, their faces set grimly as if they were standing in their doorways listening to someone trying to sell them religion. The crowd circulated in one direction, and Mary let herself be moved along at its slow pace. She stopped in front of a picture of a young girl standing by a barbed-wire fence. In the background, a woman—the girl's mother, Mary supposed—stood with her hand to her brow to shield herself from the sun's glare. She looked sad, or maybe that was just the set of her face; some people had a mournful look to them. Or perhaps the mother was watching the photographer, wondering why she wanted to take her girl's picture. But she could have been looking at something else, maybe another child she had to keep her eye on or a neighbor who was coming over to see what was happening. Mary looked at another picture, of four men picking lettuce. If you didn't know what it felt like to be bent in two for ten hours a day, you might think it was a pretty picture because a field of ripened harvest is pleasing, the way the rows lie out evenly and because it reminds you of full stomachs and good rains. In the next photograph, a man stood knee-deep in a truckload of cotton pickings that looked soft as a feather bed but which she knew were filled with burs that would draw blood if your arms and legs weren't covered. She paused before more photographs: a man holding a baby outside a shack made of bits and pieces; a boy standing in the doorway of a tobacco barn; a couple in the middle of a terrible argument.

The accretion of images in the gallery operated on her like too much noise, and for a moment she forgot why she had come all this way, why she had ridden a dirty bus that smelled of cramped sleep and useless disinfectants, why she had paid to stay in a hotel that was supposed to be clean but where a curl of someone's pubic hair greeted her when she went to take her morning shower. She could not faint. She *would* not. Someone would look in her purse and find her wallet.

Another person would make the connection. Some eager reporter would write about it in the newspaper. And how would she look then? She reached to steady herself against a wall, but a guard shot her a look. She found a tissue in her purse and dabbed at her forehead and along the sides of her nose. It was too much, being in this big room filled with all these trapped people, the ones in the photographs and the ones revolving slowly like fish in an aquarium.

A child cried out. Mary turned toward the sound, and there, across the room, hung the familiar charcoal-gray shapes of the image that shadowed her life. Time collapsed again, and she was on the side of the road with her children, exhausted from pitching the tent, knowing that it could be hours before Earl came back with the repaired radiator so they could move on from that place. She was a stocky old woman in a museum in 1982. She weighed a hundred pounds, if that, a half century earlier, watching as a lady with a limp got out of a car and asked to take her picture. She walked across the gallery and stood in front of the photograph. She remembered her children's haircuts. Just the day before, she'd taken a scissors and snipped straight across. She was pleased by the way the bobs framed their small faces. And there was the baby in her arms. Her George. Sometimes, even all these years later, she could still feel that heaviness. A watermelon might do it, or a load of clothes warm from the dryer.

She did not know what was in the minds of the people in the other pictures hanging in the gallery, but she knew exactly what she had been thinking when that picture had been taken: she had been asking herself a question, the same one she'd been asking every day since. Whenever she thought she knew the answer, she also realized that she didn't. Six times she heard the click of the camera. And each time the woman drew closer, Mary had the same feeling she had when her mother caught her in a lie. *You didn't wash out the sheets. Yes, I did. Then why are they still dirty? They fell off the line. They fell off the line and rolled around in the dirt? It was windy.* Lies to cover lies, until she was cornered and there was nothing left but to submit to the back of her mother's hand. It was useless to lie to herself any longer. She could not manage with seven children and no real husband and no work. She could not keep this very sick child alive without medicine. George let out a wretched howl. Mary felt his burning forehead and saw his misery.

The photographer went back to her car and started the engine. The wheels gained traction in the mud and she drove away. Mary imagined what would happen: They would drive back to Porter. She would go to the house during the day, when Charlie was likely to be out on the farm, so that she would not have to face him. Alma would answer the door. The girl would be confused, but all Mary would need to do to make her understand was to hold the baby toward her. Alma's arms would go up automatically the way any woman's arms would, no matter if it was her child or not, because holding was a woman's purpose. And as soon as Alma felt the heat coming off George's little body, as soon as she saw his glassy eyes and his parched lips, she would understand. Mary imagined George grown into a boy. She saw him running through those wonderful rooms Charlie had shown her that night, his keen eyes and bright laughter making it impossible for the Dodge family not to love him as one of their own.

In fact, Alma did answer the door, but as soon as she saw Mary she went back into the house. After a few minutes, an older man appeared. "I'm Theodore Dodge," he said. He stared at her with contempt. "If you're after money, you can leave."

Events were unfolding so differently from how Mary had planned. She hadn't thought she would have to explain herself.

"Please," she said. "Take him."

"I don't—"

"He's sick," she said, interrupting. "He's so sick."

The man looked down at the baby. His expression shifted imperceptibly.

"I'm begging you," she said. "He's your grandson. Please have mercy on him."

He said nothing, only turned and walked back into the house, leaving Mary standing at the door. She waited, unsure if she had been dismissed or if the open door was an invitation. Finally, he returned with Alma. She took George from Mary's arms. *"Lo siento,"* she whispered.

"We will never see you again," Theodore Dodge said to Mary.

"Never," she said weakly.

The door closed. Mary hadn't expected it to happen so fast. She hadn't been ready.

A couple stepped up to the photograph. "She reminds me of someone," the man said.

"Who?" the woman said.

"Oh, I don't know. Maybe no one. Maybe I've just seen this so many times I feel like I know her."

"She looks so . . . so . . ."

So what?

A teenager said, "We learned about that picture!" rushing toward it with excitement, as if she were meeting someone at the train station. But as she stared at the photograph, her expression grew vacant, as if she could not think of what to say next, her eagerness snuffed out by the dullness of familiarity.

"You can see it all in her face," someone else said.

What all? What do you see? She was a ghost in the room. She looked at the other ghosts in the photographs lining the walls—the farmer with dirt on his cheeks, the woman posing next to her car. None of them had known that one day they would be hanging in this museum, a single moment of their lives frozen into an indelible past like an insult you can never take back.

Mary turned again to face the picture and saw her reflection in the glass. There they were. Two women named Mary Coin. If they met on the street in the high heat of a summer's afternoon, they would be polite in the old-fashioned way to show they meant each other no harm. "Hello," they would say in passing. "My, but isn't it a wretched day?"

Walker

37.

San Francisco, California, 2011

It is a clear November day, and Walker is having trouble staying put for the remaining time left of his office hours. More students than usual have come to see him because today is the filing deadline for the senior thesis proposals. Alice will arrive soon. They are going to see a rerun of what she claims is one of the great films of the twenty-first century: *Wet Hot American Summer.*

She has been living with him since the beginning of the school year. She hates her mother, she says. She hates Harry. She hates Walker, too, only a little less than everyone and everything else. Lisette is unhappy about the new state of affairs, but she is also worn down by Alice and is relieved to have a break. Walker is grateful that in her fury, Alice has chosen him. He has enrolled her in a city school where she is repeating the eleventh grade. She goes to rehab. He tests her urine once a week, and she is not allowed to hang out with her friends at night. She and Walker eat takeout and listen to music. She shows him funny videos on YouTube.

He continues to read through his students' proposals. The work is serious and eager. The seniors have taken his introductory class and followed up with courses in narrative nonfiction and methodology.

Their undertakings are all versions, in one way or another, of his work, and he is flattered by how much they believe in him and his endeavors.

Over the last few months, he has pursued a project of his own, constructing an imagined narrative of intersecting lives—his and Mary Coin's. He wonders if he is really looking to find the truth, or if he is only trying to find a way to confront his unexpected sorrow at his father's passing, and his guilt about his children, and the essential loneliness he feels each day. In each case he has failed. He can no more prove that Mary Coin was his grandmother than he can repair himself. He hears his father's voice in his head: *What good is history?*

He turns to his computer and pulls up the photographs he took the previous year of the kids on the fishing trip—Isaac recoiling from a flapping trout, Alice caught in a private moment thinking about Walker knows not what. He resisted digital photography for a long time, knowing that once there were no paper photographs, there would be no dusty albums hidden in attics for someone like him to discover. But every age deserves its fashion and its forms, and no one can control what survives.

He scrolls back to the beginning of the file and studies the pictures of Alice when she was five and Isaac when he was two. He has an urge to see them younger, and so he finds the box of old photos he brought to the office intending to scan them. They have sat under his desk untouched for two years. He sorts through the disorganized clutter of images, looking at newborn Alice and Isaac held up for the camera, his or Lisette's hands clutching their tiny torsos. At six months old, Alice's sharp worry is already etched into her expression. And there is sweet Isaac, his gaze limpid and trusting, open to the world. Walker imagines that he can see his children's characters in their earliest photographs, and this alleviates the guilt he bears knowing that the divorce was a terrible blow to them and that his absences were small, repeated wounds. But he knows he could be deceiving himself. What if their faces are those of any children vulnerable to parental whim? If Alice and Isaac had been raised by another, happier couple, would they be better off now or just differently harmed?

Emily Muller, an ambitious senior, taps on his open door.

"Hi, Professor Dodge?" she says. He hears the upswing at the end of the sentence, the strange combination of parent-inflicted overconfidence and global uncertainty he notices in his students.

"Hello, Emily," he says.

"Just wondering if you'd gotten to mine yet."

He shuffles through the proposals, finds hers, hands it across the desk. She looks at it, bouncing on her toes a few times as if she cannot contain her anticipation.

"So you liked it?"

"It will be fine."

"I think I can uncover something really interesting. Something truthful."

"Something truthful?" he says. He looks at the pile of student papers on his desk. He wonders if he has led them all astray.

"I'm not going to predetermine anything. I'm going to let the evidence lead me," she says hesitantly. "Like you said."

Alice blasts into the office with her typical disregard for what she might be interrupting. She has dreadlocked her hair and dyed some of the knotty hanks purple. She wears combat boots and shorts. He is so happy to see her. She drops a package on his desk.

"The lady at the front said to give this to you."

"The 'lady' is Mrs. Elliot," he says of the secretary who is a whiff of old-world San Francisco propriety in a department filled with sloppy, self-aggrandizing academics.

"I guess I'll go?" Emily says.

He looks from his brazen daughter to the fearful Emily. He knows he has done her a disservice. "I'm very interested in your project, Emily," he says. "I look forward to seeing what you come up with." She backs out the door, looking pained.

"What's her problem?" Alice says.

"A surfeit of faith in her teacher," he says.

Alice looks at him quizzically. "Are you high?"

"I have never gotten high in my life."

"Bull*shit*," she says, smiling.

"Well, it's the bullshit I'm supposed to dish out. You'll see when you're a parent."

"Now you sound like Mom."

"Your mom is right about a lot of things."

"Is she right about you?"

Now they are in dangerous territory. "I don't know what she says about me."

"That you are searching for something and you haven't found it yet."

He looks at Alice. What could these words possibly mean to her? He wonders if he is as inscrutable to his daughter as his father was to him.

"Are you going to open your package, or what?" she says.

He studies the box for a moment, then finds scissors in the clutter on his desk.

"What is it?" Alice says impatiently.

He lifts out crushed newspaper that protects the contents of the package. Before he can go further, Alice reaches into the box and takes out a hat. It is made of red felt and has plastic fruit affixed to its brim.

"Who sent you *this?*" she says. Her distaste is evident, but she puts it on her head anyway. The disjunction between her purple hair and the prim hat makes him laugh. "What else is in there?" she says.

He takes a legal-sized envelope from the box. His name is written on it. Inside is a letter that informs him that James Coin has died and that his instructions were that these items be sent to Walker.

"Oh, no," Walker says.

"What?"

"Someone died."

"Who?"

Something else is in the envelope, and he pulls it out. It is a framed newsprint photograph. The glass is cracked down the center. The picture shows a man sitting in a chair with his eyes closed. He holds a shotgun in his arms.

"Who died?" Alice repeats.

Walker does and does not understand why James has sent him this box. Or, rather, he understands something, but it feels far off, like weather in another county, or history, which becomes more present as it recedes, a paradox of time.

"Dad? Hello?"

"His name was James Coin."

"How come I never heard of him?" she says.

There is another letter in the box. This one is addressed to Mary Coin. He opens it. Alice looks over his shoulder.

"Who is Vera Dare?" she asks softly.

38

Where are we?" Alice says. They left the city early in the morning. She fell asleep when they were outside San Francisco and has just now woken up.

"Nipomo."

"That's a weird name for a place."

"It's a Chumash word. It means 'the foot of the hills.'"

"Meet me at the Nipomo and we'll take a hike."

"Something like that."

She straightens up, stretches, smells her breath with a cupped hand. "Forgot to brush."

He was surprised when she agreed to take this day trip with him rather than sleep in on a Saturday. She was out late. It is April, now. She has been clean for nearly a year, so he has relaxed the rules. Last night, she texted that she was at someone named Nicole's house. This information made him feel comfortable until he realized that she could be lying, that she could be anywhere in the world. It chilled him to think that location had become a highly conceptual notion that a teenager might be crafty enough to exploit. But she came home when she said she would, and she did not smell of liquor nor did she appear to be high. She looked like a girl who had met a boy, excited and private and distracted. He and Lisette agree that Alice is doing well in San Francisco and that she can stay through her senior year. She has decided to go back to Petaluma for the summer to be with Isaac. She misses him.

The Nipomo Visitors Bureau is a lofty name for the small room in a building that also houses the mayor's office and the local Department of Water and Power. No one appears to be manning the place. A sign instructs that all purchases can be made with the mayor's secretary. A quick perusal reveals the usual fare Walker finds at visitors centers all over the country—glossy leaflets advertising the town's handful of trumped-up attractions, self-published family histories typed and copied poorly so that the text runs at a slant. There is an informational sheet about flora and fauna written by a local nature enthusiast. On the wall, a small box frame displays three arrowheads, which are meant to attest to the Indian heritage of the town, although there is no accompanying information that would prove their authenticity. Walker leafs through a glossy magazine called *Birds of Florida*, which seems to have no particular pertinence except that maybe the person who donated the magazine is a town alderman or the president of the Women's Club. Perhaps the person who owned the magazine about birds is also the person who donated the arrowheads, so that the relationship is not one of subject but of character and predilection.

"Look at this," Walker says. He picks up a secondhand book from a shelf. Published in 1952, the book is a selection of a hundred years' worth of articles from the local newspaper edited by someone named

Terence W. "Dub" Jackson. In his foreword, Mr. Jackson explains that he set about this project because of the "wonderful and adventurous history of our little town, Nipomo, California."

Alice takes the book from him, opens it to a random page, and reads aloud. " 'There was a water shortage in Nipomo. The springs were being used to their capacity, but that was not enough. Bonds were voted, and two additional pumps were bought.' " She hands him the book. "Fascinating," she says.

Walker reads another random entry. *It was reported in February that there were twenty-five prisoners in the jail and that all were healthy except for one case of pneumonia.* The book is a wonderful discovery. He will spend weeks with it.

"Look, Dad," Alice says. She leans over a glass case. "They made a stamp of her."

He peers down at the sheet of commemorative stamps. There she is. The woman, the two children—he wonders if one of them is James. And there is his father, the baby in her arms. Or maybe it is not his father—he will never really be sure. Walker knows this, just as he knows that any story told about what has happened in the past can never be certain, that there is always yearning in the piecing together of information. The story of history is the story of its telling and its retelling. There are truths lost to time and desire.

"She's worth thirty-two cents," Alice says.

He's told his daughter everything—about finding the article and visiting James Coin. About this curiosity that has latched onto him and that won't let go, so that he will spend his next year's sabbatical traveling to Tahlequah, then making the same journey west Mary might have taken. He doesn't know what the project will ultimately yield. He doesn't want to know. Not now. Because answers are inert things that stop inquiry. They make you think you have finished looking. But you are never finished. There are always discoveries that will turn everything you think you know on its head and that will make you ask all over again: Who are we?

He buys Alice a T-shirt because they both think it's funny that a town as inconsequential as Nipomo has its own T-shirt. It says "I Heart Nipomo." She slips it over her tank top. As they walk across the hall to the mayor's office, they debate whether the inclusion of the full word rather than the heart symbol is naïve or ironic. When they pay the secretary, they ask if she knows where the famous picture was taken.

"There's just fields out there," the woman says. "It's hard to tell one from another."

He pulls the car to the side of the road next to a low stone wall— the kind he remembers from the original orange groves at his family's farm, built at a time when the land was marked off by these crude structures that were nothing but rocks piled on top of one another without mortar to bind them.

"You think the picture was taken here?" Alice says.

"Could be."

She gets out of the car and he follows. She climbs onto the wall, then jumps the small distance to the ground, a bit of playfulness that makes him happy. He is with his daughter in this place. Something happened here once. Something that might have gone unnoticed but for a person with a camera.

"Tell me what it was like," Alice says.

"What?"

"Back then."

He tells her about the Depression and the farmers and the poverty. He tells her about a photographer who was sent by the government to record what was happening. He tells her a story, some of it based on facts, some of it embellished, because he wants to keep her attention and he knows how stories need to go. When he is finished, they stand quietly looking out over the fields.

"Hey!" she says brightly. "Take my picture!"

He gets his camera from the car. She climbs onto the wall again and strikes an intentionally silly pose, one hip jutted out, her chin in the air, "I Heart Nipomo" blazoned across her chest.

"Don't pose," Walker says.

"Just stand here? Like this?" She lets her arms drop to her sides. She looks disarmingly young and lovely, a vessel into which so much life has yet to flow. He lifts the camera to his face and places her in the frame. Just his girl, front and center, getting her due. His girl and this land.

"Let me see! Let me see!" she says, jumping down and running to him as he lowers the camera. She leans against his shoulder, her purple hair brushing his cheek. He brings the image onto the digital display. She falls silent, her giddy energy submerged beneath a weightier understanding. He wonders what the picture makes her feel. Does her subjectivity enlarge or diminish her? Does she see what he sees:

her singularity made symbolic? She takes the camera from him and studies the image. Her expression is solemn, as if she were witnessing something that tells her that the world she thinks she knows will only become more mysterious.

"It doesn't look like me," she says quietly.

It is a photograph, an alchemy of fact and invention that produces something recognizable as the truth. But it is not the truth.

"Who does it look like?"

"Just some girl."

She presses the trash icon. They watch as the picture slides down the screen and disappears. But it will always exist. In a cloud. In an invisible language of zeros and ones. There is no erasure.

Acknowledgments

I am indebted to the continued support and encouragement of David Rosenthal, and to the precise intelligence and refined touch of Sarah Hochman. I am lucky to have had my dear friend and agent, Henry Dunow, by my side all these years as a most trusted and thoughtful early reader. Kimberly Burns is a true believer, and I am grateful for her inventive work and her boundless optimism. Rachel Kushner has taken this journey with me, challenging me time and again with her complex and nimble mind. And Ken Kwapis never fails to help me discover what it is I'm really after.

Two of the characters in this novel are inspired by Florence Owens Thompson and Dorothea Lange, the subject and photographer involved in the making of the great photograph *Migrant Mother*. I am grateful for their lives and legacies. The letter Mary Coin writes to *Look* magazine is adapted from a letter Thompson submitted to *U.S. Camera*. Vera Dare's field notes are drawn from those Lange made while working, and from the individual and general captions she appended to her photographs.

The excellent books *Dorothea Lange: A Life Beyond Limits*, by Linda Gordon, and *Dorothea Lange: A Photographer's Life*, by Milton Meltzer, provided me with a wealth of information that was useful in constructing the life of Vera Dare.

Often, I know why I am drawn to a particular idea at the outset. But sometimes, it is only through the process of making the work that I discover what has compelled me toward a set of preoccupations. I have come to understand that it was my long-ago collaboration with the late filmmaker Richard Leacock that lies at the heart of this novel. Ricky always knew where to point the camera.

About the Author

Marisa Silver is the author of the novels *The God of War* (a *Los Angeles Times* Book Prize finalist) and *No Direction Home*, and two story collections, *Alone With You* and *Babe in Paradise* (a *New York Times* Notable Book and *Los Angeles Times* Best Book of the Year). Her first short story appeared in *The New Yorker*, when she was featured in the magazine's first "Debut Fiction" issue. Silver's fiction has been included in *The Best American Short Stories*, *The O. Henry Prize Stories*, and other anthologies. Winner of the O. Henry Prize, she lives in Los Angeles.